Dear Doug!
I hope you
this book!
the scene
is afoot!

A CASE OF MADNESS

(Or the Curious Appearance of Holmes in the Nighttime)

YVONNE KNOP

Improbable
PRESS

First published by Improbable Press in 2023

Improbable Press is an imprint of:
Clan Destine Press
www.clandestinepress.com.au
PO Box 121, Bittern Victoria 3918 Australia

National Library of Australia Cataloguing-In-Publication data:

Yvonne Knop

A Case of Madness: Or the Curious Appearance of Holmes in the Nighttime

ISBN: 978-1-922904-03-4 (pb)
ISBN: 978-1-922904-04-1 (eb)

Cover artwork by ©Ksenia Spizhevaya
Titling by Willsin Rowe
Layout & Typesetting by Dimitra Stathopoulos

Improbable Press
improbablepress.com

I dedicate this book to three fierce women who all helped me on the journey of finishing this work but passed the setting sun before it was published:

Kathrin,
my first proofreader and editor when these chapters were still in German,

Kathy,
my ever-glittering friend and support on so many levels,

Jana,
my bestie, my soulmate, my love.

They shall live on with every word I write.

Life is infinitely stranger than anything which the mind of man could invent.

Sir Arthur Conan Doyle
The Complete Sherlock Holmes, A Case of Identity

1

—◆—

The Adventure of the Noble Hermit

While strolling amid the students and scholars rushing into the University of London, I ignored the urge to check my pocket watch.

If there was ever a day to dawdle, it was today. The first day of summer that actually felt like the season it claimed to be. And the day of my personal disaster.

It wasn't a 'this train will split at the next station and you just sat down with your meal deal' disaster, but it was equally inconvenient. After decades of laboring in academia, I was about to become involuntarily unemployed. Apart from that – and this might be even more important – I was also going to die.

To delay the confrontation a bit longer, I looked for a shaded place to smoke and then took long, luxurious drags on my cigarette. A cough struggled to tear itself free from my chest, but I suppressed it. *Not now. Focus.*

Few people knew my name or my publications. But some such people existed – people who were as fascinated by a very specific man as I was, and who seemed to value my works more than I did. The man I wrote about lived in Baker Street, and he was partly to blame for my situation. Though I liked to think of myself as a charmingly anachronistic gentleman, I increasingly felt I was just a dafter in a fine suit who lurked around public buildings. Instead of engaging in modern life, I was immersed in the world of Sherlock Holmes and all things Victorian, with the natural effect of many acquaintances leaving or going extinct. It wasn't that I didn't like the company of others; it was that I struggled in the company of others. And they struggled in the company of me.

You see, the fact that I knew my dearest detective had appeared on-screen in over two hundred and twenty adaptations did not give me much hope I would find out what people did for fun. But what of fun? What about achievement? Holmes is the most filmed novel character of all time – among humans, at least; Dracula has been filmed even more often. This connection filled me with joy, and I believed it could be combined in a curious way. Dracula Holmes: he investigates at night because he's not just a detective, no – he's also a vampire. Greedy for blood and knowledge.

I finished my cigarette and stepped from the shadows only to immediately collide with a young man in the most colorful trainers I'd ever seen. In a split-second knockout victory, he fell to the ground covered in the flyers he had been holding in his hand just seconds before.

I bent down immediately to help him. "I'm so sorry," I said, quickly picking up his flyers from the pavement. At least those which hadn't fallen into the grey puddle right next to us.

"It's okay," he said, and he looked at me. His blue eyes seemed friendly though his gaze was intense.

I quickly looked down again. To my surprise, the flyers weren't gig announcements or takeaway adverts. In fact, they were promoting something very dear to my heart. "I like theater," I said, handing him back a few of the flyers. "I thought theater was dead for young people."

He smiled. "Most young people get run over by perfect strangers. That's why so few make it to the stage. *Anyway*…I'm still alive."

That he was. Alive, handsome, and holding a slim stack of remaining flyers. Slightly crumpled.

"I'm far from perfect," I remarked, thinking of the trouble I had caused him.

"I meant perfect as in total strangers," he said, still looking at me. "Though, maybe I meant it literally."

I was seized by an involuntary smile. "Do you need help with these? I used to…I work here and could take a few flyers inside." I pulled a cigarette out of the pack in my pocket and promptly lost it to the grey puddle.

"That would be nice, actually," he said, looking at the university. "What's your job?"

"Knocking out perfect strangers, mostly."

He handed me a stack of flyers. A bright smile framed by ruffled blonde hair. "Well, if that's the case, we should run into each other again sometime."

"By accident? Or…" I asked like a complete nutter. *Chit-chat is for extroverts.*

"Yes, at the charity event at the Young Vic."

"The what? When?"

He pointed to the flyers and started walking. "See you there!"

"I might be there. By accident!" I called. I gazed after him until he disappeared around a corner. Here and then gone. I wished I'd said something cleverer than "I like theater."

Back inside, I laid the flyers along the windowsills but kept one in my pocket.

"Mr Thomas?"

A distressed figure, also known as a student, was approaching me at top speed. He came to a halt in front of me, breathless.

"Daryl," I said as I proceeded down the long hallway. "You've certainly been elusive as of late."

"Is it true you're leaving?"

I tacked the last flyer onto a bulletin board. "I'm afraid so."

"Glad I caught you, then."

"You cannot catch me, Daryl. I'm not a disease."

He laughed. "That's why I loved your classes. You're hilarious."

"What I said wasn't a jo—"

"Thank you. Thanks for everything and stuff."

I stopped walking and smiled.

"Good luck in there, Mr Thomas. We all know he's a bit…you know." He waved goodbye as he headed off towards one of the lecture rooms.

I had reached my dreaded destination. I knocked and was invited in.

"Andrew, nice to see you. Sit down," said my boss. He pointed at a chair in front of his large mahogany desk. I was relieved he didn't try to shake my hand. He was no doubt a bacterial breeding ground. His office smelled of stale apple juice and mayonnaise. *The horror of it all.*

I quickly averted my gaze and fixed it on the new pictures he had hung up. Without consent, I was bombarded by his whole family. I concluded that he must have a life outside these walls. We were indeed two kinds of men. A single drawing of Sherlock Holmes hung in my office. Fictional characters are my kind of family.

"We really would have liked to keep you. After all, you're kind of an institution here," he quipped, peering at me over the edge of his glasses.

The way he rocked back and forth in his chair made me anxious. Repetitive noises or movements did that. I once ripped a pen from a child's hand and threw it over a balustrade. Of course, I could not have foreseen that the child would try to follow it. Fortunately, his mother was quick, but for this and other reasons I am banned from the British Museum permanently. I am not saddened by this. Since there is little left to steal from the former colonies, I know the exhibitions will not change significantly during my lifetime.

"Why me?" I asked.

"Mr Thomas, you know that we have to cut down our expenses."

"I know, but I would like to know why it's me." *Institutions don't get closed for no reason.*

My adversary smiled, unsettled. Lettuce remains were jammed between his teeth. "You haven't published anything for a long time, let alone participated in projects. I felt compelled to put you on the list of those we…well, can do without."

"Do without?" I wondered, pulling at the wrong end of my bowtie in the process. It unknotted itself, and I stuffed both ends into my shirt. *Keep it up Andrew. This day won't ruin itself.*

"Maybe this is a good thing. This might be your chance. You're still young and shouldn't be wasting your life obsessing over a fictional character."

By now I could hear my own pulse in my ears. I started to fantasize about *The Case of the Deceased University Director* and wondered what murder weapon would please Dracula Holmes. Probably one that left as much blood in the victim as possible. For reasons of his diet.

"This so-called fictional character is one of the most significant figures the literary world has ever seen," I protested.

"Why don't you view this as an opportunity to shift gears?"

I hesitated. "Theoretically speaking, is there any way I could stay? Keep lecturing?"

"A man like you must have other interests," he said, looking at my undone tie. "Perhaps it's time for you to go off and explore those."

"I know when Sherlock Holmes' birthday is, how tall he is, and how many steps lead from the front door to his flat. I know his cases by heart and every myth that swirls around him. Over the years, I've written volumes about him. I—"

"And what have you achieved?"

"What have I achieved?" *What had I achieved? The life of a hermit.*

"Andrew, I have to repeat myself. You haven't published *anything* within the last five years. If you want to keep teaching literature, you need publications."

"Fiction or non-fiction? I can do both," I said in a last attempt to save my reputation. Dracula Holmes, by all means, was bestselling material.

He exhaled hard. "The decision is made. You simply can't publish anything groundbreaking before you leave this office today. And that's all that could save your position, I'm afraid."

I stood up to leave. "You will regret this once I'm on the bestseller list."

"Very well then. We've found a temporary replacement, so you don't need to worry about coming in again. HR will be in touch. Goodbye, Mr Thomas," he said, finally letting me go.

I was too dazed to go and clear out my office. Instead, I shuffled back outside, lit a cigarette, and opened the top button of my shirt. In an unobserved moment, I spat a mixture of blood and saliva into a tissue. I shoved the tissue into my pocket, and when I withdrew my hand, a note fluttered to the ground. I bent down to retrieve it. *I don't know what I am and I don't know what I want. I don't know who I can be and I don't know who I was.* This slip of ancient paper was the thing closest to me. Closer than anyone or anything had been in years. Almost.

"What's up, flatmate?" a bright voice asked behind me.

I looked around. It was Mina, my personal Watson, and friend from the department. My only one, to be precise. When asked to describe herself, she's always quick to reply that she's just like her favorite coffee: dark, bitter, and too hot. However, in my opinion, size-wise she's more of an espresso. One that definitely keeps you awake. Especially if you're one of her students. She's Pakistani, free-spirited and messy, and a strict and ambitious teacher.

We found each other when we were at our lowest. I'd just finalized my divorce, and Mina was fresh out of a relationship of her own. A colleague suggested we move in together, as we'd both been looking for an affordable flat in central London. It proved to be my first bit of good luck in a long time.

We complemented each other in mysterious ways. I was a scared house cat who hid behind paper; she was a stray who went out every night. She made me leave the flat and enjoy life from time to time; I managed to give her the first home she actually wanted to return to. Since it worked for Holmes and Watson, I was convinced it might work for us too – maybe even for a lifetime. The best of friends, forever. That optimism lasted exactly two hundred and seventy-eight days and sixty-three packages of ear plugs. Stray cats like to mingle.

"Former flatmate," I corrected her, but she had long ago mastered the ability to ignore me and press on.

"So, what message did Professor Doctor Stale Apple Juice have for you? Did he change his mind?"

"Well, all I can say is that his message did not find me well."

Mina pouted. "I'm so sorry, babes."

"I need publications," I said with determination. I disregarded the *babes*.

"What for? You just got sacked."

Cigarette smoke escaped my mouth slowly. "Rache." A German word that every Holmes admirer knew.

"Huh?"

"Revenge, Mina. I need them for *revenge*."

"There, there, my dear," she said, patting me on the shoulder. This touch was a liberty, but I didn't mind it coming from her. In fact, I liked her company very much and sometimes even missed living with her. What I didn't miss, however, were carelessly stacked pans and a fridge full of takeaway leftovers that were close to taking themselves away to the bin.

"Let's go for a pint," she suggested.

"I don't know." I usually needed a week to prepare myself for a night out. There were so many considerations: googling the route, thinking of conversation starters, looking through the offered drinks beforehand, avoiding the elbows of other patrons. The endless circle of being home but wishing I could be more social and being social but wishing I were home. *The horror of it all.*

"Oh, come on! Celebrate your last day."

"Why would I celebrate a day like this, my dear Ms Advani?"

"Because you look like you need some distraction."

I remembered my hopelessly disheveled state. "He seemed to not really care about my publications," I blinked into the sun, trying to knot my tie. "Are my publications a joke?"

Mina stepped closer and tied the knot for me. "Maybe it's time you displayed some relatable emotions in your writing. Just a suggestion."

"That's not easy for me." I identified more as a typewriter than a person.

"I know." And Mina did know. Sensing what was on my mind was her superpower. Just like Watson and Holmes, we appeared to get along even when this required some tolerance of my quirks on Mina's part. I hoped that one day she would start writing about me. And that she would feature my thick black hair and mesmerizing brown eyes prominently – to distract from my dad bod. That's what young people would call it, apparently. At least Mina said so.

"I'll go for one beer." Some people are the reason you smile; some people are the reason you drink. Mina was my reason for both. The definition of a best friend.

"Very well. I just need to run some errands before we go."

"I could join you," I suggested.

Mina's eyes darted around. She was about to lie about something.

"What kind of errands are we talking about, Mina?"

"Maybe, just hypothetically, I stayed overnight at this rather hot but absolutely weird girl's place and maybe I forgot my phone charger."

"You could just buy a new one."

"No, she doesn't deserve to own my charger. It's an original Apple product. You know what she said?"

"No, but I'm sure you'll tell me in a second."

"She said strawberries are overrated."

"And?"

Mina stopped. "I use strawberry everything. Shampoo. Bodywash. Everything. You know this."

"Then maybe you weren't meant for each other."

She rolled her eyes. "Women these days, all fur coat and no knickers."

I laughed and looked at the fur coat that was hanging partway out of her black jute bag. "What exactly is that, then?"

"Fake fur. I do wear knickers, though. Right, I need to hurry before she goes back to work at that weird smoothie place. And I need to check the new comics at Forbidden Planet. *For research.*"

Her field was, naturally, comics. And her classes were terribly popular.

"Okay, then I'll run my own errand while you get your phone charger."

She smiled because she knew exactly what *my* errand would be.

Mina had temporarily lifted my mood, but the reprieve was brief. *No job. No marriage. No time left.* A cab cut in front of us, and I briefly considered taking a step forward. Mina's presence, however, kept me from doing so. No one should see a friend's body being thrown across the road and caught by a curb. I was also concerned for my pocket watch. It was really nice.

"Watch out! Tosser!" Mina shouted, throwing a gesture at the cab driver that required no translation. I signaled that she should stay calm. She, however, threw her golden rucksack in the cab's direction.

The situation was interrupted by my phone vibrating. I checked the screen but didn't answer.

"Who are you ignoring?"

"Nobody. Nobody, really."

"Is everything okay?"

"Yes. Yes, of course."

"Then at six in our pub?"

I nodded and said goodbye when we reached the intersection. I looked back to where I had envisioned my body flying through the air a moment before. There was something in my head clamoring for attention. Something I didn't want to think about. Something that eclipsed the lost job, the failed marriage.

Something I could not escape.

2

———◆———

The Doubtful Bachelor

As the train left Euston and passed a ghost station, I peered through the window. The closed stops always fascinated the child in me. They're a reminder of London's many layers, reaching from ancient times to modern day. They're tangible history. Relics of past generations. They feel like mysteries waiting to be rediscovered.

At St Paul's I got off and headed for another tangible piece of history: the London Wall. I stopped, loosened my tie, and undid another button on my shirt. The heavy evening air enveloped me like a wool blanket. Before I could even cross the road, I decided to take a detour. I ran towards St Paul and entered the gardens.

Taking a seat and lighting a cigarette, I gazed at the enormous cathedral dome. It silenced me at its sight. The majestic way it protruded into the air could convince almost any atheist there's more to the universe than we've guessed. When Sherlock Holmes and Dr Watson took a police boat to Jacobson's shipyard in *The Sign of the Four*, the evening sun shone on the cross atop the dome just as it did now. The thick summer air was broken by the dazzling light. I closed my eyes and listened to the many voices around me. Languages, laughter, and steps blended into an unmistakable melody of the big city.

I put my hand in my pocket, felt the crumpled piece of paper, and hesitantly pulled it out. *I don't know what I am and I don't know what I want. I don't know who I can be and I don't know who I was.* My fingers tapped at the end of my cigarette. The ash scattered and blew towards the neighboring bank.

Crumpling the paper back up, I looked around and took a deep breath. I didn't want to live in the past – at least not my own past – but this little bit of memory resisted being forgotten. You could hardly see the blue ink, but that wasn't important. I knew every line by heart. I briefly considered scaling the dome and shouting them from its summit. Getting myself sectioned might be the best thing I could do.

Perhaps another day.

I stood up, coughed, and tasted the blood that choked my lungs. I was reminded how little time was left for me.

Back on the road, I headed towards my favorite retreat. The day of my last lecture coincided with a slow tourist time at the Museum of London. This was lucky, because it was the place. My place.

I walked down the stairs behind the gift shop so I wouldn't have to go through half the exhibitions. Nothing destroys a creative melancholia more than the history of the ancient Romans. My destination was a replica of a Victorian high street. It was a protected area for me, which was ironic considering it was accessible to everyone. Every time I set foot in the street, a feeling of joy washed over me. You could hear music in the distance, voices echoing down alleys, and carriages passing by.

I strolled past the lovingly recreated shop windows and was finally where I wanted to be: a bar opposite Rattenbury & Co.

I sat down and closed my eyes. Apart from me, there was no one in that section of the museum – at least no one living – so I was free to look like a lunatic. It was almost as if I were perceiving smells, listening to familiar chatter, and living in that time. I relaxed myself into the illusion. A man in a fine three-piece suit strolled along the shops with his young fiancée, who was fascinated by a pair of white gloves in one of the windows. Music from a barrel organ filled the air. At the corner stood a man selling papers. He had a huge sign around his neck proclaiming the news: Holmes Presumed Dead. The policeman on the opposite side of the street was distracted from his job for a moment reading this dreadful news. A horse and carriage almost ran him down when he walked towards the newspaper man. It was a delight to watch the scene. I wasn't sure why I was attracted to this world, but maybe it was my longing for a place where I didn't feel as foreign.

It may have been a childish habit, but whenever I needed to think, I went to the same spot. Each thought that grew there and each question that crept up my throat stayed in that space, and I kept coming back to revisit them. To revisit one, especially. No one knew this thought. Not even Mina, with her psychic superpowers. It wasn't about my job or Sherlock Holmes. It was: *I'm going to die.*

I had asked myself for weeks whether the cancer would get me or whether I would beat it to the punch and die by my own hand. All I needed was my doctor's confirmation to know for sure. Either way, the outcome was as sure as eggs is eggs.

Somewhat reluctantly, I got up and headed to meet Mina. Another trip through the Underground artery, another dance to avoid brushing shoulders with fellow travelers. Mina was waiting in front of the pub.

"Got the comic you wanted?" I asked as I finished my cigarette.

"Yes." She pulled a shirt out of her bag.

"How is it you always go in for comics and always come out with anything but?"

"Just because you always stick to your shopping list when you visit dusty old bookstores doesn't mean the rest of us can't be spontaneous."

I laughed. "Well, the shirt does have words and pictures on it, so I guess it counts."

I opened the door to the smell of stale beer and old carpets, which tickled my nose. I much preferred the tobacco smell of original editions of *The Strand Magazine*.

The moment we sat down at a table in the back corner, Mina threw her phone charger on the table. "Sherlock, make a deduction."

"I can't make a deduction in a room full of people, Watson," I said, taking the charger regardless.

"You always could, and you can now."

I smiled and examined the cable. "Easy. Someone chewed on it. And since I'm hoping it wasn't your date, she must have a pet. A small one. A hamster?"

"Guess again."

"Gerbil?"

Mina laughed. "It was a rat."

I threw the charger in her direction. "Please stop dating people, it's a mess!"

"How will I know which chocolate is the best in the box if I don't try every single one?"

"You read the description on the back of the box like any decent person, and then you decide."

"Boring. Also, some descriptions don't reveal the complete ingredients."

"I fear I'm lost a bit here," I said, noticing a sticky spot on the table. *Pubs.*

"What I'm saying is I couldn't care less about ingredients or descriptions or whatever. You're alive, human, legal, and we have consent? Enough for me."

"What a giant pool of options."

"That's the fun of it. I couldn't imagine missing out on *that*." Mina looked around the room. "I've been wondering…" she said without looking at me. "And I hope you don't take this personally."

"Is it about Holmes?"

"No?"

"Then I won't."

She paused for a beat. "I've been wondering what your favorite chocolate is. In the box. One with a liquid core or one that contains nuts?"

"What do you mean?" I asked, knowing exactly what she meant. I wanted to take a few peanuts, but instead I overturned the bowl. Dozens of peanuts rolled towards their freedom while I tried to catch them. *Pull yourself together, people are watching.*

She laughed. "Nothing, my dear, nothing."

I carefully put a few peanuts back into the bowl. Those who had landed in the sticky spot stayed where they were. "Do your parents know? Or anyone in your family?"

Her smile disappeared in an instant. "No. Not their business. I mean, I wish I could tell them."

"But?"

"I just don't want to. Okay? Change of subject, please." Mina fumbled with her watch.

Trying to talk about Mina's family never lasted longer than one question and sometimes one answer. Her walls would go up. Again, I touched the sticky spot and pulled my hand away quickly. "So, what's going on with David?" I asked. "Given your little adventure last night?"

"We're no longer a couple," Mina said, avoiding eye contact and scowling. She scanned the room and fixed on a screen showing a football match.

"Yes, I know, but we never really talked about it," I said.

"I needed to sort some things first, mentally, you know." She folded a napkin on the table. "He cheated on me," she said without looking up from her fingers.

"Oh, that's not very fortunate."

"No. Not at all. He goes to work every day, and I think everything's fine. But instead he fu–"

"I'm sorry," I interrupted, knowing I would be unable to find the right words for this conversation. I wanted to say whatever she needed to hear. I wanted to do the things friends are supposed to do. But I just couldn't figure out how. I looked over my shoulder at one of the TVs. It wasn't football at all; it might have been rugby.

"I just…I just cannot believe that this is it. These are our lives.

You, alone in your flat, unemployed and frustrated. Me, alone in my flat, employed but still frustrated."

"We were frustrated when we lived together," I remarked.

"Happily frustrated together, forever," she corrected me. "You're the only one I know who loves old black-and-white films as much as I do. We do have things in common."

"What a great couple we are," I said, smiling. "We could set up a shared flat again, since we're both in need, and watch *Casablanca* every night." Indeed, financially it would have been the best idea. London is terribly expensive. Even if you're not the type to indulge in things nobody really needs. But if you are, you can eat at the French restaurant Le Gavroche, where you get a three-course meal for thirteen thousand pounds. Why not snag a bargain in Knightsbridge and buy a flat for the reasonable price of one hundred and thirty million? If you want to make a really good investment, get a haircut at Stuart Phillips for twenty thousand. You can even get a limited edition PG Tips teabag that has diamonds sewn into it. I like to drink my tea with milk, not coal, but perhaps I lack sophistication. Plus, I can't sell my liver yet, as I'm still using it.

"Oh, I'd love that, but may I remind you of the doormat incident?" Mina asked.

"It was not a doormat. It was my antique rug and you ruined it with your sticky drink abomination."

"It was an innovative cocktail made from everything in the fridge and I regret nothing." Mina fingered a strand of her hair, looking closely at it. "No reason to throw me out, though." She selected a new strand and examined it in such detail that she squinted. "I held your hair back when you were sick."

I blinked slowly. "I have short hair."

"If you had long hair, I would have done it I did hold back your tie once."

"That was a great deed," I said. "I actually miss having you around. I'm glad I'm not alone tonight."

We sat in silence for a moment, each of us lost in our thoughts.

When I snapped back to the present, I spoke slowly, cautiously. "Because there is this thought I have. That it might be good that everything has come to an end." *If you only knew what end.*

"So, how are you?" she asked. "You seem quite calm considering what happened."

"Everything's fine," I lied, picking up a lonely peanut from the bowl. Nothing was fine. It hadn't been for months, but if you could bury yourself in mountains of work, at least you didn't have to think about it. Now I'd have time for myself. *The horror of it all.*

Her fingers traced the edge of the pint glass. "What are your plans now?"

"I don't know, but I'm sure I have to get rid of Holmes." I was surprised by how true this felt.

"I'm sorry, babes. But maybe now you have time for that novel you always wanted to write. That one about Sherlock Dracula."

"Dracula Holmes," I corrected her. But the truth was that I didn't have anything interesting to write about. Nothing had really happened within the last couple of years; a dreadful diagnosis and being sacked hardly made a good story.

"Oh, yes. Show Professor Doctor Stale Apple Juice that he made a mistake by sacking you."

"I'm gonna make him an offer he can't refuse," I said with determination.

"The good old Godfather never was wrong." Mina looked at me, drained her glass, and slammed it on the table. "Next round on me!"

"Thank you, I think I should go home now."

"Not at all, Dandy Andy! This is the best evening I've had in a long time, and I'm just starting to enjoy it."

I laughed whenever she called me Dandy Andy. "Good. One more, then I'll bring you home."

"Will you come up for a coffee?" she asked.

"No."

"Why?"

"I only drink tea, you should know that."

"I have tea, too."

"Mrs Robinson, you're trying to seduce me. Aren't you?"

"Maybe." She might dismiss it as a joke, but I knew the offer had been serious. She'd offered before – after a few drinks. "You're quite a gentlemen, huh?"

"Naturally," I replied, emptying my glass. "But upon reconsideration, I'd love to come up to yours for something to drink."

"Perfect! Then I can show you what I've bought for my brother. Everything they had was in pastel colors. God, I hate pastel."

"Your brother?"

"I'm going to be an aunt. You remember?"

"Oh, right," I said. "That's beautiful." A family was something I'd wished for but was more and more certain I'd never have. I had never met a family with two fathers. I'd seen them on TV, yes, but never in real life. And, of course, I lacked what would be most important – a partner.

"You haven't properly dated anyone since Christine, have you?"

No, I hadn't, and I didn't want to discuss it. The marriage had seemed like a way to fix all my problems; it did not. "Work is the best antidote to sorrow," Holmes said. My work was the ladder that helped me climb out of the ditch from time to time, and now someone had nicked it.

"Why did you get a divorce?" asked Mina, without turning her gaze away from the bar.

"She deserved someone better."

"What was the real reason?"

"We didn't get along."

"Are you sure you didn't bore her to death with facts about Sherlock Holmes, Mr Wikipedia?"

"It should be made clear that this man prefers a factual and precise language that can appear dry to most human beings. There's a quote from–"

"Siri, delete Wikipedia," Mina said to her phone.

We laughed.

"Surely you've had offers, though," Mina continued.

I shook my head. "I'm not that popular anymore."

"Oh, nonsense!"

"I'll be forty next week, Mina. I am socially awkward, old-fashioned, and easily disgusted by ninety percent of what people do. I talk about Sherlock Holmes all the time. Oh, and I'm unemployed now."

"I know. You're quite frustrating. But for whatever reason, you're also strangely adorable."

"Thanks for noticing. I call this my special charm." I got out the theater flyer and put it next to her glass.

She examined the paper closely. "You do know that this is a charity event?"

"Yes. We could go? If you have time."

"You, Andrew Samuel Thomas, want to go to a big, crowded *charity* event? Who is the sexy actress you clearly want to get off with?"

"I don't want to get off with anyone." *And she is a he.*

"Speaking of events, would you like to go to Pride with me this weekend?"

"I'm busy, I'm afraid." I said it by reflex.

"Busy with what? Cleaning your vinyl?" She emptied her glass. "Come with me. Help me do some networking for my organization."

"Isn't your organization dead?"

"Well, nobody seems to be interested in helping socially marginalized researchers *yet,*" Mina said, "but this seems like the right place to find a face for it. Gain us the needed attention. I made this thing my pet issue. If I fuck this up, my career will be over. Well, not my career, but my reputation, which is the same. As you know. So. Come on. Pride?"

"I'll see." I didn't have an aversion to Pride – just to crowded places and bright colors. However, it was important to Mina. And I found myself wondering if the attractive stranger from earlier that day was a fan of parades.

"One more?"

I nodded and pushed a few pounds towards her. Mina pushed

them back at me. "I said this round is on me. You keep your money." She got up and strolled to and from the bar.

"And you? Now that David is done with?" I asked.

"Little flirt here, little flirt there. Little disasters like last night. I need some distraction."

"Would he be a good distraction, over there?" I pointed to a man by the front door.

Mina glanced at him and turned back to me. "He looks like he wants to show young children the bunny in his car."

"Good observation. Call Scotland Yard. And what about him?" She looked towards the table beside ours. "I think he's married."

"Either that and he wants to cheat, or he's divorced."

"How do you know that, Sherlock?"

"Do you see the lighter stripe on his ring finger?" I said. "There must have been a rather permanent ring there recently."

Mina looked at me in amazement. "Not bad."

"And her?" I pointed to a young woman behind the bar.

"How can anyone look so good?"

"The right genes, I suppose." I shrugged and swiped my index finger through the remaining salt in the peanut bowl. "There's another potential distraction back there," I said, pointing to a man leaning against the bar. He was wearing a grey suit and had his jacket draped loosely over a chair. He raked his hand through his hair and looked over at us. I quickly looked away.

Mina gawped. "He looks good!"

I nodded in agreement and hoped she didn't notice. "I say, that's your distraction for tonight. I'll forgo the tea." I got ready to leave.

"That's a pity."

"Oh come on, I'm really no competition. Me or a successful businessman with an athletic figure and dreamlike hair?"

Mina smiled and looked back at the man. "Is he married?"

"I don't see a ring, but that doesn't mean anything. Oh god, he's coming over."

"What?" asked Mina, burying her face in her sweater.

I tried to indicate that he was now standing right behind her, then riveted my eyes on my pocket watch. "I see my last bus arrives in five minutes. I must hurry. Can I leave her with you?" I smiled at the attractive distraction.

"I'll keep my eye on her," he said, taking my seat.

Mina gave me a look. Either she liked my matchmaking skills or she wanted to kill me. It was probably a bit of both.

I shook a cigarette from my pack and exited the pub, leaving my phone on for my walk. London is a different city by day and by night. She has two faces. It's no secret that away from the tourist attractions, the place is bristling with drugs, and an unobserved purse disappears faster than a chocolate bar in the hands of a two-year-old. I call London the Janus city, and her changing appearance affects my own nature – sometimes in unexpected ways.

3

The Man with the Bleeding Face

My hands were strangely numb, my walk more cursive than straight, and I barely noticed anything of the world around me. I tried to orient myself and decided to take a small detour to the bus station to rid my blood of some alcohol. Only one thing is more degrading than throwing up on public transport. Talking.

When the illuminated Admiral Nelson became visible in the distance, I became painfully aware of the fact I had gone in the wrong direction for miles. I tried to calculate a new route and headed east. Rather, I thought I was headed east, but instead I stumbled north and even further away from my home.

I had just weaved through the city center when I heard loud voices in the distance. I slowed my steps. My breath condensed in the air. I tried to inhale slowly and exhale quietly. A group of men stood grunting around something in a small side street. They were in a rage. Like animals, they were circling whatever it was. Shouting. Beating. Cursing. Spitting.

I approached them carefully and pressed my body against the masonry of the building behind me. The wet cold crept up my back. The numbness slowly disappeared from my fingers. Only then did I realize the beasts were not cornering an object, but a man.

I recognized his colorful trainers immediately. It was the young man with the theater flyers. He looked anything but alive. Like a sack filled with rice, he tipped from one side to the other with each kick. I felt a cough coming and tried to suppress it. I reached for my pocket watch. It was just before one.

My courage was, if not missing, not great; but I wondered if I hadn't learned something from Sherlock Holmes. It was not too late to be a brave man. I wished I had learned something else from him, however. Baritsu – a term most likely referring to a martial art called Bartitsu – would have been particularly helpful in that moment. A special feature of this kind of self-defense is the use of walking sticks or umbrellas as weapons. I didn't have an umbrella with me that night, but I've been advising everybody to carry one ever since.

I buried my cigarettes and my watch deep in my pockets and walked quickly towards the group.

"Piss off!" I shouted, and at that moment I found it a great relief to bellow vulgar words through central London. I had already learned a lot from Mina in that respect: if you want to make your voice heard, try vulgar language. Not always suitable, but mostly effective.

"What did you just say?" called one of the men. He was now moving quickly towards me. Somehow, I hadn't expected that. I considered backtracking, but unfortunately I lack that skill along with Baritsu.

"I said that you should leave," I replied.

He spat on the ground and laughed. "He says we should leave this bugger alone!"

"I didn't use that word," I corrected quietly, wondering why I had to act like a know-it-all in this particular moment.

The man puffed himself up, walked over to me, and smashed his forehead against mine. I staggered back and fell to the ground. I'd always thought that wouldn't work in reality, but the fact that I was lying on the pavement suggested I might not always be right.

With a grin on his face, the man stood over me. "Are you one?" he asked before spitting on the ground again.

My reply was interrupted by a kick in the kidneys. My body burned with pain. I screamed and bent double on the ground. My elbow landed in a gob of the man's spit. *The horror of it all.*

"A what?" I finally gasped.

"A poof."

I looked at him and shook my head.

The man shifted restlessly from one foot to the other. He glanced over his shoulder at the rest of the pack. "It's worse than that. He thinks he could get other men to fuck him in the ass."

I decided that further correction was needed. "Strictly speaking, you can't persuade…someone to be a…to be gay…and the practice you name isn't necessarily what…gay men…only gay men…do," I remarked, breathing heavily. I've never been able to keep my mouth shut. It usually got me into trouble. Even lying on the ground, I still thought it was one of my best qualities.

"You're a smart man, huh?" he asked, and before I could answer the question affirmatively, he grinned and stepped on my pocket watch. It must have fallen out when I dropped to the ground.

"Oi, let's go. I hear the pigs," said another member of the group, and the pack became visibly nervous. The man above me nodded, spat again, and turned his back to me. They moved away, but not without kicking their victim one last time and shouting, "Poofter!"

I waited on the ground until the group disappeared around the corner. Unfortunately, the sirens disappeared with them, and my hope for help faded. My head was in pain, and the alcohol had gone. When I got up, my pocket watch dangled from its chain. I didn't have to look closely to know the glass was broken. A wistful feeling came over me. I quickly pushed it aside and pulled out my phone. Luckily, it had survived the fall and the kicks. After dialing the emergency line, I lit a cigarette and closed my eyes briefly. I tried to understand what I had just witnessed, but I couldn't. My legs trembled as I walked over to the man who was crouched on the ground.

"Are you able to get up?" I asked, kneeling next to him. Only then did I see how much blood he had lost. He looked at me, eyes wet and face slick with red, and hesitantly shook his head. The blood dripped from the tip of his nose. I scanned our surroundings. Far and wide, there was no one to see. How could it suddenly be so lonely in a city of millions?

He straightened up and touched his head. His blond hair was soaked in blood and smeared with dirt from the road. I took a deep drag of my cigarette and threw it aside.

"What's your name?" I asked.

His blue eyes looked at me again. Through the blood surrounding them, they appeared luminous and penetrating. His skin was pale and lifeless. He was in his mid-twenties, perhaps, and not particularly muscular or skinny. Clearly neither of us was in the shape for street fights. After just a quarter of a second eye to eye, my breath became shallow. It felt like someone was pushing my head underwater. His eyes pinned me down as I drowned, and I tried to gather my wits. *The poor man's been beaten. Stop swooning at him.*

"Have we met before?" he asked, dazed.

"The university. Earlier. Seems like we did run into each other unexpectedly again. As planned."

"Glad you're here."

I smiled.

"Matt," he continued, coughing. "My name."

"Okay, Matt. I called an ambulance."

He closed his eyes and collapsed.

I sat behind him to support him, too focused to hesitate or feel revulsion at holding a bleeding stranger. His cold, soft body leaned heavily on mine. I wrapped my arms tightly around him, and although I was shaking, I felt an unknown calmness in myself.

My career hadn't prepared me for street brawls, and reading about Baritsu didn't mean I could fight. No book could have readied me for this evening: no lexicon, no Sherlock Holmes case, no Bible.

"Hey, you have to stay awake," I said.

His eyes opened again.

"No mates waiting for you at the club?" I tried to smile and held him tighter so he wouldn't tip to the side.

24

He slowly shook his head. "My…he's gone home."

"I just left my friend in a pub. She'd met someone else, anyway. Did you know those men?"

"No," he replied weakly.

His blood stained my trousers. The only thing radiating warmth at that moment was the red liquid slowly leaving his body. The air around us began to take on a metallic smell.

"I'm sure your friend would be disappointed to see you've ended up with someone else in your arms tonight," he said, and I felt like he was trying to smile. "But it's good that you didn't go with her."

For a moment I thought he was back to complete consciousness, but then he closed his eyes again. A drop of blood made its way across his pale cheek to his lips. Despite the cold, he was only wearing a black t-shirt. There was a tattoo on the inside of his upper arm.

Hoping to soon hear ambulance sirens, I took off my suit jacket. It would at least keep him warm, I thought. I glanced around. The club we were sitting in front of appeared to have closed long ago. A CCTV camera on the corner was angled so that it missed the exact spot we were occupying. I carefully draped my jacket over him, trying to move his head as little as possible. He was unresponsive.

I took his cold hand in mine to comfort him, and I made sure he was breathing. I watched the blood slowly make its way down the road and disappear into a drain.

His grip on my hand loosened, and finally the lights of the ambulance and police lit up the darkness. I took a deep breath.

The medics cared for the stranger. For Matt. I stood next to him, covered in blood and looking on in dismay. I wondered what would have happened if I hadn't been there at the right time and had the courage to intervene. He wouldn't just have died; he would have suffered a miserable death.

"Good evening," said a policeman.

"Not very," I replied.

"I'll need your details, and we'll have to speak to you again tomorrow. For a witness statement." He took out a small notebook, and I gave him my contact information and a brief description of what had happened.

"Where are you taking him?" the policeman asked one of the medics.

"To the University Hospital."

The policeman nodded.

Once I'd finished speaking, he looked around. "Just horrible. Every night it's the same. Someone looks at someone's girlfriend for too long, and boom…"

"This was something else."

"Was it?" he asked, adjusting his cap.

I lit a cigarette and looked up. The sky was so clear you could see Ursa Minor above.

"Well, in any case…" The policeman put the notebook away, wiped his nose, and handed me a business card. "Tomorrow morning you report to Scotland Yard."

Holmes makes it clear from the beginning that he is not happy with the work of Scotland Yard, to say the least. In his eyes, they lack the ability to bring together facts, leads, and an open mind. They seize upon the obvious and stop there. They're missing what Holmes calls the value of imagination. And they're too slow.

The ambulance and the police disappeared into the night, and I was left at the scene. The sudden silence crushed me. I was at loose ends. Returning to the real world after such an adrenaline rush felt impossible. But perhaps it was all over besides the witness statement. An extraordinary event that would fade into an ordinary night over time. Brawls were so common in this city, and this story wasn't material for my next publication. After all, Holmes hadn't arrived on the scene.

I tried thinking of the firmament, far away from everything that was happening. This usually reassured me, but it wasn't working. I was about to become self-reflective. *Heaven forbid.*

I started walking towards home, but kilometers later I was still thinking about the stranger.

"Got a penny for me?" asked someone with a broken voice. It

was a beggar I'd noticed outside Euston a few times but always passed. I stopped. My hands reached for my wallet, and I grasped a ten. The man accepted it gratefully.

"Is that blood on your clothes?"

I nodded.

"What happened? Can I help you? You punch someone?"

"No. Actually, yes," I replied.

"Boys will be boys. You can't change them."

"I guess so."

For some reason I sat down, and the man pressed a bottle of booze into my hand. We both stared at the empty street. Every now and then a cab drove past us and broke the silence.

"I failed in everything," I said.

"Typical suit with a tight tie, what?"

"Sure. Something like that."

The sky was still clear. I thought I could see the sun rising, but it was only the illuminated buildings and streetlights.

"So go on, what happened?" he asked, looking at my shirt.

I watched two cabs pass by and followed the lights until they could no longer be seen.

"There was a man. They beat him to porridge. I helped him."

"A hero, huh?"

I shook my head, took a drag of my cigarette, and felt a painful pull in my throat. The emotions I'd tried to suppress all day came to the surface.

"No reason to cry, bub," the man said. He handed me the bottle again.

My emotional filter was completely disabled. The tears ran down my cold face. They left a salty taste in my mouth, and I rinsed it away with the bitter liquid from the bottle.

"I'm not a hero. I'm not even a human being." *I'm certainly dramatic, however.*

"Superman isn't human either," he said.

I smiled and wiped my tears away with my shirtsleeve. "Alcohol is an asshole."

"Cheers to that." He lifted the bottle into the air. I passed him a cigarette. "You're okay," he said.

"Thank you, that's very kind."

"Why should I be unkind? We're all the same."

I picked a pebble up from the road and rolled it back and forth in my palm.

"We're not all the same," I said.

The man regarded me. "The only things that set us apart are how we treat people and how people pigeonhole us." He pulled his jacket shut. "We don't get to decide who we are. Others decide that for us. We are born as human beings. Flesh and blood. Then they tell us who we are and what value we have and what we have to do."

Maybe he was right. Maybe I knew it and was secretly afraid of it. "Getting cold," I said, rising to leave.

Five minutes later, I looked around and saw the University Hospital towering over me. I decided to walk to the station and wait for the Underground to open in the morning. The alcohol had wiped every thought of dirt and blood from my mind, so I wondered why the few people I passed stared at me.

The memory of the beaten man resting in my arms simply would not leave me. I could almost feel him, see him, smell his blood. That softness, that coldness. Those blue eyes. How badly was he hurt? My steps slowed until finally I stopped altogether. It was as if something held me to the spot. I searched for the flyer in my pocket and, while taking it out, pulled the old note, my eternal companion, along with it.

I looked over my shoulder. *I didn't choose to be the way I am; nor did the stranger whose life I might have saved.* The homeless man was right.

I turned around and walked to the hospital. As soon as the doors opened, the woman behind the registration desk stood up. "I'm okay," I said from a distance. She sat down again. "Has an emergency arrived the past hour?"

The woman sucked her teeth. "I can't give that information out,

I'm afraid. Unless…" She put on her reading glasses and looked at the computer. "What's your name?"

"Andrew Thomas," I said nervously.

"You're not a relative, then?"

I shook my head.

"Then there's nothing I—"

The doors to the emergency room opened. "You always meet twice," said a figure approaching me.

I recognized the policeman immediately. "How is he?" I asked.

The policeman sighed. "You can wait in the hallway. The doctor already gave me a piece for not sending you here as well." He filled out a form on the registration counter and handed it to the woman. "All right, that's it."

"You can go over there. I'll let the doctors know," the woman said, pointing to a door.

I sat down in the hallway beyond and waited anxiously for the doctors to appear. It was as if I were rooted there, staring at my broken watch. I let it dangle back and forth between my legs.

My phone vibrated. It was Mina.

"Andrew," she whispered, "it's perfect."

It was good to hear her voice. Tears started pricking my eyes again. "Is the distraction with you? You're even more drunk, aren't you?"

A giggle at the other end of the line. "He's in the living room. I'm in the bathroom. What should I do now?"

"No idea. Talk?" I asked hesitantly, peering down the hallway.

"Should I go back in wearing nothing but my knickers?"

"Which ones are you wearing?"

"You had your chance. Let me check." She giggled again, and I heard her putting the phone down. "Oh no. I shouldn't go out in these."

"Then go in naked," I suggested, lost in thought, restlessly tapping my fingers on my leg.

"Naked? Really? Okay."

"You're mad," I said. There was finally a hint of a smile on my face.

"No, I'm happy with a twist. Why are you still awake?" she whispered from a distance.

"I'm in the University Hospital."

She picked the phone back up. "What happened?"

"Can we meet tomorrow? I need to talk to you."

"What happened?" she repeated, her tone going serious.

"Let's talk tomorrow."

"I'm worried now. Are you okay? I can come over after…or let's meet tomorrow and watch one of our favorites? *Casablanca*, maybe?"

It filled me up with warmth to know I had her in my life. "I'm all right. I'll come around tomorrow. Please, don't worry. Have fun tonight. You deserve it. And don't forget your charger."

I hung up and continued to stare along the white hallway.

The story of Holmes and Watson also began in a hospital. A former colleague of Watson's told him about a stranger who worked in the chemical laboratory and was looking for a flatmate. It was the start of something unforgettable. *Maybe this is the only way I can meet people.*

A door opened. I jumped up. "How is he?" I asked eagerly.

The doctor had a serious look on her face. I had no idea that this was the beginning of a story which would end all that I was.

Again.

4

—◆—

The Return of Sherlock Holmes

I rushed towards the doctor.

"Is he all right?"

"He's going to be okay. He's lost a lot of blood, but he doesn't have to go to the intensive care unit. Fortunately, he doesn't appear to have any serious head injuries. He has one large puncture wound to the back of the head and several severe bruises. He would probably have bled to death without you."

I'd been holding my breath and finally exhaled. "Could you give him my number? I was the only witness. The police already have my details, but I would like to talk to him." *Smooth.*

The doctor handed me a pen. "But it's probably going to take some time for him to be able to make calls again."

I nodded and wrote my number on a piece of paper. "Can I go?" I asked uncertainly, feeling that I didn't really want to leave.

"Do you feel all right?" the doctor asked. "I could examine you. You're certainly in shock."

"Thank you, I…I'm well. I just need to eat something." In fact, I felt horrible.

The doctor fetched some water from a dispenser in the hall and sat down next to me. With trembling hands, I accepted the cup and forced a smile on my face.

"Can I?" she asked while touching the cold stethoscope to my chest. "Let me get something to calm you."

"I don't need anything," I lied, emptying the cup.

The doctor stared as if she knew there was something very wrong with me. I wished I could say: *I have lost my will to live; I need help.* But I couldn't.

"Get some sleep," she said with a sorrowful look on her face, already retreating.

Out of habit, I looked at my watch; its hands stood still. With slow steps, I left the building.

When I finally arrived home, I bent down, picked up my mail, and skimmed through the pile of paper. My doctor's letter, which I had been waiting days for, had not yet reached me. Instead, there were just more useless takeaway flyers.

I filled my bathtub with cold water and put my clothes in. I would probably never get the blood out of the wool trousers completely. It was then I realized I didn't have my jacket. This was one of my favorite suits. I looked wistfully at the sad, wet bundle in the tub. I tried to spread the fabric out; the water turned bright red. A metallic smell hung in the air. For a brief moment, I thought about coloring the suit black, but I'd always remember. It took some time to reach into the cold, dirty water and take the heavy wool into my hands. *I can't bin it. I have to bin it.*

Something soft touched my arm. My eternal companion swam to the surface. I took it, spread the paper carefully, and put it on the heater. Smeared with someone else's DNA, it lay there, its blurry words shouting: *Get rid of me, the past is not a place to stay in for too long.*

Some might say looking back is a waste of time, but I strongly believed that the past still had things it wanted to tell me. You could learn from it, laugh at it, and cry about it – though you could not live in it. I knew this, yet I clung desperately to my home there. The past defined the man I was.

My own thoughts had overwhelmed me again. It was because I

paid attention to every little one, no matter how negative, thinking to myself: *Ah there must be something to it.*

Once again, I knelt in front of the tub and reached into the broth of dirt and blood. My hands swiped the fabric. I looked at my arms, where I discovered small traces of blood. They were inconspicuous, almost transparent, and lay like a veil on my light skin. I salvaged the theater flyer and laid it next to my eternal companion to dry.

I winced. The endorphins coursing through me were doing little good. I didn't feel many of the so-called happiness hormones at that moment. My body was in terrible pain.

Clad only in my underwear and a dressing gown, I entered the kitchen, took a beer from the fridge, and lit a cigarette. I closed my eyes and let the smoke slowly glide over my lips. My pulse finally slowed down, and the metallic smell in my nose gradually disappeared. However, before giving myself some rest, I checked my phone one last time to see if Mina was all right. She'd left a voice message. The phone felt cold on my ear. "Hey, Dandy. Just wanted to let you know I got home safe. Hope you did too! Love you, babes." Positive news, *finally.*

I wandered into the living room and over to my music collection. When I was little, music was the only thing that could touch me. It miraculously brought forth emotions I'd buried deep in my heart. Even if I could only hear the whispering of something past, music was able to form a clear voice out of the whisper. She dug long-forgotten notes from the back corners of my mind and played them for me again. In fact, Holmes and I had one thing in common when it came to emotions: the love of music. If I heard good music, I felt alive. Unfortunately, the music I liked was made by people who were very much un-alive or would be soon, so I was somewhat concerned about the art form's future.

I chose a CD of Chopin's piano pieces, sat down, and tried to wipe away a bloodstain on my arm with some beer. I stared into the room. It was so quiet that every time I took a drag of my cigarette, I could hear the paper slowly burn down. Apart from the blood, it had turned out to be a beautiful evening. I was pleased that even more bottles of alcoholic liquids were waiting for me in the kitchen. I had finally found a strange inner calm, so I relocated to my study and sat down at my typewriter. There must be something to write about. Anything. I lit a cigarette. The blank page stared back at me. So much for my revenge publication.

A short while later, I had just closed the door of the fridge when I heard noises coming from the living room. They sounded like the steps of someone wearing hard-soled shoes. Then I heard a cup being gently placed on a saucer.

My heart stopped.

Whoever was playing a prank on me had definitely chosen the worst moment possible. I was sporting bloodstains, I'd just lost my job, and above all my best suit was ruined.

My left hand gripped the beer bottle. I took a deep breath and carefully approached the door to the living room, quietly opening it and slipping through. On closer inspection, I could not discover anything strange, so I reluctantly ventured further into the room.

The light from the streetlamps illuminated my bookshelves and the well-known drawing of Holmes' struggle with Professor Moriarty at the Reichenbach Falls. The picture showed a scene from "The Last Problem," the final case in the volume *The Memoirs of Sherlock Holmes*. The fight ends with the fatal fall of the two men. But as it turns out, Holmes is not dead at all. Instead, he leads a life under a pseudonym and spends some time in Tibet, among other things. This concept had become more and more interesting to me: to fake death and start again. To die without dying. A trick I wanted to learn.

In this light, the picture always achieved its best effect; some evenings I just sat there in the dark and looked at it. In the right mood, I could even hear the sound of the water clearly. It made me marvel at one of the most glorious men who had ever lived. Yes, lived, because of course he existed, and Doyle was in fact Watson. After his retirement, Holmes returned to rural Britain and became a beekeeper. Everyone knows this.

I was turning my thoughts from the picture to my typewriter again when I heard an unfamiliar voice say, "You forgot your jacket in the hospital."

In terror, I let the cold bottle fall from my hand. For the second time that night, I wasn't ready. The bottle shattered on the floor, and the beer pooled around my feet. I held my breath and hesitantly turned towards the voice.

My face must have been whiter than porcelain when I saw the stranger in my living room. But no – he was no stranger after all. I recognized the distinctive pale face immediately. Apparently, he wasn't busy beekeeping at all. He sat hunched on my reading chair and pierced me with his gaze. I was petrified as he calmly lit his pipe. My eyes blinked rapidly. I could smell tobacco and a fireplace. I didn't have a fireplace.

Maybe I was already dead.

"What's going on, old friend?" he asked, staring at me.

5

A Case of Madness

"I–"

"Sit down," Holmes interrupted me, pointing his pipe at my sofa.

Old friend. I wouldn't have thought he'd say that. Certainly not after everything I had written about him. I pressed two fingers against the artery in my neck to make sure I was still alive. There sat Holmes, straight from the imagination of Sidney Paget, calmly smoking his pipe.

I sat down, too, and hoped the illusion would disappear. My first meeting with Sherlock Holmes and I was in my underwear and an old dressing gown. I didn't know if this was the best or worst thing that could ever happen to me.

"What…how…" Scraps of words tumbled from my mouth.

"Surprised?" he asked, turning away briefly. His face was brightly illuminated, suggesting to me that he was in front of the fireplace at his Baker Street flat.

"A little bit, yes. After all, you're not real."

The Holmes in my living room had neither dark nor grey hair – it was a mixture of both. But his nose was unmistakable. A number of people had claimed I had the perfect Holmes nose, but when I looked at him, I realized that his was straight and pointed, whereas mine was tiny and round.

"It's an honor to meet you," I said. *Why not politely converse with your hallucination?*

"I'll take your case," Holmes replied without hesitation. He crossed his legs.

"What case?"

"Yours."

"I don't have a…case."

Again, his gaze seemed to pin me down. *I'm not one of his clients,* I thought. *I'm a researcher, and he's my subject – not the other way around. Oh, and he's not really here. That too.* I figured I may as well light a cigarette.

My Holmes looked back at the fire. That I did not have.

"You always eat dinner alone, you take people home late at night when you're drunk, and you send them away before dawn. You let them sleep on the hard sofa after you're done with them, while you sleep safe and sound in your bedroom."

"I…this is not…it's just that…" Hearing it out loud was shocking and embarrassing. But he was right. I was a master of impersonal naked encounters.

"You avoid all manner of relations when you are sober, and you have a meticulously maintained appearance. Your face is without blemishes, and your hair is faultless. Your hands…"

"What's wrong with them?" I looked at my pale fingers and well-manicured nails.

"Nothing. I'm just observing."

Again, he stared at me.

"When you entered the flat tonight, you lit a cigarette. You never smoke in your flat. That means you must have been very upset about something, apart from the blood on your clothes. You're afraid of something. Something just happened. Something that has shown you exactly that – that you are afraid. You have realized you are actually afraid for your life, contrary to your own logic. But why now? The first step will be to understand this fear."

Of course he was right. I shut my lids briefly and saw the blood and blue eyes in front of me again. The gentle face bathed in red. I heard his soft words. I felt his slowing breath. The body that had rested on mine. *Why am I so afraid?*

The fact that Sherlock Holmes was sitting in the armchair in front of me proved what stress and alcohol could do. I didn't have to be a famous detective to deduce that.

"There is no case to solve here," I said, flashing an unsettled smile.

"You consulted me," Holmes replied.

I wondered why a creature of my own imagination was being so persistent. If I was thinking him up, the least he could do was stop working against me.

"I didn't consult you. You just turned up."

"Sure?" my visitor asked. There was the hint of a smile on his narrow lips.

It was hard for me to think clearly, and I didn't know what to do next. With every drag of my cigarette, I inhaled deeper, hoping to calm down. It could be no coincidence that this rational observer appeared on the very evening my orderly life was thrown into disarray.

"We're going to need a good strategy to trick your stubborn head," Holmes said, pulling his knees tightly back to his body.

Or simply drugs. I suspected someone of sprinkling cocaine on the peanuts in the pub.

"I'm actually very happy," I said. "Perfectly fine. Your services are not required. I'm just going to need a few days of rest, and then everything will be back to normal."

"Sharing a secret means getting rid of something. The space that the secret has occupied in your head can be used for something new," Holmes said. He continued smoking his pipe.

I didn't understand a word of this. *Am I being psychoanalyzed by Sherlock Holmes?* It almost seemed that my rational, academic self had defected and was now sitting opposite me. Again, I looked at the blood on my arms. I wondered who the man on the street was.

I knew his name but nothing else. Except that he liked theater too.

The clock on the shelf showed it was already after four. Since I no longer had a job and was therefore divested of all responsibilities, I didn't care about the hour. I decided to pour a gin and listen to music with Sherlock Holmes until the sun rose. I chose Mendelssohn's Violin Concerto in E minor, Op. 64, to the delight of my guest.

Felix Mendelssohn-Bartholdy was an important figure in the Victorian era. Watson was so impressed by Mendelssohn's compositions that he asked his flatmate to play some pieces for him on the violin. When I asked Mina, she fled our flat in despair. Sherlock Holmes, however, loved the violin. He owned a Stradivarius, which I knew from a quick internet search was more expensive than all my possessions combined. He famously bought it from a pawnbroker in Tottenham Court Road for a few shillings. My own memories of learning to play an instrument are rather traumatic. Piano. Many neighbors were harmed in the process.

My visitor closed his eyes. There was still a hint of a smile on his face. With a sudden clarity of purpose, or perhaps the fog of drunkenness, I thought, *Why not. Let's solve my case. I'll see if I can pencil it in.* Although I didn't know at that time exactly what the case was, I trusted Holmes' instincts more than those of any other person, including myself.

I could have observed him for hours. As he sat listening to the soft sounds and gleefully smoking his pipe, his every little movement captivated me. My grandfather had also smoked pipes. I remembered him sitting in his armchair every Sunday after church, calmly smoking. He didn't talk much, but when I spoke, he listened and smiled from time to time. He was the father I would have liked to have, but he died when I was only eight years old. My parents did not allow me to attend the funeral. They were afraid a child might disturb the burial.

My head hurt, my hands were wet, and my mouth was dry. I had a hangover.

Shivering and struggling to sit upright on the sofa, I noticed I was still in my dressing gown and underwear. There was ash on the table and I was annoyed that I'd smoked in my flat. I equated this behavior with complete loss of control, and this mental connection made me remember my nocturnal visitor. Those endorphins must have done something. I had a conversation with Sherlock Holmes. He'd seemed a bit off, but he'd looked just like I had imagined him. And I had been imagining him all my life.

I got up from the sofa and tried to balance my body. It wanted to go in a different direction than my head commanded, so I had to hold on to the living room door. There was clearly enough alcohol left in my system to have me zigzagging the rest of the day. I directed my feet to the bathroom and was greeted by a bathtub full of bloody water. *Oh. Right.*

When the mixture had finally disappeared down the drain, I took the shower head, washed away the last blood remnants, and put my sodden clothes in the bin. The smell was so outrageous I had to turn my head away and gag. In doing so, my eye landed on the heater.

I bent down and picked up the little note, which was by now brown. The words were blurrier than ever, but I still knew exactly what they said and muttered them quietly to myself: *I don't know what I am and I don't know what I want. I don't know who I can be and I don't know who I was.*

As I undressed, I found bruises from the fight. I'm opposed to physical violence, and seeing a man suffer like Matt had made me feel awful. My Dracula Holmes fantasies were always violent – probably an outlet for feelings I had never learned to properly deal with. However, I could never physically harm anyone in real life. I still think of the innocent bee I accidentally killed with my bike when I was six. I named her Bumble, and a funeral was held.

I got into the shower and closed my eyes, letting the warm water run over my face and envelop my body. Thoughts drifted through my mind like ghosts, and for the first time in over fifteen years, I remembered his voice. I hadn't heard it for so long that at some point it had just disappeared. But now it was as clear as if he were standing right in front of me again: *I wish someone could understand what I am, what I want, who I can be, and who I was.* There are people in our lives who we will never escape from. They are burnt into our minds and control us whenever we are weak. Some for the better, some for the worse.

Getting rid of my secret was easier said than done. I didn't know how or when to start. It was too heavy, as simple as it was. I'd been pushing it away for years, and I wanted to keep doing that until it just didn't exist anymore – until the day of my death. Why open the case? Even the most enthusiastic Holmes fans wouldn't read *The Man Who Fought with Himself*. Or should it be *A Case of Madness*? It was no case at all.

I switched the warm water to cold. It helped me think more clearly. My desire for control fought with my doubts. Control meant safety; doubts meant pain. I breathed in deeply, still rattled by the previous evening. Again, I saw the blood running down the street and the blue eyes penetrating me. I felt his shivering body on mine and the grip of his fingers getting weaker. Why did I suddenly care so much about a stranger? I had never believed in fate, yet the proceedings of that night were the biggest sign I had ever seen in my life.

But of what? I had no idea.

After drying off and wrapping a towel around my hips, I confronted myself in the mirror. I was about to apply my shaving foam when I was interrupted by a persistent knocking at my front door.

"Thank heavens! You're alive!" said my neighbor opposite once I'd thrown open the door. He seemed genuinely surprised to see me.

"Why wouldn't I be?"

"Because of all this mess," he said, gesturing along the hallway. The grey stones were smeared with blood, there were cigarette butts lying everywhere, and to top it all, there was an imprint of a bloody hand on my door.

"Oh, that…" I said casually. "I…uhm…I went fishing."

"In London? In the middle of the night?" He clutched his phone and appeared ready to call in emergency services.

A violin playing a quiet melody met my ear, and I remembered my visitor. The other one. I carefully looked over my shoulder into the flat.

"Is there someone holding you captive?" whispered my neighbor. "I can call–"

"What? No…" I looked over my shoulder again. A shadow moved along the wall behind me. I swiftly closed the door halfway.

"Are you sure you're all right?"

"Look, I have kind of a thing going on here. So, let's talk some other time, if you don't mind." I was still peering nervously into my flat.

"A thing?" he asked suspiciously.

Great, now I look like the kidnapper.

"All good. I'll take care of this," I assured him, pointing vaguely at the blood and cigarette butts. Thankfully, he left without interrogating me further.

Thinking I might have forgotten to turn off the music the night before, and hoping that I hadn't really seen a shadow, I went into my living room. When I saw who was standing in front of my window, I was relieved the towel was still wrapped around my hips. My heart raced. *I'm fully conscious. I haven't taken any medications. There can't be* that *much alcohol left in my system.*

There wasn't any reasonable explanation for what I saw and heard. Holmes was still here. And he was holding a violin.

I listened to the melody and identified the music as "The Tales of Hoffman" by Jacques Offenbach. I remembered how Sherlock Holmes had tricked his adversaries in "The Adventure of the Mazarin Stone" by pretending to play this piece in another room. In that case, the music actually came from a gramophone, so Holmes was able to listen to a conversation that led to the resolution of the case. I stared at him and forgot that he was an illusion. He played the melody to the end and turned to me.

"Any news about the case?" he asked calmly, putting the violin aside.

I shook my head and made sure that the towel stayed where it was.

"The nucleus accumbens in your brain is currently highly active, probably due to adrenaline and cortisol, and your hypothalamus is rather active as well."

I didn't get a word of that. "What exactly is this about?" My towel slid down, but I grabbed it before I could reveal anything I didn't want to show my literary hero. After all, it was only the second time I had met him; we ought to take things slow.

"You've looked at your phone at least four times since waking, your heartbeat is increased, you cannot organize your thoughts, and your mood is fluctuating."

I leaned against the door frame. *How does Sherlock Holmes know what a mobile phone is?* My brain seemed to be running amok, and I cast a questioning gaze at my visitor.

"It's obvious," he said, taking the violin in his hands again.

Obvious that I've suffered irreparable brain damage from the brawl.

He was about to play his violin again when he said what I didn't want to hear. "You're in love."

"I'm not," I replied. Almost before he'd uttered the sentence.

"When you have eliminated the impossible, whatever remains, however improbable, must be the truth."

Maybe I'm in a nice coma. I couldn't even tell if I had ever been in love. I should have been. After all, I was married once. "Love means nothing but chaos and suffering."

"And that's where you are wrong, my dear Andrew."

"I would have to get hit by a bus to change my mind about that."

"A bus?"

"Yes, a bus. A giant London double-decker bus."

"That's arrangeable."

"What?" I looked at him, confused. "No, Holmes. No. Just let it be."

"Love means seeing beauty that blooms, even amidst the chaos and suffering."

"Norbury," I said with confidence. A word that Dr Watson used when Sherlock Holmes had overestimated himself or put too little effort into a case.

Holmes appeared insulted. He put the violin aside again and walked towards me. "You tap the door frame nervously. You blink more than usual, and your pupils are dilated. You're lying."

It was clear that from now on I would have to monitor my body language and facial expressions to hide things from this man. *From this man I'm hallucinating.*

"But I also see you are concerned...no...you are afraid," he said, almost hesitantly. "As I explained last evening, you have certain fears to conquer."

"Your brilliant mind hasn't figured out anything else in the past eight hours?" I was feeling slightly superior. I crossed my arms, but the towel slid down again. So much for superiority.

Holmes' grey eyes lit up. "We will solve the case," he said firmly.

"What case exactly?" I asked, but he disappeared as suddenly as he had arrived. I had lost my sanity and the towel around my hips.

6

—◆—

The Dancing Men

I checked my phone again and threw it on the bed. Sherlock Holmes was wrong – however ridiculous this sounded to me, the man was never wrong. Often, his deductions were merely conjectures, but they mostly turned out to be correct. Sherlock Holmes displayed a self-confidence I would have liked to possess. To be fair, he wasn't keen on being with people either, but still.

Some people claim that his deductions and conclusions, even his cases, are completely far-fetched, eyebrow-raising, and illogical. These people do not understand the principles of fiction. Maybe my obsession makes me think like that, but no one complains about *The Hobbit* being a bad book because Hobbits don't exist.

Because Holmes had been right about certain things that morning, I was already devising several ways to get rid of him. I didn't want anyone, even Sherlock Holmes himself, roaming through my thoughts. To make matters worse, this Holmes was a creation of my own mind, so he would inevitably know what could be found in the hidden corners of my brain and heart. *I could move flats, but he might follow me. Perhaps I could simply tell him to go and never come back?* He seemed like a man of good manners, so I was sure that he would understand. I laughed. *I'm preparing a speech asking my own mind to leave me alone.*

In my tired state, I returned to my study. There was definitely something to write about now, but I felt unable to put it down on paper. Instead, I decided to enlist Dracula Holmes to help me take my revenge. I began to type: *Dracula Holmes – By Andrew Thomas. The fleeting fog revealed a skinny figure at the Florentine fountain.* Again, I stared at the page.

The sound of my phone ripped me from my thoughts. I rushed to my bedroom and felt a slight disappointment.

"Hello, Mina."

"Andrew…" said a suffering voice at the other end.

I noticed my heart beating faster and took a breath to calm down.

"You sound catastrophic," I said.

"Shit, I have the worst hangover ever, and you know what's even worse? I looked at the present for my niece again. They wrapped it in pastel paper. Pastel, Andrew. The world is against me."

I walked to my closet and reached for a tie. Pain shot through my body. I grabbed my side and remembered the agonizing kick in the kidneys I'd sustained.

"You have to drink a lot of water and eat something," I said, taking a dark blue suit and a matching vest out of the closet. "And pastel isn't bad. At least for a baby."

She sighed. "I can't move."

"You can. You just called me," I replied. The blue suit wandered back into the closet, and I chose a fresh grey instead.

"The beautiful man in the suit wasn't perfect," Mina whispered, as if these were her last words.

I tried to put on my socks while keeping the phone stuck between my head and shoulder. At my age and with my aversion to sport, this amounted to a gymnastic exercise.

"I can see your old pattern," I said, getting a cramp in my calf. I tried to stretch out my leg and lay down on the bed.

"You're coming by today, right?" she asked. "*Casablanca?*"

I took a deep breath and massaged my leg. "I have to go to Scotland Yard today. Because of last night. And then I have to get my things from the office. And I'm still waiting for a call." I hoped she wouldn't ask whose call I was waiting for, because I wasn't able to explain why I was waiting for it at that point.

"Scotland Yard?" Her voice suddenly sounded clear and awake.

I breathed in deeply. "That's where you have to go after a crime, don't you?"

"Why all the effort?"

I tried to put on my sock again. "I'll find out right away."

"Are you the new Batman of London?"

"No, I'm poor." The sock was finally where it should be. "I'll come by later," I promised.

"Bring your phone charger. And coffee. Just describe me when you order it."

I laughed. "Dark, bitter, and too hot, I remember."

"Exactly!"

She clearly knew how to get what she wanted.

After getting dressed and having breakfast, I made my way to the address the policeman had given me the previous night: No. 8-10 Broadway, in a side street off Victoria Street. Those who committed a crime went to jail, and those who witnessed or wanted to report a crime went to the building with the well-known rotating sign: New Scotland Yard.

I was just walking down the steps to the Mile End station when my phone vibrated. It was an unknown number. I climbed up a few steps and answered.

"Hi…this is Matt…uhm…Matthew Lewis." He stopped speaking, and for a moment there was an unbearable silence on the line. "I don't know what to say now."

I didn't know either.

Around me, tourists chatted and buses passed. I plugged my right ear with my finger to hear him better.

"Hi, Matt," I said, and we fell silent again. I must have looked like Colin Farrell in *Phone Booth*, because I received numerous concerned and confused glances. I swallowed hard.

Matt laughed. "I suppose I should apologize for so rudely fainting in your arms."

"That's probably my natural effect on people." I grabbed the cigarette pack in my pocket and tried to get one out single-handed. I failed and dropped several on the steps.

"I really must thank you," Matt said. His voice was calm and had something impish and cheeky to it. I wouldn't have guessed he had been severely injured the night before. "What's your name?"

"I'm well, thank you."

He laughed out loud. "Your name. What's your name?"

"I'm sorry." My breakfast began to dance in my stomach. "Andrew…Andrew Thomas."

"Well, Andrew, are you going to visit me in hospital? I should get to know my savior." He laughed again.

I hesitated. Holmes had said getting rid of my secret would make room for something new. I repeated this in my head but didn't know what to do, let alone whether a meeting with Matt would help me with my questions. My hands began to sweat.

"Still there?" asked Matt.

"Yes, yes, of course. I can come over. I just have to do something first." I was almost proud of my quick acceptance. Usually, I was as spontaneous as a bus schedule.

"Put on your best dress, we will dine in the fanciest hospital in London," he joked.

"I've…but I've only got suits?"

"I meant dress as in attire," he said kindly.

"Well then, I'll come by later," I replied before abruptly hanging up.

Phone calls were always a trial. Introverts text. *There is nothing that isn't textable.*

My hands were shaking as I put the phone back in my pocket. For a moment I stood there in a bubble, hearing and seeing nothing around me. It was as if life in London had stopped, and I was light as air. Then I heard voices, sirens, and music. Reality came crashing down. My cough was getting worse, the blood I coughed up was growing darker, and I wanted to decide: suicide or cancer.

I thought I had known the answer. But now something was ignited in me; something was trying to convince me to continue, no matter how hard the path ahead might be.

I took out my eternal companion and looked at it in awe. *I don't know what I am and I don't know what I want. I don't know who I can be and I don't know who I was.* The words echoed in my mind.

I climbed into a full carriage on the District Line, one of the oldest of London's Underground system. Even as a child I could remember all the stops because of the tiles. They were designed differently in each station, with symbols representing the immediate vicinity. Warren is an outdated English term for labyrinth, so the Warren Street station has a kind of puzzle on the wall, which waiting passengers can solve. I wondered what an Andrew Thomas Street station tile would look like. *A nice pen?* I got out at Euston. Despite its current bleak appearance, it's the second oldest station in London. Arguably, the oldest is Deptford, built in 1836. I wondered if Holmes had ever been.

I made my way out of the crowded Underground and lit a cigarette. In Westminster it feels like people are stacked on top of each other. You hear loud voices shouting from all directions in different languages, and no one looks at you. Those who begin their visit to Westminster Bridge with a bag will most likely finish it without one. If you dislike human interaction, you should avoid Westminster – simply because of Parliament.

I struggled through the mass of people, trying not to burn anyone with my cigarette. The crowd pushed me to the side, and I was forced to walk along a wall until a bright orange booth blocked my path.

"Do you want to donate?" a young woman asked, approaching me.

I took a step back. "No, sorry…I'm in a hurry."

"You can never be in too much of a hurry to help others." She flashed an optimistic grin that made me nervous.

"I'm in a hurry. I have an appointment," I said, but I stopped regardless. My hands rummaged through various flyers, pins, and pens. I like pens.

"Even with a small donation a month, you can help. We're fighting the stigma of HIV and helping people who need medical assistance."

"I can't be late," I explained, absently grabbing a few pens. I succeeded in knocking almost all the flyers to the ground.

"Education is key," the woman continued.

I bent down to pick up the flyers and put them back on the table. "Yes. Yes. Indeed. Does it cost?"

"A small donation, yes."

"Define small," I said, finally putting four pens into my pocket.

"That's totally up to you."

I wanted to leave with my pens immediately.

"You'll get more pens," she said, laughing.

My face turned hot, and I had to laugh too.

"Why not take a flyer with you and get back to us?"

I nodded and accepted the offer. Then I hustled away as quickly as possible, my face still burning.

Sherlock Holmes and Dr Watson rarely visited Scotland Yard. Instead, they met with police officers in Baker Street or at crime scenes whenever a particularly difficult case had foiled the authorities. This is further proof of the brilliant spirit Holmes possessed. When the police could find no way forward, he was consulted. I was summoned that day because I knew something – not because I was a genius, and not because I was on a quest for justice and enlightenment like Holmes. I was, however, anxious that the facts should be presented exactly as they were.

Inspector Lestrade was probably the most famous police officer in the Holmes cases. His relationship with Holmes can best be characterized as a mixture of respect, love, hate, and friendship. A relationship that was similar to my own with Holmes. But whereas I was trying to keep the great detective out of my head, Lestrade had grown to appreciate Holmes' approach, despite making a sarcastic comment every now and then. I'd often wondered what the inspector's first name was, because the only reference to it appears in "The Adventure of the Cardboard Box." In that case, he ends a message to Holmes with the words: "Your very devoted G. Lestrade." I'd always bet on George because I like the sound of the name.

I entered New Scotland Yard and stopped at the front desk. "I'm here to give my testimony."

The woman behind the desk looked at me sternly. "Who summoned you?"

"I…erm…" *I summoned Holmes, but who summoned me?*

"Did you get a card?"

I pulled out the policeman's business card and slid it towards her.

"Wait. I'll call him," she said, picking up the phone.

I tapped my fingers on the counter.

"Inspector Riley is on sick leave. Inspector Adams will go through everything with you. Room H201."

I thanked her. She nodded grimly and returned her focus to the documents on the desk.

I started searching for the room and had to wait at the lifts. I couldn't be in a lift filled with people – or worse, filled with one person. After five minutes I finally found one that was empty. To my surprise, my search then led me to a kind of open-plan office. I scanned the sea of name tags.

"Mr Thomas?" a tall woman asked, reaching out her hand to me.

I nodded but ignored the outstretched hand.

"DI Adams. Please follow me." She pulled her hand away.

Hands are a veritable biotope for countless bacterial species; if they've touched a computer keyboard, the biotope is twice as large. I wasn't obsessed with washing, but I never liked shaking the hands of wild strangers. The fact that I had bathed in a stranger's blood the night before sent a shiver down my spine.

The DI's office was at the end of the large room. As we walked, we were accompanied by eyes peering over computers.

"Please sit down," she said, closing the glass door with a loud thud. "May I offer you a drink?"

I shook my head and fumbled for the chair. The peering eyes had made me restless, but I was determined to relate what I'd witnessed without embarrassing myself. Visions of Holmes dazzling the police danced through my head. *That's aiming a bit high.*

She sat down opposite and pushed a document over to me. "Please see if all the information is correct. Date of birth… address. Don't forget the signature."

I nodded, went through everything carefully, and signed.

"Can you show me exactly where you were when you discovered what was happening?" she asked, pointing to a map laid out on the table in front of me.

I tried to remember which street I was coming from when I'd heard the voices. The fact that I couldn't remember was unusual. And embarrassing.

"Did you arrive after the fight started?"

"Yes, yes, of course," I said, staring further at the map.

"There is no reason to be nervous, Mr Thomas," she said, and her calm voice and smile helped a little.

From the corner of my eye, I saw a third person appear. He was leaning against the wall. I looked carefully to the side and swallowed. *Not now. Not in a police station.* Trying to ignore Holmes, I focused on the map.

"Are you okay?" asked DI Adams. She stood up to fetch a glass of water for me.

"I am." *And I'm going to appear excessively normal if it's the last thing I do.*

"I'm glad you're not one of those bloody reporters trying to blow up this case." She set the water in front of me. "These days, everyone wants a bit of fame. Anyway. Do you know where you were?"

I took a sip of water and wondered what she meant about fame. *Mafia boss?* Meanwhile, my memory was still at large.

"Was the street narrow or wide?" asked Holmes from the left.

I tried not to glance at him. The street was more of an alley, I remembered. I began looking for the narrowest street near the crime scene.

"The entrance to the club was facing this street?" added Holmes in a calm voice.

I thought about it and came to the conclusion that it could have indeed been this street. My finger tapped on the map.

"Good. And then you saw exactly what?" the DI asked.

I smelled tobacco and looked carefully to the side. Holmes was still leaning against the wall, but now his eyes were closed and he was smoking a pipe.

"Mr Thomas?"

"Oh…excuse me. I…I…I saw four men standing around something. It wasn't until I got closer that I saw it was a man. He was lying on the ground and was apparently unconscious."

"Did you know the man?"

"No. Well, I'd seen him earlier in the day. Putting up flyers. Just outside my university. Well, my former university."

"So do you or do you not know him?"

"No, I don't. Not really. He likes theater, I think?"

"This information is not relevant to the interview," noted Holmes.

"Okay, we can move on. Did you approach them?" the DI asked.

"No. Well, yes, I was trying to draw attention to myself. Only one of them came over to me, though."

"Can you describe the man who came over to you?"

My brilliant spirit could of course not. It was almost as if the memories of the night were blurred, if not partially erased. I looked tentatively in the direction of Holmes.

"The man hit you with his head. Did he have to stand on his toes? Or did the blow come from above?" he asked, scratching his forehead.

"He was a little smaller than me," I said as my memory of the man returned. I was just trying to describe him in detail to the DI when she pushed a photograph towards me.

"Is this him?" she asked.

I looked closely at the picture. "That's exactly the man. He broke my pocket watch."

I heard a groan from the left.

"It's very valuable," I said.

"Life is too." She took the picture back. "What about the others? Can you describe the other men?"

I looked helplessly to my left, but Holmes was gone.

"No. Unfortunately not," I said.

"That's a shame. The one in the photo was captured by CCTV near the crime scene."

"What sort of sentence will he get?"

"He'll probably be charged with grievous bodily harm."

My fingers started tapping nervously on the back of the chair, making the sort of repetitive noise that usually set me on edge. I took a deep breath, trying to stop images of the beating from reappearing in my head. Unlike my Dracula Holmes fantasies, these images were real and therefore horrifying.

"Is there anything I can do for you?" the DI asked as she stood up. She opened the door and smiled. "You saved a life."

"That I would ever experience this…" I said, rising.

Her gaze followed me as I left the room. "I hope this won't get bigger than necessary. They're all going nuts already," she said in a muted voice, pointing at the rows of desks outside her office.

"Why exactly?"

I was struck by her questioning glance.

"Well, why am I here?" I persisted. "I gave my testimony yesterday. Why a witness statement at all?"

"You really don't know?" DI Adams was astonished. "Yesterday, you saved a member of a very well-known family. The media is full of it."

"What family?" I asked, fearing I might have saved a royal.

DI Adams pointed towards the exit. "I've said too much. Good day, Mr Thomas."

I nodded and left, passing the sea of eyes again. They stayed on me as I waited for the lift, and I was relieved to step into it. Just as I'd said to myself that I would never go for a drink with Mina again, the lift stopped. I pressed the buttons, but they didn't do a thing. *Of course this would happen.* I had to laugh.

My gaze fell on the mirror. In the lower right corner, there were sketches of stickmen. Not any stickmen. They were the dancing men from one of Holmes' cases. In it, a landlord consults the famous detective because his wife's been receiving mysterious messages which consist only of dancing men. The little stick figures drive them to despair, and only one person can solve the case.

It had been a long time since I'd last dealt with the dancing men, but as Holmes noted in the case, what one person can invent can be unraveled by another. I inspected the stickmen. My heart raced as I tried to remember how to read them. My inner geek was more alive than ever. Gradually, the trick of it came back to me, and I deciphered the message. I was sure that Holmes wanted to tell me something, given how well we'd worked together in the interview. Finished with praising myself, I couldn't believe what I was actually reading. The dancing men represented two words: *blind idiot.*

The lift opened, and three non-stickmen looked at me inquiringly. The sketches were gone from the mirror. Laughing, I left New Scotland Yard. I had just been insulted by Sherlock Holmes, which in my case meant I had just insulted myself.

As soon as I set foot in the full streets again, I lit a cigarette. I looked up into the bright blue sky and decided to take a detour through St James' Park to get to the Green Park station. To be precise, it was a significant detour, but the ultimate destination was my former workplace, and I knew there was a meeting until at least one o'clock. For obvious reasons, I really didn't want to see any faces I knew. I pinned my hopes on a mass lunch exodus.

I pushed my way through the crowds and approached the place I had worked in for over twelve years. There were still some pictures and documents in my office that I did not want to leave to the university voluntarily. Mina had eyed a wonderful drawing of Sherlock Holmes. In it, he was sitting huddled on an armchair and smoking a pipe with his eyes closed. This drawing was not an original by Sidney Paget, but it was a precious copy of *The Strand Magazine*, housed behind glass. I would have given it away under no circumstances – except over my dead body. Even then, I would probably try to take it with me. I didn't know why Mina was so keen on it. She barely knew Holmes.

I quickly put the picture she loved so much in the box with everything else, closed my office door a final time, and looked around for the department's secretary to hand her the keys.

While walking outside I thought about my visit to Scotland Yard and got incredibly nervous. The fact that the media was involved unnerved me. I wondered whose life I'd saved. Who was the bleeding flyer man in colorful trainers? I was about to find out.

7

———

The Deputy Mayor Mystery

My mouth got drier and drier as I approached the hospital, and my fingers nearly crushed the cardboard box in my hands. There was cold sweat on my forehead. It was either fear or food poisoning – but by no means was it what Sherlock Holmes had claimed. I bet on food poisoning. *Bloody chicken wrap*.

At the traffic signal, I thought about turning back and making an excuse, but when it turned green I was dragged along by the crowd. Once a London crowd is in motion, it's hard to escape, especially with a heavy box in your hands. As recently as four hundred years ago, the Euston Road area consisted of fields and farmland. The busy thoroughfare was originally designed to move sheep and cattle to Smithfield Market without having to use Oxford Street. It's hard to imagine cattle being driven past the expensive shops, though today's crowds are similarly herded between the buildings and railway stops.

Before I walked into the hospital, I paused and straightened my tie. While doing so, I thought of another explanation for recent events: hypnosis. Someone in the pub must have hypnotized me. I picked the box up again, pressed it firmly to my body, and let my feet carry me into the giant glass building.

"I'm looking for Matthew Lewis' room," I said at the registration desk.

A young woman with blond hair glanced at me. "What's your name?"

"Andrew Thomas."

She bombastically typed on her computer. "You're not on the list."

"But I rescued him," I said hesitantly.

"What?"

"I called the ambulance last night."

"Sorry!" she said, bombastically.

"You're the man who called the ambulance?" asked a warm voice.

I turned around. In front of me stood a tall, Black woman who looked like an advertisement for the fair sex. Her black hair reached to her hips, and her eyes were without doubt the second most beautiful I had ever seen in a woman.

"Hi, I'm Beverly, but please call me Bev," she said, reaching out her hand.

I quickly battled my aversion to handshakes and won. "I'm Andrew Thomas."

"Have you seen? The case is breaking the internet."

"How can one break a non-physical thing?"

She looked at me, confused. "Well, it's going…viral? You know? It's…" She searched for a word. "Popular?"

Bev swiped around on her phone and held the screen under my nose. A quick Google search indicated that the case was indeed much discussed. Though it was hard for me to find my way through the confusion of text, I pieced together that this had hit the morning news. Apparently, *The Sun* wanted my contact details. *The Sun?* I was slightly disgusted.

"So, I created a virus?" I asked.

Bev laughed. It seemed I had a natural if unintentional talent for stand-up comedy.

"No, it just means that this news spread *like* a virus." She quickly and correctly guessed my level of technological engagement. "You know, everyone is talking about it," she explained, tapping the screen. I was up to date again. I briefly considered asking Mina to instruct me on social media use. I had to be closer to death than I had feared.

"Do you watch TV?" Bev asked, scribbling something on a piece of paper. It looked like a sign and a name.

"No. Not too often. I work a lot. What's this?" I asked as she handed me the paper.

"This is Matt's Instagram."

Although I didn't know what to do with it, I put the paper in my pocket and hoped to be enlightened later.

"Are you friends?" I asked.

"I live with him."

"Oh, so you're his girlfriend?"

Bev laughed. "Oh my god, no. He's single, well, kind of, if you're concerned."

"I am concerned, but not about this."

"Take this form," said Bev. "Show it, and they'll let you in."

I looked at the form in confusion. "Why do I need this?"

Bev stared at me in amazement. "Otherwise, anyone can just march in. Which is not exactly in the interest of Matt or his family."

I remembered the words of DI Adams and finally grabbed my chance to find out what made Matthew Lewis so special. Besides his blue eyes.

"As you might have gathered, I'm not highly familiar with social media or modern media in general…" I started cautiously.

"Oh, you want to know why there's so much fuss about a boy you picked up on the street?"

Not particularly, but yes.

Bev pointed to a screen in the adjacent waiting room. The man on it was none other than Michael Lewis. I had to swallow. No one in England could get around reading one of his books at school, and he described himself as the most important export the country had ever produced. His wife was probably his biggest competition in that regard. She was none other than the CEO of one of the most luxurious hotel chains in the world. Saying they were wealthy and well-known would have been an absolute understatement. In terms of exports, they certainly outranked Marmite, anyway.

"His parents are grateful to you. But don't expect them to contact you. They're busy. As usual."

I nodded. Too busy to meet the man who saved your son's life? *Soap opera material.*

"But Matt will be happy to see you," she said, patting my shoulder before walking to the exit. I considered following her for a moment. But it was time for me to meet the man I had saved. Properly this time.

As the doors of the lift closed, I could clearly see the signs of last night in the mirror. My hair still looked like a mess, my eyes were red, and my skin was unnervingly pale. In a state of pure panic, I pressed the button for the ground floor once the doors to Matt's floor opened.

"That picture was drawn during the very curious case of Mr Jabez Wilson. I remember well," said a familiar voice, and the lift stopped.

I dropped my box in terror. A few documents scattered across the floor, but luckily my precious picture was unharmed.

"Please stop popping in like this," I said.

Holmes stood smiling, arms crossed, in front of me. "I was with you the whole time."

"You weren't. I haven't seen you since…" *Since you questioned me at a police station? In front of the actual police?* I knelt down to pick up the papers, trying to reassert reality.

"Not seeing something doesn't mean it doesn't exist," Holmes said. He looked at the blinking lift buttons and pressed them all at once. A loud noise rang out.

"You're such a smart one." After depositing a few documents back into the box, I quickly wiped the framed picture with my sleeve. It was much dirtier than I would have expected, so I had to rub my arm against my leg to get rid of the beggars' velvet.

"You will meet with the man now?" He'd bent down and was

riffling through the rest of my disorganized documents on the ground, raising an eyebrow from time to time.

"The man is named Matthew Lewis." A strange feeling came over me when I uttered his name. "But I've just decided not to go."

"That won't bring us forward," said Holmes, still examining my work with an arrogant look on his face.

"What do you mean exactly?" I continued dropping the lost papers into the box.

"Well, you have to find out."

"Is all this even necessary?" I had the feeling I wouldn't be able to shroud myself in ignorance for much longer. This made me anxious.

"If it wasn't necessary, you wouldn't have consulted me."

"I didn't–" I fell silent at Holmes' stern look, remembering that we had already discussed this point. *I might have conjured you up, but that doesn't mean I need your help.*

"I believe you're in great need of my help," he said.

I jumped. Had he responded to my words or my thoughts? The latter was unnerving, even for a hallucination. *Don't think anything weird.*

"You know, if everyone could analyze themselves as well as they can analyze others, we would all lead better lives," Holmes said. "But most of the time we are strangers to ourselves. The person you should know best is often not even recognizable in a mirror." He gazed at the picture of himself.

The Sherlock Holmes cases are full of contradictions, and so is the protagonist himself. I might know his cases by heart, but the man is still a mystery to me. He is sometimes a savior, maybe even a hero, and sometimes a depressive drug addict.

"I know myself well," I said, contradicting him.

"If you hold your watch in your hand, you know it. You know what the material feels like, how it is designed, and you may even recognize the sound of the ticking and be able to distinguish it from that of any other watch. You are used to this watch; you take it with you every day. But the really interesting thing is inside it. Only when you open it will you learn how the watch works, what hidden mechanisms power it, what sound it makes without its protective glass. Do you really know yourself?"

I thought of my broken pocket watch. Although it was destroyed, I still kept it with me and would have never thought of doing otherwise. Leaving the watch behind would have equaled the loss of a whole life path. What Holmes didn't understand was that I knew myself but didn't want to. I knew exactly what was behind the glass: my antagonist. And that antagonist couldn't be held captive for much longer.

"Do you really know *your*self?" I asked Holmes.

"Knowing oneself is the first step towards leading an honest and peaceful life."

"You haven't answered my question."

"What was it again?"

I finally picked up the box. *Don't think that I'm naïve, Holmes.*

"A really complicated case," I said, to trick him back into the conversation, but when I looked up from the picture in my box, the detective had already disappeared. I was still able to perceive the scent of tobacco, and I closed my eyes for a moment.

The doors opened again. Time to make a decision. Whatever I was doing there, it was as if an invisible force pushed me to do it. This force held my shoulders and propelled me meters further down the hallway. The smell of food and disinfectant was overpowering. With each step, my shoes produced a squeaky sound on the shiny PVC floor.

There was a policeman in front of the door to Matt's room, and I handed him the form Bev had given me. I nodded; the policeman nodded. A fine example of positive non-verbal communication. He put the form in a folder and gestured at the room. I heard my heart beating and thought of Sherlock Holmes. Behind the door could hide answers, or questions that would help me find the right answers. No matter what I might expect, it could change me. And change is unsettling. *The horror of it all.*

I put the box down. My hand grasped the door handle. I

hesitated. I let go of the handle. It was wet, and I tried to dry my hand on my trousers. The past twenty-four hours had been an experiment in how much I could bear; this was too much. I took off my jacket, put it over my left arm, and nervously ran my fingers through my hair. Then I grasped the door handle again. I felt the cold metal, gently pushed it down, picked up the box, and – someone opened the door from the inside.

I almost fell into the room, barely hanging on to my box. *Don't step on Holmes!* When I finally stood upright again, my eyes met those of Brayton Hughes, the deputy mayor of London. The look on his dark/pale/ face must have replicated the one I had when Holmes appeared in my flat.

His face suddenly lit up. "Oh, I'm sorry, I should have recognized you."

"Me? Really?"

"Do you have a second?"

"Yes…" I said, still clinging to my box. He shepherded me out of the room.

"We shouldn't blow this up unnecessarily," he whispered. "It's better the offenders get a verdict of not guilty. The media is already full of all this. We cannot have any details coming out or anybody sniffing too closely. You understand?"

"Not guilty?" *Who do you think I am?*

"Listen. Whatever amount…"

The box started to slip through my fingers. "I'm afraid I'm the wrong person."

"Fifty?"

"Pounds?"

"Fifty thousand, if the case won't make it to the broader public," he said, looking around nervously and rubbing his nose. "You were the best lawyer I could find."

I couldn't reply. I just stared into the dark abyss of his soul to signal that I was the wrong person.

"I'll get back to you. And track down the weirdo who found him that night. He shouldn't talk to anyone." Brayton held his phone to his ear and turned around to walk away. "Hi…no…I was in a meeting…will be there in five…yes…"

Track *me* down? Little did he know that I'd barely left a trace on the world. *Untrackable.* I had to pause for a moment. *What the hell is going on?*

8

—

The Thoughtful Actor

"Hello?" The voice belonged to Matt. I cautiously stepped back into his room. "Hello," I replied, trying not to appear startled to see the exact person I was expecting to see. *This time.*

To my astonishment, he had no bandage on his head, apparently no broken bones, and nothing else that would suggest what had happened last night. The only things that struck me were his bloodstained and swollen eyes.

"Sit down," he offered, pointing to a chair next to the bed.

I regarded the side table, which looked like a flower stand at a petrol station. There wasn't room for a single additional blossom. If it were me in that bed, there would only be a pack of grapes on the table – from Mina. I wondered how great a choking hazard grapes were for hospital patients. Dracula Holmes would have enjoyed such a case: *The Green Death.* The blood would taste sweeter.

For a moment we just stared at each other. Unable to endure his gaze, I glanced at the greeting cards next to the bed. One said: *It's a pity I won't inherit.* A strange kind of humor. I liked it.

"You saved my life," Matt said suddenly. It sent shivers down my spine.

"It was a matter of course."

His eyes glistened with tears. "I don't even know how to thank someone for *that*."

"Well, they surely don't make cards for such an occasion."

He smiled at my joke. "No, really. I could be dead now. So, thank you, although the words don't do it justice."

"I should tell Tesco's to sell cards that say thanks for saving my life."

"They should."

I remembered my strange encounter. "Even London's highest politicians come to see you. The deputy mayor? That's incredible." *And he offered me an incredible amount of money.*

"I'm glad he had a minute for me for once," Matt said sharply.

"So, you know each other?"

"If you ask him, no. If you ask me, yes."

I was puzzled.

"I think it's best if you don't mention you saw him here to anyone. I bet he's already paid the right people to sweep this under a rug as quickly as possible," Matt continued.

Stay out of this, Andrew.

"I wish he could just tell the truth, but I guess it's fine in his position to lie."

Not your business, Andrew.

"I guess I just have high demands."

"Are you a couple?" I interrupted. *My inner Mina is speaking.*

"If you ask him, no. If you ask me, maybe."

"Well, *I'm* not a secret at all. I broke the internet," I said.

Matt laughed shyly, covering his teeth. "We did. I started this."

"Technically, the uneducated gentlemen who beat you up started it."

"Or maybe the fact that they think I'm gay. They beat this insecurity right back into me."

His eyes got wet. I'd never met anyone who seemed to have so few boundaries. We barely knew each other, yet he was sharing intimate thoughts and details with me. It made me feel uncomfortable, but I also felt that I somehow cared.

"Aren't you…because you and–" I stopped, then peered intently at the door.

Matt suppressed a laugh. "Oh, they're all wrong. I'm just partially gay."

"Partially?"

"Well, let's say that although I've only dated men the past few years, dating a woman is still within the realm of possibility for me. At least ten percent or so. *Anyway*, they will never understand."

"I understand," I said. I unbuttoned my collar and loosened my tie. "Why is everyone going crazy about this?"

"The media seize every opportunity to make money. And then my family do the same." He sounded angry and disappointed.

"Have your parents come over to see you yet?"

"Ha, no. My dad is in New York with his girlfriend, and my mum is somewhere in Bali with her *friend*."

"Where did all the cards come from, then?"

"The family I choose," he said, smiling at the cards. "*They* certainly don't mind being seen with me."

"I wonder why so many people even care. The media and everyone."

"What do you mean?" Matt asked.

"Things would be so much easier if people minded their own business. If you can't be who you are because of…reputation or what have you…something is very wrong. Either with the person who's afraid to tell the truth or with the world." The moment I said this I knew I had crossed a boundary. *Not your business.*

"I guess Brayton and I are a perfect example," Matt said. "I mean, he's a Tory and he's Black. He surely can't be gay as well."

I glanced at Matt and was arrested by his gaze. "Your life seems…" I searched for a positive word for what I was trying to say. "It seems quite eventful."

"I've been on a boat in the middle of a storm since I can remember. There has always been something. I don't know life on a calm and peaceful island." Matt sighed. "We stick to what we know, I guess. As troubling as it might be. But who knows, maybe one day, by chance, my ship will wreck on the shores of such an island. I surely don't know how to navigate it there, though."

Silence filled the room. There was something so very true about his words. However, I felt I was an island in need of a shipwreck. *Castaways have to become your friends, right?*

I was about to make my excuses and leave when Matt spoke again. "Bev, my housemate, said that the scratches on my face would ruin my career."

"Oh. With the flyers…are you in theater yourself?"

"Underwear model."

I struggled for words.

"Just a joke. Yes, I'm an actor. I studied at the Royal Academy."

I was astonished; it was almost impossible to get accepted to this institution. Maybe his father's name had helped him, but I was still impressed. The man who'd nearly bled to death in my arms, hardly able to speak a word, was in fact a man of character and talent.

"That's wonderful," I said. "Why acting?"

"I guess it was the sensation of being someone else. The feeling of being in someone's skin and not my own."

I wanted to ask why but considered it inappropriate. "That must be a wonderful thing. How long have you been doing it?"

"Since I can remember, actually." He carefully felt his wound. "I always loved to play dress up and stuff, so my mum made sure I could use that creatively instead of becoming a cross-dresser. My mum's words, not mine. And you? We've established you like theater, but what do you do for a living?"

I was amazed by his memory. If he could still recall what I said to him after his brain was shaken like a ketchup bottle, he indeed was an incredible man. "I am…was…a lecturer," I replied.

"What subject?"

"Literature. I did a lot of research on Sherlock Holmes."

"Oh, I've never read any of those stories."

They aren't stories, they're cases. Usually people who said they'd never read a Holmes case lost all my respect, but this time I almost didn't care.

"Maybe I should read some," he added.

A broad grin overtook my face. "You should. Definitely." I would have liked to tell him that Sherlock Holmes was the reason I was sitting there, but my hallucinations didn't seem like an appropriate topic. "There's also a famous play about Sherlock Holmes," I said instead.

I could barely speak without bringing in my knowledge of Doyle's master detective. Others were constantly talking about football, politics, or television, but I couldn't stop throwing my literary opinions at everyone's head. People around me got so bored they'd deliberately avoid making any comments I could conceivably connect to Sherlock Holmes. To their despair, however, I always found a reason to talk about him.

"I didn't know that," Matt said. "That's embarrassing for an actor." He hid his face behind his hands.

I'm doing it again. Shut up about Holmes. "Actually…it's not so important if–"

"No, tell me more. As soon as we're talking theater, I'm interested in everything someone has to say about it." He poured a glass of water and looked at me patiently. There was something about him that made me want to crawl into bed beside him.

"Sir Arthur Conan Doyle and William Gillette wrote it, in 1899. Very long ago," I began, smiling. *That last bit didn't need pointing out.*

"I think I know the name Gillette," Matt replied, lying back again.

"They were friends and co-wrote *Sherlock Holmes: A Drama in Four Acts.*"

"Elementary," Matt said.

I had to laugh. "The famous phrase 'Oh, this is elementary, my dear fellow' actually only appeared in this piece and never in the classical canon." I was sure that I had crossed the know-it-all line.

"It's stupid to name a whole television series after that, then," Matt said.

The modern audience loved their modern Holmes. I, on the other hand, was too narrow-minded to accept him. That said, I had to acknowledge when a new depiction of Holmes was particularly apt. I just never would have admitted it out loud.

"It's ironic, though," he said. "I got beaten up just two days before my job is over. And it was the day you lost yours."

"So, you got a side job?"

"No. I'm in a TV series. My character will die tomorrow. *Anyway*, better him than me, I guess."

"I don't watch a lot of TV," I said.

"That's good. I honestly have no idea where to go from here career-wise, to be honest."

I pulled the flyer he had given me the day before out of my pocket. "That charity thing, maybe?"

He rubbed his face. "That's at an impasse, too, I'm afraid. It's not going in the direction I had envisioned."

I thought of Mina. "Just like my best friend. A project of hers, that is. So, I know what you're talking about."

He propped his legs up on some pillows and looked at me. "I'm going to read Sherlock Holmes for you, and you're going to help us raise funds at our charity performance."

I nodded and had no idea why. Mina would check my pulse if she knew I had agreed to actively raise funds for something. She would probably order a coffin if she knew I'd done so without asking what it was. This would require the brain space that was taken up by my secrets. I feared I would soon be greeted by Holmes' dancing men again. I might even begin shaking people's hands spontaneously.

Matt's phone vibrated, and his face flushed. "Sorry," he said, his expression turning grim the moment he looked at the screen.

"You can answer the call. I really don't mind."

He accepted the call and closed his eyes while speaking. "Hi, Mum. No, I don't think I need that right now. No, really. Of course, I'm still in hospital. As I said, I really don't...okay, bye."

I gave him a questioning look.

"My mum. She's in a shop and wants to know if I need a new yoga mat."

70

"You do yoga?"

"No. I hate yoga."

"Then why didn't you tell her?"

"I can't. I don't want to be mean," he said. He was smiling, but I could tell something was bothering him.

"What does your tattoo mean?" I asked, hoping to change the subject to something lighter.

He stretched and turned so that I could look at the inside of his upper arm. "A secret sect," he said dryly.

My face must have turned paler than it already was. Matt laughed out loud. "Why do you believe everything I say?"

I would have liked to give an honest answer, but instead I smiled, unsettled.

"It's a rocket."

"So, that's the symbol of the sect?"

Matt laughed again. I had said something that someone actually found funny. I smiled.

"Do you listen to rock or pop music?" he asked, and my smile disappeared. Modern theater, rock and pop music: my personal nightmare. I could only shake my head.

"You're making a face like I just told you I'm a murderer."

I pulled myself together. "Is this a band symbol, then?" I asked, trying to mask my apparent disapproval.

"It's for the Rocket Man."

I stared at him blankly.

"You know? Elton John," he added.

"The one from *The Lion King*?" I was desperately hoping to land another joke.

Matt rolled his eyes, and his face grew serious. He took a deep breath. "Brilliantly talented pianist, alumni of the Royal Academy of Music, founder of the most important AIDS charity, with nearly five hundred million dollars raised, fabulous icon of the seventies, supporter of many new and unknown artists, and one of the most important musicians and songwriters of all time. But *anyway…*"

I wasn't the only one who had a passion for something. Unlike me, however, Matt wore his passion on his skin. He pinned me down with his blue eyes. I shifted on the chair again.

"And *The Lion King*," he added.

We both laughed, and I felt relieved.

"Sorry, I can become very defensive of people I admire," he said.

I smiled. "Rarely happens to me. I might be like Holmes in that regard."

"Well, he cared about Watson a lot. Didn't he?"

I shrank in my chair.

"What's in the box?"

"Oh, these are the remnants of my old life," I looked wistfully at the cardboard.

"Your old life?"

"I've lost my job, and that's all that was left in my office. The job was…it was really everything that interested me. The books, the words, the knowledge."

"And what is your new life going to be?"

Hallucinating literary figures. "I don't really know yet. Definitely confusing."

"Everything falls into place at some point. Just wait. What's the picture? There in the box?" Matt pointed to the image of Holmes in his armchair.

I took it out and handed it to him.

"Is that him? Sherlock Holmes?" he asked, and I nodded. "A beautiful picture."

"It radiates calm. A calmness and contentment."

"Is it valuable?"

"To me. It's actually a magazine. You see?" Of course, I had always dreamed about owning an original Paget drawing. He created more than three hundred and fifty for the Sherlock Holmes cases, but most of them have been lost or destroyed. Supposedly, only about thirty of the originals still exist. Most of them are to be found at the University of Minnesota. Yes, the biggest Sherlock Holmes archive in the world is in North America. This is thanks to John Bennett Shaw and the astonishing collection of Sherlock Holmes memorabilia he bequeathed to the university. I visited the archive one January and didn't want to leave. Tim Johnson, the archive's curator, said I could come back anytime. I told him I certainly would, as long as it wasn't in January. It took my fingers approximately eight weeks to thaw once I'd returned to balmy London.

"That has to be old."

"It is," I said as he handed the picture back.

"It's brave to just drag it around London in an old cardboard box."

"Then at least I have an eye on it."

Matt sat up and was visibly in pain.

"Is everything okay?"

"Yes, actually I got away very well. This is the worst of it." He showed me two stitched wounds on the side of his head. "We should have a drink on you."

I felt flattered. "Thank you, not necessary."

"What! You saved my life. They would have killed me. Why don't you come to my house once I make it out of here? Say, tomorrow?"

I quickly calculated the sum of shared housing and artistic types: hippie communes and drug use. Nothing to do with me. Holmes and Watson lived in a flat together, but I imagined that shared living had changed dramatically in the 1960s. I didn't know if an evening in an artist's house was something I could survive. As much as I appreciated that the man in front of me was a member of the Royal Academy, I thought all artists were mad.

I was just preparing to refuse when I saw Sherlock Holmes standing behind Matt. *So much for madness.* I fixed my gaze on Matt again.

"It's a capital mistake to put up a theory before you have clues," Holmes said, and my eyes drifted involuntarily back to him. "Twisting facts will not take us any further. We are in the middle of a case. To give up now would be a futile effort." Having made this pronouncement, he disappeared again.

"What are you looking at?" asked Matt. He turned towards the window.

"A…a…bird." *And you're looking at a madman.* "I'd like to come by. Tomorrow," I added. "If you're sure they'll let you out so soon? Where do you live?"

"Oh, you're going to feel comfortable there." He laughed. "Camden. Right in the thick of it."

I rubbed my face with my hands, hoping that Holmes would show up to save me.

"Not your sort of place?"

"Not precisely."

Camden is home to Camden Town. Camden Town features Camden Market. This assemblage of stalls and shops is in the immediate vicinity of an Underground station and always teeming with people. I marvel at how they can withstand being packed together so tightly. The place is disorganized, colorful, and hip. In other words, it's one of Mina's favorite areas.

"I'll survive," I said, noting another tattoo under Matt's hospital gown. "But I don't drink very much."

"We'll see," Matt replied, winking at me. "*Anyway*…if I introduce you to my friends, you won't be able to get around a few drinks."

"Why?"

"Without you, they wouldn't have me anymore."

"Maybe someone else would have walked by."

"Maybe not."

Matt sank back into the pillows and closed his eyes. His face had soft features, unlike mine, and he was almost smiling in his sleep. He must have been heavily medicated; I couldn't otherwise explain someone falling asleep in the middle of a conversation. It was an uncomfortably intimate thing to do. I propped my head on my hand and watched him, feeling as though I were in my special place at the Museum of London. The questions I always left there had found me. I churned them over in my mind. Matt didn't seem to struggle with thousands of questions or fears; he seemed full of answers. I was impressed by the person in front of me. Typically, only fictional characters impressed me.

I got up carefully and collected my box and jacket. Looking at

Matt again, I stopped and put everything back down. He was a sleeping beauty. Thankfully I had pens in my pocket. I wrote him a little note and placed the pen next to it. As a present. Everyone loves pens.

Outside the hospital, I put the box between my legs, lit a cigarette, and looked at the crowded road. In "The Red-Headed League," Sherlock Holmes asks Dr Watson for an hour of silence, saying the case contains a three-pipe problem. Clearly, my life had become a three-pipe problem. Or a ten-cigarette problem, at least.

"Okay if I join you?"

I looked around. "Still here?" I asked Bev, wondering if she had waited for me.

"Here again. I grabbed some things for Matt. How did it go?"

"Well, it was good. I might come over to your house for a visit."

She smoked thoughtfully for a moment, considering me. "You're a bit different from the rest of Matt's friends, aren't you?"

"Am I?"

"I suppose you might meet the rest of them, so I should warn you," she said, laughing.

"Why? Are you all criminals?"

She looked at me as if I were from another planet.

"What should I know, then?"

"Let's see. Matt and I live together, then there's Michael and Toby, they're rather boring, but then there's Liz too." She laughed again. "Do everyone a favor and please shake hands with Liz."

"If I don't?"

"You don't want to know. Let's just say Liz loves to pick a fight."

"Why?"

"Liz is…special. If you manage to make them like you, you have a friend for life. If they don't like you, you won't see Matt again."

"They?"

"Yes, they. Liz. We named Giorgio after Liza Minnelli because of a stupid argument they were to blame for, and they kept that name. A variation, anyway."

Who? What? Where? "I'm a bit lost here, I'm afraid."

"Oh, sorry. They identify as non-binary. So, we say they and them instead of she or he."

"I don't quite understand, but I'll do my best to remember."

"You'll do it even though you don't understand it?"

"Yes. I may not understand it, but I respect it. They do sound really special."

"Because they're non-binary?" Bev asked defensively.

"No, because they decide who can or cannot be friends with Matt based on a single handshake. That *is* special, isn't it?"

Bev laughed. "Absolutely. You are too, just in another way, I guess."

"That's it, I suppose."

"Matt also has his weaknesses," Bev said, smiling.

"And they are?"

"Oh, I'm giving away secrets now, but what I can tell you is that I hope you're single."

"Why?"

"You're just his type."

I liked to hear this.

"Or, better said, you're his parents' type."

I did not like to hear this. "His parents' type?"

"I don't want to spill all the tea before you get to know each other, but all I can say is that his parents are absolutely done with all those Grindr dates and weird, closeted middle-aged men with attachment issues."

That second one's hitting a bit close. "I thought he's with the…deputy mayor."

Bev's face turned stone cold. "Oh, so you've met the phantom?"

"Brayton Hughes is a phantom?" *A proper Holmes case, finally.*

"Well, he doesn't like to be seen with Matt, if you know what I mean."

"No."

"It's complicated, to say the least." She paused for a moment. "However, you are eloquent, well-dressed, and absolutely gorgeous.

Matt just lets himself be treated like a choice again and again. And there you are, rescuing him in the streets of London. Hell of a date you would be."

Oh, yes, hell of a date.

"I have to go in and be at Matt's service. The usual," Bev said, turning to the door. She was just about to go through when I summoned all my courage to ask her a question I had never asked anyone before.

"Bev?" I said, and she turned around again. "Can I meet Matt again like…this?" I looked at myself in the window and gestured vaguely at my reflection.

"The suit is okay. You have a good figure, good posture – and hello, long legs. But please leave the tie at home."

"Why?"

"It's pretty, but try to be a little bit casual. You sure you don't want to date him?" She smiled and walked into the building.

I knew I'd better talk to Mina about it. Her easy way of living extended to casual wear. If she couldn't help me, I didn't know who could. But I needed to talk to her about something else – something more important than collar buttons.

I needed to tell her who I really was.

9

———

The Man Inside the Closet

The train to Hackney Central was overcrowded with young alternatives. They were strikingly if strangely attired. I got the sense they were bursting with passionate interests, and I wondered if those interests were as varied as their fashion choices. Most of them were on their phones. Did they blog about every band, every artist, every idea they encountered? Was that how people met now? *If I joined social media, what would I blog about? Sherlock Holmes? Ties?* I struggled to name a third option. *Pens, maybe?*

Mina lived in a small flat under the roof of an old house. It was unrenovated, otherwise she could not have afforded it. A rarity in the London property market.

I balanced my cardboard box and its sensitive contents as I walked through the streets. The Victorian buildings attract many artists and students, and no ordinary goods are consumed here: the chocolate is fair trade, the curry vegan, the beer brewed at home. I stopped at one of the many coffee suppliers, bravely put the cup in the box, and went on.

After a few meters, I reached the Victorian house where Mina lived and rang the bell. After being buzzed in and climbing the interior steps, I was greeted by an open door.

"Come in," she muttered, grabbing the coffee out of the box.

She took a sip. "Ooh! That makes me come to life!" I thought that her face did indeed regain some animation.

Her flat was, strictly speaking, a room converted from an old industrial space. To make it look bigger, it was painted completely white, including the wooden floor. The only natural illumination came through four skylights.

Mina had a penchant for everything colorful. I liked dark colors: black, grey, and sometimes dark green. While I found Mina's vivid cushions somewhat beautiful, I felt an aversion to the neon Hindu god figures that adorned all the walls. In her flat, everything was mixed with everything. There was hardly an item without frills and luxuriant ornaments. On an old wooden box stood various colorful flowerpots with half-living inhabitants; next to this display was a porcelain cockatoo. In our shared flat, our different tastes had culminated in a Sherlock Holmes bust decorated with Mardi Gras beads and red lipstick. The contrast summed up our different personalities well – except the clash had, in some way, actually looked kind of nice. However, to me, her flat resembled an opium den in an old film and was thus something I couldn't live in.

While walking into the living room, Mina pointed towards a small package. "Does this look pastel to you?"

"Shockingly pastel," I said as I followed her.

She made herself comfortable and yawned. "You got a charg–?"

I tossed the phone charger in her direction.

"Thanks for that."

"You should start buying them in bulk. So, why wasn't it perfect, your date?" I asked, making myself comfortable in an armchair.

"I'm more interested in your night."

I kept looking at her, hoping to get an answer to my question so I wouldn't have to answer any of hers.

"Okay." She stretched out on the sofa. "He got a call."

"From whom?"

"His wife!"

"No!" I opened my eyes wide. "That's…not good." I tried

to suppress my laughter. "Though we did mention that was a possibility, if you remember. So really–"

She muffled another laugh and tucked the blanket around her legs. "Well, we were already in his flat, so…frankly, my dear, I didn't give a damn."

"Was the wife gone with the wind or out picking up some milk?"

"Oh, he has a special flat, you know. In the city. For special friends."

"I should have known," I said, rolling up my sleeves and relaxing into the conversation.

Before her engagement, Mina had a habit of bestowing her charms on anyone who liked her. She was simply able to convince them all, and she seemed to have fun with it. For this reason, I was surprised when she got engaged to David after only a few weeks. But I was even more surprised that he seemed to be to blame for the separation, because Mina was by no means a saint. Anyway, it seemed she had returned to her old habits.

"As if you've never had a dodgy one-night stand," she said.

I shook my head. Holmes knew about my nightly visitors, but I didn't want anyone else to. Although Oscar Wilde thought that the best way to get rid of temptation was to give in to it, I was absolutely not convinced. Taking people home never made anything better for me. That said, Mr Wilde and I were more alike than I would have suspected. I discovered this when I first read him. In fact, Doyle and Wilde met during their lifetimes. Not because Doyle believed in fairies but because their careers briefly intertwined.

Mina looked at me with disbelief.

"You know I can't deal with most people," I said quickly, hoping to avoid more questions.

Mina laughed. "Shit, you're a bad liar. I remember you once came back to our flat around nine in the morning looking like you'd had a fight with ten raccoons. She must have been wild! Or a raccoon…"

I couldn't resist a smile. Then my gaze fell on the porcelain cockatoo again. I wondered who'd had the courage to produce such an item, let alone sell it. I would have enjoyed writing a case called *The Bird That Killed* for Dracula Holmes. I imagined him searching for a murderer who used just such a porcelain cockatoo to bludgeon his victims. No. Perhaps the indignity of such a weapon was too great.

"I can't imagine it," she said, stretching out on the sofa again.

"What?" I asked, still fascinated by the cockatoo.

"You on top of someone. Sweating, moaning."

I hoped the bird would come alive and eat me. "You shouldn't be trying to imagine that," I replied. The horror of this conversation. *The horror of it all.*

"Oh, come on. Tell me."

I shook my head. "I don't talk about those kinds of things with anyone."

"You and your decency. Are you still a virgin, or what?" she joked, slowly sipping her coffee.

"No. I was married."

"Oh, right. I forget sometimes."

The cockatoo and I continued to stare at each other.

"I just know which topics are appropriate and which aren't."

Mina rolled her eyes. "Bummer. How's your revenge publication?"

"Not quite finished yet." I rolled my tie around my finger. "Say, Mina. What is this Instascam?"

Mina laughed. "You mean Instagram? Since when are you interested in the internet?"

I shrugged. "I'd like to create an account."

She put the coffee cup aside and patted the sofa. I walked over and sat down next to her. "Do you have a fever?" she asked, pressing the back of her hand to my forehead.

"I just think I should adapt to the modern era. Regarding future jobs, this is good."

"Adapting to the modern era?"

"Yes."

"Well, let's make you an Instagram account," she said, rising to fetch her laptop from the desk. "Do you even know what kind of platform this is?"

I shook my head as she settled beside me again. I still considered the temporary separation from my typewriter in the summer of 2006 the death of my artistic soul. No, I did not know what kind of platform Instagram was.

"It's like any other social media, basically."

"Right. Social media…"

"Don't worry, it's not so social. Contact without real contact. Actually, it should be exactly your thing," she joked, opening the internet browser and clicking an icon. With another click, we faced the new account box and filled out my basic details.

"You're going to need a username to post stuff here."

"Just use my name."

She typed it in. "It's gone. You need something different."

"But that's my name."

"Maybe, but there are probably hundreds of people with your name."

"If it's my name, I should be allowed to use it," I insisted.

"You can't have the same name as somebody else."

"But I do have the same name."

"Well maybe you shouldn't have been the last person on earth to join Instagram."

I pondered. "I can't think of anything else."

Mina took a big sip of coffee and typed: *holmesoddflatm8*.

"No. That's abominable. Is that a name at all?" I asked.

"Now it is," she said with a laugh, saving it.

I wasn't Holmes' flatmate – and I certainly wasn't his "flatm8." He was mine, and without paying rent. I would have preferred Dr Watson. He seemed a little more reserved and grounded to me.

"I already don't like this site," I said, leaning back.

Mina looked at me and pulled on my tie. "Oh come on, you asked for this. So how would you describe yourself?"

I clasped a pillow to my stomach. "Smart, talented, intelligent," I said.

Mina typed: *know-it-all, bore, potential killer.*

I slapped the pillow on her head.

"Why are you in such a good mood?" she asked, grabbing the pillow and throwing it at me.

"Write 'Boring Baker Street irregular and potential killer,' please."

Mina continued to type. "Why do you want to sign up here so suddenly?"

"Because…I…"

"So, the usual reason people have. You want to stalk someone."

"No," I lied, avoiding eye contact.

"Okay. Who are you looking for?"

"Nobody."

She looked at me sternly. "I can't find them for you if you don't tell me. You want to try doing this on your own?"

I sighed. "Maybe, so, potentially, the man whose life I saved yesterday."

"Now we're talking, babes."

After a short period of silence, Mina dared to ask about the previous evening. I told her what I had experienced. My heart beat almost as fast as it had that night.

"It's horrible. Good that you were there. Who were they?" she asked.

"I don't know."

"I hope they lock them up."

"I hope so too."

"And who was the man?"

"His name is Matt. I visited him in hospital earlier. He's doing surprisingly well. My pocket watch is broken."

"Your old man's watch? How will you survive now?"

Obviously, this loss was trivial compared to what Matt had gone through, but I was still angry. And I felt a pressure on my stomach as I thought about what I wanted to say to Mina. Though I'd arrived in the middle of my life, I felt like an eight-year-old about to confess something to his father. But the madness had to end before more fictional characters showed up in my flat and forced me to do things.

"What's his name?"

"Matthew Lewis."

"There's definitely a lot of people with that name," Mina said, typing in the search box.

I thought about the note Bev had given me and pulled it out of my pocket.

"That's probably his name there."

Mina took the note in her hand. "Matt the Cat?" She laughed.

I, too, found the name a little strange for an adult man.

"Then let's look for the kitten, Dandy Andy."

I peered nervously at the screen. Looking at his pictures, a cold sweat broke out on my forehead. He was undoubtedly handsome, but also shockingly younger than me. We scanned his pictures; his clothes were ordinary, yet every outfit seemed to have a twist – mostly in the form of colorful trainers. Not really my taste, but they fit him.

"Luckily, you saved the kitten. This is not any Matthew Lewis; this is Matt Lewis."

My organs stopped functioning for a moment. "You know him?"

"Of course! I mean, he's not uber famous, but if you have nothing to do besides binge-watch granny soaps in the evening, he is."

"He said he's on TV every day. I thought it was a joke."

"I'm devastated to tell you it's not. He's in *Westend Street*. He plays a minor role, but yes, he is in it. I guess you'll be famous now too!" she exclaimed with a devious laugh. "Isn't his father Michael Lewis?"

"Oh yes, the Michael Lewis who said that British literature was reborn with him."

"I think it's his modesty that sets him apart," Mina said.

"Indeed."

"But he's a master of his trade," she added.

84

I had to agree with that as well. While people couldn't get enough of his writing, many couldn't handle his character. I hoped that Matt hadn't inherited any of his father's traits, because they were notorious in Britain – and probably outside Britain too.

Mina was starstruck. "Audrey Lewis is his mother."

"Well aware of the fact."

"She's the sixth-wealthiest woman in the world."

"She won't be if she continues to buy yoga mats for people who don't do yoga."

Mina shot me a confused look. "It seems like you know them well already. How did you and Matt get along?" she asked, astonished as she clicked through his profile. She stopped at a picture showing Matt half-naked with a tar-like liquid being poured over him in the middle of Trafalgar Square. "I mean, you met him and now you're searching for him online?"

"Holmes and Watson understood each other too."

"You follow him now."

"Follow? Who?"

"Well, the kitten. Now you can see everything he posts."

I had to admit to myself that this site had its merits.

She kept clicking through the pictures. "Don't tell me that charity event we talked about is his?"

I nodded.

"And you know him now?" She connected the clues. "He's my solution!"

"Your what?"

"My organization. He could be the face that helps stop my organization from bleeding out."

"No, please. I don't want him to think I'm taking advantage of this situation."

"Okay. Okay. Sorry."

"Can you see who follows him?" I asked.

"Sure. Is there anyone particular?"

"Brayton Hughes. The deputy mayor."

"I know who he is…let me see… No, he doesn't follow him."

"Curious."

"Why?"

"Nothing. Just curiosity."

"What is this really about?" she asked, closing the laptop and sinking deep into the pillows.

I felt the blood rushing through my veins. It was suddenly difficult to breathe, and I started to sweat again. My legs bucked up and down. I had to get rid of one of my secrets and make room for something new. I knew it had to be in that moment, and I knew that Mina had managed the unimaginable: she had befriended me. I trusted and loved her like nobody else.

"I'll be back," I said, rising and walking quickly to the bathroom. I splashed cold water on my face and breathed in deeply. The situation was no longer avoidable if I wanted to finally lead a different life. *What life? Why go through this when I'm not even planning on a future?* I had always run away from feelings, and the urge to just jump right out the bathroom window was overwhelming. I looked through the glass and concluded that jumping wouldn't be an option. I didn't want the first time I opened up to someone to be my autopsy.

"Feelings are the enemy of clear thinking. In order to think clearly again, you need to know and control your feelings. Your profession requires clear thinking."

I looked in the mirror. "You again?" I hissed at the reflected image of Sherlock Holmes in Mina's bathtub. He sat with his knees pulled up to his chest, fiddling with a rubber duck that resembled the Queen.

"Hello," he said calmly.

"What are you doing here?"

"Helping you solve the case. You're on the verge of your first breakthrough."

"Am I?" I rubbed my face.

"Things that are easy are neither exciting nor worth the effort," Holmes noted.

"Can we please agree that you won't just show up out of nowhere?" I asked.

When I turned around, he was gone. He'd had a point, however much I might disagree with some of his theories. Even so, I couldn't find the courage to go back in and tell Mina my secret. I searched for my eternal companion. *I don't know what I am and I don't know what I want. I don't know who I can be and I don't know who I was.* The crumpled note was by now nearly torn apart. I remembered the moment I had gotten it. I had to open up to Mina.

Back on the sofa, I began. "We're friends, aren't we?" My hands were sweating. I saw in Mina's face that she understood whatever I wanted to say was costing me a lot of effort. My fingers searched for my cigarettes.

"Of course we are. Should I look away? Maybe you can say it if I look away?"

"No…I…"

"Do you want to say it to Peppa?" she asked, pulling a little pig out from under a pillow.

I laughed. "No. Thank you. I…you have certainly wondered why…why I always reject your offers, even though we understand each other so well…"

She looked amazed and also a little shocked. "Because…because you're in love with me?" she asked.

I swallowed. "No. Well, yes, I love you, but not in a lover way." I felt like I was going to have a heart attack.

"Okay, not because you're in love with me. But because…" She waved her hands in the air.

"I…I can't." I dropped my head in my hands, rested my elbows on my knees, and tried not to breathe. At that moment, I didn't know what was worse: saying it or showing someone that I had no control over myself. Somehow, saving a man's life and talking to a fictional detective had pushed me to reveal a truth that was excruciating to me. My face felt hot. I was scared. As long as I didn't say it, it wasn't there; and you didn't have to worry about non-existent things.

"Take a deep breath, babes. Don't stress about anything before there's even stress to stress about," she said in her calmest voice.

I looked at her, confused.

"The motherly advice that I, as your former flat and soulmate, want to give you is that it's not good to stress about stressing over stress that probably doesn't need to be stressed about." She sighed. "Hope I will never be a mum."

"Yes, please, it's stressful," I said. I started to bite my nails.

"You don't have to tell me anything, Andrew. If you just wa–"

"I'm not attracted to women." It burst out of me, and I didn't dare look up from my hands. For a moment we said nothing, and I heard the blood rushing in my ears.

"Oh! Right! So, it was a male raccoon then!" Mina exclaimed.

I was grateful for her humor, which eased the moment. I should have known I could count on her for that. "A wild racoon from Bournemouth," I said, lightening up for a moment before I looked at my fingers again. My shirt stuck to my wet skin.

"Thanks for opening up to me."

I rubbed my face and sighed.

"You know me, you know that I date everything with a pulse. Screw what others think. I know, easier said than done, but you're still you," she added. "Really, Andrew. Don't feel bad about it. We will get through this, together. Like Sherlock and Watson would."

I raised my head and folded my hands under my chin. Not even being compared to Holmes and Watson cheered me up. I wanted to say something, but my lips wouldn't move. It was as if they were glued together.

"Why now? Why are you telling me?"

I put my head back in my hands. "I think because of last night. This situation. He was almost beaten to death because he's what I don't want to be."

"What don't you want to be?"

"What I don't want to be," I said.

"Which is?"

I hesitated.

"Gay," I said.

We looked at each other for a while.

"Why? Why don't you want to be gay?" she asked.

I took a deep breath and played nervously with my tie. "I…I am completely unknown to myself. I think I'm scared."

"Of what? I always thought you were very happy with yourself," she said.

"I…I never have been."

"There's nothing to be afraid of. No one likes you anyway – except for me, of course."

I smiled at her joke. "I always thought that if I didn't have contact with anyone, it wouldn't matter."

"It just makes you go mad. I know that myself."

I already knew it too. "I'm scared," I repeated, feeling this unbearable pain in my throat.

"You're really scared," Mina said. She looked at me in amazement.

I was scared for my life. With every breath and every step I took, I was afraid of the future. But that was a secret I would keep for myself, as much as Holmes might urge me to reveal it. The first step was taken, and I dared not go any further.

"He's not been out of my mind since yesterday."

"Matt?" she asked.

I nodded. Whatever it was, our encounter had conjured up Sherlock Holmes and put me in a situation I'd never dreamed of.

"You know, it doesn't necessarily make life easier, but damn, you lead a life that's honest, and that's the most important thing, isn't it?"

"I'm not so sure," I said.

Mina took a deep breath. "It's so frustrating. Others shouldn't care."

"They really shouldn't, but they do. They always do. Imagine your parents knew about you. That you're…"

"Pansexual is the term."

"That you're pansexual."

Mina swallowed and lowered her head. "I want to tell them."

"Why?"

"Me giving you advice about not giving a shit but hiding my true self from my family…I need to finally tell them. They're coming down in a few days."

"How will they react? What do you think?"

"God knows. I see a chance my mum will be understanding. But my dad? No. Never."

"Why is that?"

"He's conservative and old. He grew up in Islamabad. I guess that's enough said."

Mina rarely showed her vulnerable side – something we both had in common. We had just mastered completely different ways of living behind a protective wall.

"If he loves you, he will understand."

"Love. Yes, right," she said, rubbing her face. "Did you ever tell your parents? Or am I the first one you've come out to?"

I hesitated. "My family knew."

"But if they knew…"

"They made it more than clear that if this information should ever make it past the doorstep of our house, I would regret it my whole life. I decided to keep quiet."

"That doesn't give me much hope with my parents."

"I know. I'm sorry." I cleared my throat. "I will be there for you, whatever happens when you tell them."

She put her head on my shoulder. "Thanks, babes," she whispered.

"Of course, I'm your friend." I stared at the ceiling. "I think I like him a lot. Maybe even a bit more than I like you," I said, and she smiled.

"How dare you." She crossed her arms. "Does he like you back?"

"We had a nice conversation about theater, but he seems to be in an on-and-off thing with a man." I had to hold back the urge to blurt out his name. "I'm actually not sure if he likes me in the way I like him."

Mina sat up again. "On-and-off thing? Better be careful there."

"I will. It's weird how quickly one person can change everything. What a lovely and inconvenient coincidence it was to meet him."

Mina sighed. "It must be fate. Of all the gin joints in all the towns in all the world, he walks into yours."

"We should watch *Casablanca*."

She looked at me. "Will we ever stop doing this?"

"Absolutely not."

Before I could even finish my sentence, Mina had turned on the TV. "That we would ever end up like this…" she said.

"Life is infinitely stranger than anything the human spirit could invent," I replied.

"Did Holmes say that?"

I nodded.

"There's something to it," she said.

Suddenly I was smiling and happiness overflowed within me.

"I knew there were living cells left in you," she joked, putting her head back on my shoulder. Then she whispered the first words of *Casablanca*.

Back outside, I breathed in the cool evening air. It tickled my lungs, and I coughed. Blood came up; I could taste it clearly. The warm glow of Mina's company faded away. There were no stars in the sky. It was as if they had all fled and left me alone. I lit a cigarette and took a drag. Now that one of my secrets had been revealed, I almost felt lonelier than before. Mina and I were more deeply connected, but the rest of the world had moved further away from me. I was floating somewhere between heaven and earth, somewhere no one could reach me. Not even the missing stars. I wanted to jump on the back of Ursa Minor and ride along the firmament.

Some raindrops fell on my face, and I put my jacket over the cardboard box to protect its contents. It was hard to believe that everything I had done at the university fit in something so small. I had experienced so much there, and there were uncountable memories of that place. I had liked working there, I supposed. And I had certainly needed that work.

Despite the rain, I did not hurry. Walking a city after dark, watching people, and soaking up the atmosphere – these things form a distinct pleasure. During the day, London is often alien and distant, but at night the city is like a close confidant. Everything is bathed in a strange orange light, there are only a few people around, and it's ghostly quiet. It's as if the city envelops me at night and tries to tickle the longing out of me. Discovering a city by the glow of streetlamps is particularly appealing, and not just for aspiring vampires. In every city I've ever been to, there has been an almost mystical atmosphere at night. The most beautiful thing is to have the whole city and its sights to yourself.

Victoria Park is closed at night, so I had to take a detour along Grove Road. This street bisects the park, and it's not my first choice during the day, because I prefer the way through the park itself. Unlike other large parks in London, Victoria Park is rarely overcrowded. Admittedly, it's not one of the top destinations for tourists. Especially if they have only a few days in the city, people prioritize Hyde, Green, or Greenwich. But Victoria Park has been open to the public for almost one hundred and seventy years. It has attracted millions of visitors from all over the world, and it always attracted me.

A place I love even more than that, however, is the Columbia Road flower market in the East End of London, near Brick Lane and the Spitalfields markets. It's overcrowded, but the sight of the flowers is too beautiful to be ignored, so I find myself battling the throng. My favorite flowers have always been lilies – a flower connected to luck. In retrospect, I should have probably bought more of them. Or maybe Sir Arthur Conan Doyle should have planted them. It was 1930 when he collapsed in his garden, holding a flower in one hand and clutching at his aching heart with the other. It is believed that his last words to his wife were: "You are wonderful." *If I ever find someone who dedicates such last words to me, I shall have lived the best life.*

Back home, with my door closed behind me, I was relieved to finally put down the box. As I did so, my gaze fell upon a letter that was half hidden by my doormat. A few days before, I'd been convinced that I wouldn't care about this particular letter's contents. Now that it had arrived, however, I felt fear. Something had changed in me. I just stood there looking down at it, knowing these could be my last few minutes in the reality I'd grown accustomed to. As if on cue, I started coughing.

The letter which lay so inconspicuously on the floor would dictate the manner of my death.

10

—◆—

The Mysterious Letter

Iknelt and took the letter in my hand. It was light, yet it carried more weight than any ordinary missive. My fingers traced its edges. Before I slipped my thumb in the small opening on the side, I took a deep breath. One can only fear death if one has something to lose. Whatever it was that I could lose, its pull was strong.

Having enlarged the envelope's opening, I hooked my index finger under the flap and pulled through the thin paper. I took the folded sheet in my hand. One word. A single word that would determine everything the future held for me. I unfolded the letter and scanned it for that word.

There it was, black on white. It was as if I were holding my will in my hand. Holmes said that any truth is better than indefinite doubt, but I didn't want the truth. Not this truth.

I went to my bedroom, folded the letter, and put it under my pillow. I had already guessed what its contents would be, but now it was certain. There was no way to attribute my condition to more benign causes. There was even the inevitable appointment date – urgently scheduled. I looked at my phone and noticed a voicemail from an unknown number. The medical establishment following up, no doubt. The calls had been coming for days. I had ignored them.

I might have lost my job, but that didn't mean that I had lost everything. In fact, I felt that I had won things and would maybe win even more. I had always wondered what happens after death, and especially about what would happen after my own death. Looking around at what life had to offer, I was suddenly terrified by the thought of dying. I didn't want to die from cancer. I didn't want to die by suicide. I didn't want to die in treatment. I didn't want to die. Against all odds, I wanted to live. I wanted to live more than ever. I was curious about what the future could offer me. I wanted to see and live my future. I wanted to experience love and compassion. I wanted what every human being craved. This could not be it. This could not be all I had to show for my life. I wanted a happy ending. I wanted *my* happy ending. And all I could do about it was sob into my pillow.

Tea was my choice to calm myself down. To regain control. When I walked into my living room carrying a steaming mug, the smell of tobacco greeted me, and it cheered me up. "Good evening, Mr Holmes," I said.

"Good evening," he replied.

"I thought we agreed that you wouldn't show up like this anymore."

"It was not an agreement. You simply mentioned it."

"Yes, that's probably how it was." *Several times.* "Have we solved the case?" I asked with anticipation.

Holmes looked at me seriously. "The case? No. We're still in the early stages."

"Oh." I was surprised. After all, I had admitted my secret to Mina. One of them, anyway. And Holmes had mentioned in the bathroom that I was taking the first step towards a solution.

"Your secret was a necessary instrument. Sit down. We'll smoke together, and I'll explain it to you," Holmes said calmly.

I sat down on my sofa and lit a cigarette. An empty bottle from the night before served as an ashtray. I got the distressing feeling that I had just been tricked by Sherlock Holmes. *Who would have guessed.*

"An instrument? What for?" I asked.

Holmes crossed his legs, took a drag of his pipe, and looked at me. "To solve the case, your case, you will need confidants. Sharing a secret binds two people together. You and Mina are now connected in a certain way."

"But wasn't that the solution?"

"My dear Andrew, we both know it's not. I know what keeps you awake at night. It's the fear. You have only begun to confront it."

I leaned back and looked at the ceiling. I was up against Sherlock Holmes' cool intellect. *I wish I'd made another fictional character my psychiatrist.*

"So, the case is about my fear?" I asked cautiously.

Holmes snorted; I assumed it was a laugh. "No. As I mentioned before, your fear is part of the case. But it's not the case itself. If you can understand what this case is all about, you won't be far from the solution."

"Why don't you just tell me?"

"You have to find out for yourself. I'm only here to help you."

I thought of the dancing men and wondered how an insult scribbled on a mirror was particularly helpful. Holmes solved all his other cases; why I should have to solve one as his apparent client was still a mystery to me. *I suppose it might have something to do with the fact that I'm talking to myself.*

"What does fear mean to you?" I asked cautiously.

"For me, fear is an instinct. Something your body reacts to first. Like wild animals when they run from a predator."

"But isn't my kind of fear another one?"

"It is because you feel in the first place. You let your feelings guide you, not your rational mind or instincts."

"Just to be clear, an animal who thinks rationally doesn't get caught by the predator?" I asked, figuring I'd landed a joke. *I'm witty and pretty, Holmes!*

He folded his hands under his chin. "An animal who thinks rationally? That would be a human being."

I crossed my arms. "Why are you trying to help? And why now?"

"People like you keep me alive. Without you, I would only be a figure pressed between yellowed pages. I owe you my life. Think of it as a gift." Holmes pulled his red-and-gold dressing gown tightly around himself.

"What role does Matt play?"

Holmes smiled. "The most important role of all."

Infuriating. "You already know that?"

"Oh, it's obvious," he replied, standing up and putting his pipe aside.

"No. Not really."

"We all share the pleasures and burdens of memory."

I smiled. "That's Francesco Petrarca."

"Quite right."

I found this statement remarkable because Dr Watson often claimed that Holmes' literary knowledge was not particularly extensive. In the case "The Boscombe Valley Mystery," Holmes reads a collection of Francesco Petrarca's works on the journey from London to Hertfordshire because he doesn't want to speak a word until he and Dr Watson arrive at their destination. The fact that he was now quoting this Italian poet made me suspect he might have an interest in literature after all.

"Petrarca also said, 'Books have led some to learning and others to madness,'" Holmes noted.

I felt like he was trying to give me a broad hint. "What do you mean exactly?" I asked as the ashes of my cigarette missed the neck of the bottle.

"You'll find out tomorrow."

"And Mina? What role does she play? Why do we need to be connected?"

Holmes looked at the picture of himself and Professor Moriarty at the Reichenbach Falls. "All parties involved are key to resolving the case."

I exhaled hard. "Speaking of the case, how did you survive?" I asked, nodding at the picture.

Holmes smiled. "Well, the answer would eliminate your fascination."

"Why is it you're so against giving me answers?"

"Why is it you're so ashamed of who you are when you seem to care so little about the opinions of others?"

He'd hit the nail right on the head, and I swallowed. "I…I don't know."

Holmes didn't accept my answer. "Why?" he persisted.

"I…I don't mind being criticized for my stubbornness. I just don't–" I paused and looked at Holmes, who stood in the middle of the room smoking. "I don't want to be slagged off for something that's just me. Something I didn't choose to be. Something that is so very…so very natural."

"You fear criticism?" Holmes asked, and I knew he would keep digging until he had the answer he wanted to hear.

"I don't want to be labelled or judged for anything but my profession. They can say whatever they want about my articles or books, but about my sexuality? I don't want people to talk about it. It's something intimate, you know. But they will talk. I will be asked about it, I will have to explain again and again. I don't want to explain myself to anyone."

"Talking about your feelings isn't your cup of tea, I suppose?"

"No. I mean yes, but asking people who they have sex with shouldn't be anyone's cup of tea."

Holmes nodded. "Quite right," he said, and he sat down again.

What I didn't tell him was how my father used to talk about people like me, though I wasn't the loud, girlish, and flamboyant figure he'd describe for fun. Of course, there is nothing wrong about being that way, but his appalling homophobic remarks planted the thought that there was something wrong with me. That I was nothing but a joke. I didn't want to be a joke. I didn't want to be joked about.

"Bach or Sarasate?" asked Holmes.

"Sarasate, of course," I replied.

Holmes took up his violin and started playing. I closed my eyes and pondered what the case was really about, not knowing that I would soon meet someone who would give me a valuable hint.

11

—◆—

The Man with the Bowler

When I woke up the next day, my head seemed clearer again. Yes, the situation was grave. Yes, I had reached a point where I could not go back. Yes, I was in the process of falling apart, and not just metaphorically. But I didn't want to die. Not anymore, not yet. I wanted to die of old age, not cancer. I tried to put aside the thought and turned my focus to the previous night.

I had told Mina one of my secrets, but I was still unclear as to why. My secret felt like a blemish, a trait that was as alien to the person I wanted to be as flying is to fish. But flying fish do exist, and the day when I had to face myself had come. Nature has its whims, and I was probably one of them.

When I was fourteen, I didn't lay an eye on girls or boys. I was generally uninterested in anything with a pulse. The only things that attracted me were books. For most of my teenage years, I questioned why I was so different from the others. Everyone else was colorful fruit salad, and I was the oatmeal. The rest of the class returned to school every Monday boasting about the mad things they'd done at the weekend – whom they'd kissed, and whose bins they had blown up for a laugh. Meanwhile, I found pleasure in classical music, literature, and sorting my father's ties according to color.

It would take me a long time to understand that I focused on books and science because doing so distracted me from any kind of romance or intimacy. I eventually realized it was mainly male novel or film characters who attracted my attention. They aroused me in a way that transcended mere curiosity. My eyes were fixed on the screen or glued to words on crumbling pages. I absorbed each movement and utterance. Men's bodies were different from women's. They were angular, sometimes hairy, sometimes soft, and sometimes hard. I would sit watching TV in the dark living room of our big house late at night, looking around again and again, fearing my parents would catch me. But I couldn't name where the fascination came from. Nor why I felt I needed to keep such things secret.

I was nineteen when I met a boy in one of my university classes. When he suddenly stopped coming to class, I felt that something was missing. When he came back, I felt an unknown warmth and nervousness. I was irritated by my reactions, and that was when it dawned on me: *I like that boy. I like him the way other boys like girls.* I knew I was gay. But I knew my father would not approve of this, and I didn't mean to tell him. Or anyone. Ever. But that didn't work. He knew and he was furious.

Thinking I had to play a certain role and find people who matched my created self, I hid who I really was and never stopped. I continued this until I couldn't tell what was me, and what was the man I dressed up as. But I wasn't alone in my hiding place: I had Sherlock Holmes. And I couldn't deny that my obsession with him went beyond scholarly fascination and artistic appreciation. For me, he was the perfect image of a human being: well-dressed, calculating, and clever.

While I knew from an early age that I would write about Sherlock Holmes, Holmes himself only discovered his purpose as a young man. When he was about twenty-one, he spent his vacation with his university friend Victor Trevor, whose father was enthusiastic about Holmes' skills and encouraged him to become a detective. My vacation with a university friend only encouraged me to never go on any vacation with any friend again. Getting to know someone's bathroom routine? *The horror of it all.*

I met Christine, the woman I married, at a conference. She was beautiful and eloquent, and her intellect surpassed mine. She was also enthusiastic about Sherlock Holmes, which was probably the reason I saw a soulmate in her. She showed me that contrary to all my expectations, I might be able to love a human being. Unfortunately, I couldn't love her the way a husband should. We were rarely physically close, but emotionally we were fused. Sometimes I missed her, but I couldn't just show up at her door. Not after everything that had happened. Even telling her about the cancer was impossible, though I felt she should know. Seeing no other way out of our marriage, I had told her a cruel lie: that I had found another woman. That decision was one of the stupidest of my life. But even as our marriage dissolved because of my secret, I wouldn't have considered telling her the truth. She had asked too many questions that were too uncomfortably close to reality. I had to distract her. I often blamed myself for the fact that I couldn't return her feelings. As much as I loved her for the person she was, every intimate encounter was like a cold bucket of ice water to my libido – the ultimate proof that I was not attracted to women in any way. The experiment had failed.

But every double life will sooner or later be revealed. So it was with the good Effie Munro in the case "The Yellow Face," and so it was with me. In both cases, a man from Baker Street was responsible.

With these regrets swirling through my mind, I huddled deeper under the blankets, ignoring my alarm. Until the afternoon I was sacked, every day had been exactly the same, be it a weekday or weekend. I was always up at seven. In this way I was unlike Holmes, who had no fixed daily routine when he was on a case. All he did was work. Sleep and a balanced meal were optional. When he was close to solving a case, he usually relaxed a little, perhaps performing chemical experiments or playing the violin. If, on the other hand, things weren't going so well, he did what I did when I was nervous: he smoked and didn't sleep.

My phone vibrated. I looked curiously at the text message. *Come around this afternoon at three. I'll send the address later. I would be very happy. Matt.*

I stared at the screen, tossed the phone to the side, and hid under the blanket again. A few seconds later, however, my phone was once more in my hand.

Thank you for the invitation. See you later. Andrew.

My thumb hovered hesitantly over the "Send" button. I didn't know if I was ready to go to hippie hell, but curiosity about my case's meaning made me fire off the message despite all doubts. I caught myself waiting for a response, although it didn't require any.

To distract myself, I decided to give my revenge publication another shot. The typewriter greeted me like a prophet of doom. It was a fruitless project, but at least it gave me something to focus on. The sound of each typed letter sparked a feeling of ultimate joy: *Dracula Holmes – By Andrew Thomas. The fleeting fog revealed a skinny figure at the Florentine fountain. My tired eyes seemed to wickedly betray me, but there he majestically stood with his long coat fluttering in the dazzling moonlight.*

The buzz of my phone startled me. Mina was trying to reach me, so the dazzling moonlight had to wait.

"Hello, Mina. Long time, no talk," I said, slightly disappointed that it wasn't Matt.

"Hey, still gay?"

I sighed with a broad smile on my face.

"What are you doing today, babes?" she asked without giving me the slightest chance to say anything.

"Going to Camden to meet Matt, apparently."

Silence on the other end.

"You still there?" I asked.

Mina made a weird high-pitched noise, followed by something that sounded like jumping around.

"What's wrong?"

"I'm happy for you!"

"I'm not quite sure what to expect yet."

"Dandy Andy! Take condoms with you!"

"This is…I'm not going to–"

"I want all the details later. Everything! The hotter, the better."

"Never. So, what are your plans?"

"I have a meeting to save my organization. Is there any chance you could ask him to–"

"Mina, I don't know him well enough to ask for such a favor."

"Yet. We will see. I'm at the office now. So, hear you later!"

"Okay, bye."

"Condoms," she whispered before hanging up.

I finally dared to take a look outside. People rushed across the street with umbrellas and anything else they had at hand positioned over their heads. I had stopped carrying an umbrella myself because I usually forgot it somewhere. It was particularly painful when I forgot one from James Smith & Sons, a wonderful shop with Victorian flair on New Oxford Street. They've been selling umbrellas there for almost two hundred years, and I carelessly left mine on the Underground.

After a shower, I stood in front of my closet. I remembered what Bev had said outside the hospital: if I didn't want to look like a clown, I should dress a bit differently than usual. She hadn't said it directly, but that's how it came across. I put on a suit, left the ties in the closet, and came to the conclusion that I looked absolutely ridiculous. The next step would have been a t-shirt under the suit. The thought of it sent a shiver down my spine. Going without a tie was a big enough first step. My suits were my protection from the outside world.

Like Sherlock Holmes when he wasn't busy solving a case, I started the day with breakfast and a newspaper. But it was no daily newspaper for me. Why deal with politics and business when you could just as well read *The Baker Street Journal*, a quarterly publication devoted to all things Sherlock Holmes? While my eyes scanned the text in front of me, I bit into a piece of toast with jam. In all the chaos of the past few days, I finally had a moment of calm, and I wanted to enjoy it as best I could. Classical music played on the radio, the tea tasted fabulous, and I was the only one in the room. Being alone has something beautiful about it; it's just that no one wants to be lonely. I was about to take another bite of my toast when I heard a familiar voice. The toast dropped to the plate.

"We have no time to lose," said Holmes, who was sitting opposite me in pajamas and a dressing gown.

"I need a moment of rest," I replied. I picked the toast up off the plate and turned back to the *Journal.*

"You're in the middle of a case."

And my very late breakfast. "The case can wait," I said, chewing.

"Trust me when I say it can't," Holmes disagreed.

Annoyed, I put the newspaper on the table and got up. The plate with the rest of my breakfast went in the sink.

"You seem irritated," Holmes remarked as he lit a pipe.

"Well observed. No one but you could have figured that out." I fished the toast out of the sink, threw it in the bin, and inhaled deeply. "Sorry, Holmes. It's just, I don't know if I should go on."

"Absolutely."

"I'm heading into something. Matt and I...we live in two different worlds. That's a fact," I said, sitting down again.

"As I said when solving 'The Boscombe Valley Mystery,' nothing is more deceptive than an obvious fact." Holmes smoked his pipe and looked at me. "An obvious fact blinds us so much that the idea of what might be dies. Now go out and solve the case, my dear Andrew. Before it becomes fact that you..." Holmes sounded unexpectedly anxious.

"That I what?"

"Have lost."

"I can't lose anything."

"You can. More than you can ever guess."

"What can I lose?"

"The answer is the case."

I rolled my eyes. "You and your strange case," I mumbled. *And if you say I consulted you one more time, I'll smack you, hallucination or not.*

"It's your case, and you consulted me," he said.

"Right, that's it. Out. Shoo." But he was already gone. I was clearly desperate for any kind of help. Since I didn't know many people, I seemed to have made up the best help I could get. *I need to work on my visualization skills.*

My eyes fell on the clock, and I jumped up to hustle to the Central line. It's the most frequented line in the city, and it's the only one to run east – west through central London. It stops at all of the major tourist attractions and is usually completely overcrowded. Within seconds of a carriage door opening, the smell tells you if it's going to be a pleasant trip or a hellish one. Usually, I just count the seconds until the doors open again. To my surprise, it was fairly empty that day. I still decided to stand, and I did the same on the Northern line to Camden Town because I preferred not to touch the cushions. With so many germs and bacteria, the Underground is a planet of its own. I've never understood how people happily place their lunch on seats that haven't been washed since Thatcher.

I stepped out in the street and lit a cigarette. Just in front of the station were several men and women playing music. I was sure it would be Britpop or something from Amy Winehouse, given the area. After her death, she became a kind of saint of London. But I was surprised to hear jazz instead – something I could like. In fact, it sounded like they were playing Louis Armstrong's "Basin Street Blues." I stopped, smoked my cigarette, and kept listening. Some people danced slowly to the music, and some just stood swaying back and forth. The general public and I seemed pleased.

The rain had stopped, causing haze to rise from the streets. It was a strangely warm and humid climate. I took off my jacket, rolled up my shirt sleeves, and continued to watch the musicians. For a moment, it seemed to me that I wasn't in London at all, but in a remote place. Some police sirens quickly reminded me of my location, however. I took a few pennies out of my pocket and put them in the hat at the group's feet. I had to smile, because I wasn't used to doing this.

I continued down the road towards Camden Market. A confusion of smells invaded my nose: food, cigarettes, and incense smoldering in front of a shop. No house resembled another, and oversized sculptures clung to some exteriors. I looked at the small map I had taken with me as a precaution and made sure I was in the right place. Unfortunately, I was. All right, I would go straight to Matt, have a short conversation, and go home again. Under no circumstances would I be in this part of town at night. We all have our limits.

As I stopped to light another cigarette, I noticed a strangely dressed man. He was medium in size and wearing an unusually old-fashioned long coat. On his head sat a bowler, under which grey hair poked out. I watched him kneel in front of a junction box. Out of curiosity, I got closer. The man was not just kneeling in front of the box; he seemed to be copying something that was depicted on it into a notebook.

I felt like I knew the man from somewhere, but I wasn't sure where. I decided to speak to him in hopes of satisfying my curiosity. Carefully, I stepped closer. When I was almost standing behind him, the man stopped his scribbling and looked around nervously. Before I could say a word, he rose and quickly walked away. I was about to follow him, but from the corner of my eye I saw something very familiar to me: more dancing men.

This person in the bowler had to be someone Holmes knew; his clothing could have been illustrated by Sidney Paget himself, and the figures on the junction box made the connection clear. But why would an acquaintance of Holmes be copying down symbols that Holmes himself had left for me? Admittedly, in the case of the dancing men, it wasn't Holmes who wrote these messages – he just decoded them. They came from the pen of a spurned lover whose promised bride had gone to England without marrying him. However, I had naturally assumed that anything I was hallucinating, stickmen included, must be the work of the great detective. But this was incorrect. The stickmen on the junction box weren't from Holmes, and the ones in the Scotland Yard lift probably weren't either.

I remembered that it was up to me to solve my own case and

pondered how I could put together the facts I knew into a whole. It proved more difficult than expected. I had not been jilted, nor had I ever been promised to a woman who emigrated to another country. So what was the reasoning behind it all?

I knelt in front of the box, as the man had done, and began to decode the stickmen. I was utterly absorbed. Some passers-by stopped to see what I was doing, but they soon noticed I was staring at a white junction box. Or what was a white junction box to them, anyway. I puzzled out the meaning, but when I finished, I wasn't enlightened. It was a phrase I must have heard or read at some point, but I didn't remember where or when. I checked a second time and came to the same conclusion: *the rest is silence.*

Immersed in my decoding, I didn't realize that I was almost smoking the filter of my cigarette. I threw it to the ground. My inability to place the phrase unnerved me. It certainly wasn't from Doyle's pen. I didn't like not knowing something, especially when I clearly did know it. I wondered who the man with the bowler might be, and I remembered that Dr Watson wore such a hat in many of Sidney Paget's drawings. I smiled. It was quite possible that it was him. *If only we'd spoken.*

Though spotting Watson uplifted me, I knew it meant I was closer to madness. Just how close would soon be revealed.

12

—

The League of Extraordinary Folks

The further I walked down the street, the more ordinary it looked. I checked the map again. The building in front of me was an unusually narrow brick house with no front garden. Without the exact address, I would certainly have missed it because it almost disappeared between the other houses. The house was roughly three meters wide and slightly skewed. I walked a few steps past it so I couldn't be seen through a window and lit my cigarette with shaking hands.

A raindrop hit me right on the tip of my nose. I stayed outside as if rooted, just staring into the distance, so that my hair got soaked and stuck to my head. My skin became visible through the fabric of my shirt, and the remainder of my cigarette resembled a sponge. Still, I didn't move.

One hand clutched my eternal companion, and the words hammered my brain again. *I don't know what I am and I don't know what I want. I don't know who I can be and I don't know who I was.* I was determined to write this story anew. The thought of taking my life was more distant than ever, and I wondered how this idea had ever made its way into my mind. I was going to decide the path of my life – not a disease. It was me against the cancer now, and I was determined to win.

I threw the sponge aside and walked towards the house. Something in me wanted to escape, as I had always done. My heart skipped beats. As I caught fragments of my own reflection on the lacquered black door before me, I saw how my shirt stuck to me and my hair hung in my face. I sighed and rubbed my sleeves over my hair to dry it, which made me look like I shared a hairdresser with Boris Johnson. When I rubbed my hair again, the door opened.

"What are you doing standing out in this rain?" asked Matt.

His black sweater hung on him like a huge blanket, and his hair was tousled. He had a unique light charm, wearing effortless clothes tastefully garnished with one gold watch that was probably worth more than my flat. I looked past him into a long hallway. It contained a jumble of bicycles, books, newspapers, empty boxes, and jackets. Just as I had imagined a shared house in this area to look. But it smelled better.

Matt looked weak and insecure, but he continued to smile. He was smaller than I remembered, and he looked far from recovered. With slow steps, he led me down the hall. I didn't like seeing him that way. It reminded me of how I'd felt on my mother's bad days.

Something touched my leg and I stopped. I looked down at a tiny black furball with ears. "What's the cat's name?" I asked as I bent down to stroke them.

"Oh, that's Hercules," Matt said, laughing.

"A cat named Hercules?" I asked.

"I know it's stupid. My cat is a girl," he said, still laughing.

I followed him into the living room, where he immediately lay down on the sofa and wrapped himself in a blanket. Hercules jumped up and curled herself next to him. I took a seat on a nearby armchair.

"You look different," he said, and he grabbed his chin.

I mimicked his motion. There was stubble on my face. "I've been busy the last few days," I said. I was sitting there with a frantic heartbeat, stubble, a wet shirt, and no idea what I was doing. Other than making a fantastic impression.

My legs jiggled up and down. "I'm surprised they've let you go."

"Let's say they did."

"What do you mean?"

He avoided eye contact with me. "I wanted to see Brayton, as he made it very clear he couldn't come to the hospital again. It would make things too obvious. *Anyway…*" His lips smiled, but his eyes didn't.

"Where is he now?"

"Not here. In fact, I haven't seen him since yesterday."

I didn't usually want to punch anyone in the face, but I knew that if I ever saw the deputy mayor again, I would. My ability to properly read people was lacking, but I was sure he wasn't a nice man. "You don't look completely recovered yet, Matt."

"Oh, it's just the bruises. I'm fine."

The wet shirt stuck to my back, giving me a chill.

"Take a blanket," Matt said, pointing to a stack next to the chair.

"Thank you, I'm okay," I replied, continuing to freeze. I looked at him and wished I could crawl into his sweater. It certainly had room enough for two people. It was as if he were hiding in it. "Have you ever noticed a strangely old-fashioned man with a bowler in this area?" I asked.

"There are all sorts of strange birds here, but I've never seen a man with a bowler, I suppose. Should I?"

"By bowler, I mean a hat," I remarked.

"What else would you mean?" Matt rose from the sofa and buried his hands in the long sleeves of his sweater. "Tea? I just made some," he continued, walking towards the hallway.

I nodded and followed him. On the way, I noticed a record player and smiled. Another point in common.

"Suppose he was there. Why did you notice him?" asked Matt. He took the teabags out of the pot and reached for two cups.

"Ask him about the quote," a familiar voice said behind me.

It was hard to resist the urge to turn around. Instead, I made a flapping gesture with my hand behind my back to signal he should leave us alone.

"The quote might bring us closer to solving the case," Holmes added.

I put my hand on my neck and casually turned around. An absolutely normal thing to do. Holmes was dipping a chocolate bar into something that looked like nacho cheese sauce, which by now also covered the tip of his long nose.

"Ask him," he said, chewing in delight.

I turned around again. "Does the phrase 'The rest is silence' sound familiar to you?"

Matt poured some milk into the tea. "Of course. Why?"

"What is it from?"

He laughed a little. "Really?"

"What? What is it from?"

"Well, Hamlet. As a literary scholar, you should know that."

I grasped my cup and peered over its edge, embarrassed. Matt took a sip of his tea and fixed me with his gaze. Just like on the evening when I'd found him, his eyes seemed to penetrate me. He put his cup down.

I almost choked on my first sip and tried to suppress the urge to cough while trying to look absolutely in control. My eyes turned wet.

Matt added milk to his tea. "I would say that after 'To be or not to be,' it's one of Shakespeare's best-known quotes."

I got smaller and smaller behind my teacup. "Is it?" I asked hesitantly.

He nodded and slowly walked back into the living room with his cup. "What does this have to do with the man?"

"That line, it was written on a junction box, and he copied it down." I wished I hadn't mentioned it. I sounded mad.

"That's really weird. Sometimes people use the phrase to mean that you can't say a word about a difficult thing."

Trying to walk and drink at the same time, I nearly choked on my tea. *Again.* "How's the preparation for your charity event going?" I asked, clasping my warm cup.

"I haven't been in the right frame of mind to really focus on it," he said.

I remembered the friendly man with colorful trainers I had met in front of my former workplace. The man sitting in front of me was far different. A night could change a whole person, it seemed.

"It might sound stupid." He paused. "But I feel I'm doing what so many are doing and have done before. People don't seem very interested. They do come to see me or the other actors and actresses, but *anyway*, I doubt they come for the cause."

"How can you tell?"

"We have the publicity, but we don't raise much money. And I'm afraid that what I plan to do is too niche."

I took a sip of tea. Properly this time. "But if you have the publicity, you might have the power to make something niche interesting."

"My flatmate, Bev, is a researcher in the field of molecular medicine, and because of her skin color and other things that are not for me to tell, she faces obstacles and marginalization again and again. There should be equal opportunities for all academics. I would love to focus some theater gigs on that."

I almost dropped my cup. "Actually," I started, not knowing how to say it, "my best friend, Mina, set up an organization last year to help researchers from marginalized groups, but they never really got attention and now they're close to giving up on it."

"Are you joking?" Matt asked, looking at me in astonishment.

I shook my head.

"Seems like Mina and I are a match. We should get in touch."

"I can ask her. I bet she'll be surprised to hear about you." *She won't be.*

"Thanks so much." He took a sip of his tea and got up again. "Should I put on some music?"

Only now did I notice the size of his music collection. His question wasn't a question after all, because before I could answer, he was already reaching for a record.

"I want to show you a song," he said. "I know my taste is a little different from yours, but…"

Fearing we'd listen to 'Your Song' while he stared at me – an unbearably intense proposition – I winced and tried to nod casually. When I looked at the record Matt had chosen, I was surprised to see a painting by Patrick Procktor on the cover. He was a painter I had always admired, whose life was marked by far more tragedies than mine.

"I like the cover very much," I said.

Matt looked at it and smiled the way I did when I looked at *The Strand Magazine*. He was more like me than I'd ever imagined.

"As you might guess, it's a song by Elton John. It's called 'Tonight,'" Matt whispered.

I wanted to say something to change the subject – Holmes, pens, tea, anything that could calm me – but Matt held his finger to his lips. I stayed silent and listened to the music. To my surprise, I heard sounds I liked – piano and an orchestra. The tea slowly warmed me up as the music, which began quietly, continued to build. The sun broke through the clouds and dazzled on the wet terrace tiles. The thought of my disease crept into my mind again. There were so many things I still wanted to experience.

The sunlight gained strength until it shone brightly into the room, and I blinked at Matt. He lay stretched out on the sofa, eyes closed, with his arms crossed over his chest. Hercules purred softly next to him. The music filled the entire room, and the air was suddenly heavier than before. The dust danced in the light. I had felt like I was drowning when I met Matt, but now I felt like I was floating. I felt so much at once, yet it was as if I drifted without any senses. I gazed at Matt and admired the way his uncombed hair looked in the sun shining through the window. His hands looked pale and soft, just like his cheeks. As I clutched my cup, I noticed a strange pressure on my body. I was overwhelmed by a feeling that took away my breath. In my imagination, I lay close beside him and touched his lips with my finger. My body finally warmed up. A bit too much and too fast, maybe. *Concentrate on your tea.*

"What do you think?" he asked.

I almost dropped my cup. "The song is beautiful."

"I know. That's why I showed it to you."

This intimacy was briefly overpowering. I looked around, composing myself. The room was untidy. Books, sheets, and newspapers everywhere. You can never own enough books or records. It was the kind of mess I might even allow in my own home. I was actually quite comfortable.

"*Anyway*...I have something for you," Matt said hesitantly before rising and leaving the room.

I heard him walk up the stairs and come down after a few moments. Hercules followed. Matt stopped on the steps several times; he really shouldn't have absconded from the hospital.

"After I escaped, I got something for you. To thank you for... you know," he said, looking at a small box in his hand.

"You shouldn't have done that, Matt. You belong in a hospital bed."

"Look at it first."

I carefully opened the box. "Matt, that's too valuable. I know how much these cost. I..."

"Nonsense." He lay down on the sofa again.

I gazed at the shiny metal of the pocket watch and carefully took it out of the box. The cold metal warmed up in my hands. As I held it to my ear, I heard the quiet, soothing ticking.

"Do you like it?" asked Matt.

"Yes, very much so." I looked at the details of the clockwork. "A savonnette. I really like this one. The lid is beautiful."

"If I had known beforehand how much you knew about watches, I wouldn't have bought you one."

"Why?"

"Who knows, maybe I would have made an absolute mistake."

This pocket watch was anything but a mistake. I was just about to say something when we heard the front door shut with a loud bang. This was followed by violently aggressive footsteps.

Matt grinned. "That's definitely Bev."

I can't handle two people at once.

Bev stormed into the living room. "I see you escaped successfully in order to please the phantom again, Matt." She looked at me and her jaw dropped. "Matt, you didn't mention we'd have a visitor *today*! I'd have prepared a proper welcome."

"Can I blame the drugs?" Matt joked.

Bev marched up and squeezed me into a hug. I bore it as bravely as possible, which is to say I turned into a plank of wood. Olive, maybe. It has a very interesting pattern.

When she finally let go of me, she took off her jacket and turned to Matt. "What do you think about my new shirt? Got it at Liberty for a bargain."

"Really nice," Matt said. "It really suits you."

"Is there tea left?" Bev asked, walking out of the room just as quickly as she had come in.

"That's our lovely Bev," Matt said softly, smiling. "I don't know about the shirt though."

"Don't you want to give her your honest opinion?"

"I don't want her to be cross with me. You look a bit ruffled. *Anyway*, did she frighten you as much when you met at the hospital?" asked Matt. He took off his sweater, and the shirt underneath pulled up. My eyes fell on his belly, then his black belt and large silver buckle.

I didn't realize Bev had returned to the room. "You are the man of the hour," she said. "Matt has already told me a lot about you."

I reprised my role as a plank of wood.

"Has he?" I'd rarely been informed that I was the topic of private conversation.

"I didn't say that much," Matt replied.

Bev put her hand on Matt's chest. "That's what you claim." She turned to me. "I don't want to spill all the tea before he tells you, but yesterday, when I visited him in hospital, he said–"

"I don't know what she's talking about," Matt interrupted.

My face was terribly warm. "How did you get to know each other?" I asked, to save us all from embarrassment.

"At school. We didn't really get along. Then a few years ago we met again in a bar. I was no longer Jacob, but Beverly. From that moment on, he was my anchor," Bev said, smiling at Matt. "Sad that you'll leave London soon."

13

———

The "Bum Verano"

My heart dropped. *Leave?*

"Oh, Matt hasn't told you?"

I shook my head.

"Today I booked a one-way ticket to New York to live with my father," Matt said. "Bev leaves soon for her internship at the Centre for Molecular Medicine in Oslo, *Westend Street* kills off my character *today*, Brayton and I are such a roller coaster that I can't deal with it anymore. So, I'm leaving. I'll find roles in New York. I need to start anew."

"Closer to Hollywood is all I say," Bev said.

Matt sighed. "Actually, I think it will be the end of my so-called career. But I need some time for myself. There's going to be nothing to keep me in London anymore."

"You can really give up your career like that?" I asked curiously. *I'm surprised they didn't have to drag me out of the university.*

"For my mental health? Yes," he replied, looking out the window.

The sun continued to shine through the stuffy air. My hair was drying, and I was starting to feel like I should leave. My heart was already too invested in this; I knew I shouldn't sink deeper. He was leaving, and I was sure I hadn't made the same impression on him as he had on me. The strange feeling of jealousy and sadness continued to spread like a disease. I really liked the man who sat before me. "May I use your bathroom?"

Bev looked confused. "Well, yes, sure. Upstairs. First door to the right."

I nodded and went upstairs.

"You need to go downstairs immediately," Holmes said. Fortunately, he'd waited until my fly was zipped to materialize.

"Holmes! What is it with you and bloody bathrooms?"

"I thought modern people met in bathrooms to talk."

"Technically, yes, but with consent."

"You need to hurry."

"Why?"

"You need to listen to Bev and Matt," he said, dipping his index finger into some kind of sticky glitter. "That's absolutely not my business, Holmes."

He applied some of the glitter to his arm. "It might be of interest. They are talking about you."

I paused. "Then maybe this is my business after all."

"I suppose."

I left Holmes with the glitter and went downstairs carefully. The voices in the kitchen made me stop in front of the door.

"Oh, I agree. He's a good-looking gentleman, your savior. But he's a bit off." Bev's tone was muted.

"It's weird, I know. I'm really drawn to him, though," Matt replied.

"You've just met. You don't know him really."

"Yet," Matt added.

"Maybe, but don't you want to resolve things with Brayton first? And don't forget you're leaving in a month. Better to not get invested."

"I know, I shouldn't. But I don't really know how to resolve anything with Brayton."

"Don't tell me you still have feelings for him."

"I don't know. Andrew is…since I met Andrew, I'm not sure."

"What is it about him?"

"He has an awkward charm I somehow really like."

"Awkward indeed."

"No, he really is charming."

"So was Brayton, and Kian, and–"

"Yesterday, in the hospital, he listened. It was the first time in ages I felt that someone was genuinely interested in me. Not sex, not money, not fame. Me."

"Honey…be careful, though."

"He reads."

"These are your standards now?"

The doorbell rang. I rushed into the living room and sat down, trying to regulate my breathing.

"Oh, it's about time," said Bev as she and Matt emerged from the kitchen.

"For what?" asked Matt.

Bev looked at him incredulously. "Well, now you're here you can join us, right?"

"What do you mean?" asked Matt, but Bev was already at the door. "Oh no," Matt whispered, rubbing his face with his hands. He looked at me, stricken. "I'm sorry. I completely forgot when I invited you…"

"Forgot what?" I pre-emptively turned into a plank again. *At least move your eyes to seem alive.*

Matt just looked at me anxiously and apologetically.

I heard a loud voice coming from the front door, but it spoke so quickly that I couldn't understand a word. Matt shifted to the side of the sofa and exhaled heavily.

A short, very tanned, and muscular person walked into the room. I didn't know if I should be fascinated or shocked that people with Liz's style existed outside of television. These weren't clothes; this was proper runway material. But it wasn't only their high-fashion appearance – it was also the way they moved and talked. I was speechless. They balanced a gift in their arms that seemed both too big and too heavy for them.

"Hi, girls! Matt, you made it out! And who is this?" they asked, turning to me.

While Liz was wearing a glittering ensemble and gesturing theatrically, Matt sat poised in his seat, smiling cleverly like a boy and watching the scene unfolding in front of him. I gathered all my courage, stood, and went to shake their hand.

Bev announced my identity. Liz made a strange noise and dropped the gift. Ignoring my outstretched hand, they fell about my neck. I was both relieved at their acceptance and petrified by their physical enthusiasm. Suppressing the urge to push them away, I survived until they let go – after giving me a kiss on each cheek. I wondered if at some point I would simply turn into a tree.

"I heard *all* about you. A gentleman and a scholar. And a hero! Have we met before?" Liz asked.

My heart jumped. "I doubt it."

"I'm pretty sure I saw you at the Admiral Duncan last week, darling. A big, strong man," Liz said, turning to the others. "How could I forget. No wonder you invited him."

"I don't know this place, I'm afraid." *Go to a gay bar once and of course this happens*

"No?" They looked at me from top to bottom. "Maybe if you imagine me on heels that reach to heaven and blonde hair styled up to the Gods?"

I shook my head knowing I indeed remembered them. How could anyone forget their presence.

"Does my stage name Conny Lingus ring a bell?" Liz asked.

Bev rolled her eyes and sighed. "Leave that poor man alone, Liz."

"I... I am alright," I stuttered. *Breathe Andrew, breathe.*

Liz picked the gift back up. "Are you all coming with me, or are any of you pregnant?"

A pink hurricane had swept through the room and my head. I sat down on the chair again. My comfort zone had just been assaulted. I belonged at home, listening to my music, sitting behind my desk, tapping on my typewriter.

"Listen, Liz, I forgot all about it, and I've invited Andrew over without realizing," Matt began. "I can't go, I'm sorry."

"You mean it's not why you snuck off today?" asked Liz. "Don't tell me the phantom has anything to do with this. Has he?"

"Stop calling him that. It's complicated enough," Matt said.

"What exactly?" Liz insisted.

Matt took a deep breath. "A man in his position cannot be openly gay."

"Patrick Harvie, Ruth Davidson, David Mundell, Justine Greening, Anthony Bacon, and many others would like to disagree. It's not about his position, honey."

"That doesn't make it better," Matt said.

"You mean you seriously won't go to Michael and Toby's baby shower?" said Liz. They put the gift down on the table.

"Liz, it's been stressful lately," said Bev, taking Liz into her arms. "Let's ease up on him, he's been through enough. Give me a few minutes and we can go." She untangled herself from Liz and left the room.

"Honey, look at you. Your pretty face looks grey and sad. Maybe you should still be in hospital?" Liz asked Matt anxiously.

"I decided to leave. Maybe it was the best decision after all," Matt replied. He smiled at me.

Liz shook their head. "No, darling, the best decision was to order a Bum Verano."

Matt laughed shyly.

"Isn't it Rum Verano?" I asked.

"Well," said Liz with a smirk. "*Someone* was too drunk to properly read, so *someone* ordered a Bum Verano."

"Great times when you still worked at the Black Cap." Matt had a broad smile on his face. "*Crazy* times."

Liz laughed loudly and looked at me. "You know, I even gave him his own stage name back then. But I could never convince him to join the art of Drag."

"What was it?" I asked curiously.

Matt giggled. "I went by the gorgeous name of Bikinki Bottom. Which tells you all you need to know about me."

I couldn't hide a smile.

"You've always been a party girl," Liz said, taking Matt's hands. "So, you might as well come along to the pub tonight."

"I'd love to come along," Matt said, although he was undoubtedly not in the shape for it.

"Well, then the visitor comes along?"

"Me?" I gawped at them. *There's not enough tea in the world for this.*

"Of course, you, gorgeous. We have to celebrate the best fathers on earth." Liz shook their head and followed Bev upstairs.

"Don't you think you're better off at home with tea? To be honest, you look like you need rest," I said quietly to Matt.

He hesitated. "I know. I just don't want to let my friends down."

I got up to go, but Matt rose and approached me. "*Anyway…* sorry about all this. I absolutely understand if you don't want to be with me. I mean with us," he said. "But you're welcome to come along."

I wanted to reject the offer, but the thought of being by his side for a little longer led me to agree. "I'm sure one drink can't go wrong," I replied, holding my new pocket watch firmly in my hand.

14

—◆—

The Sign of the Five

As I walked down the street with Matt, Bev, and Liz, I realized I had never really gone out with a group. We looked like we'd escaped from a circus. Bev was the glamorous trapeze artist, Matt was the handsome magician, and Liz was simply a carnival of a person. Meanwhile, I looked like the circus' harried accountant. People probably wondered what had brought us all together. A circus, obviously.

I was given the honor of carrying the unwieldy gift, so I couldn't smoke a cigarette. Consequently, my nervousness didn't have a release valve, and my emotions started to pile up. But since this seemed like something that might help solve my case, I stayed focused. In retrospect, perhaps I just wanted to find an excuse for the part of me that was feeling happy and excited instead of anxious and overwhelmed.

"This is quite heavy. What's in it?" I asked.

"Everything a baby needs," Liz said.

"Lady Gaga?" Bev joked.

"No, and anyway it would be Beyoncé," Liz replied.

"You're a living cliché," Bev said. She had just put into words what I had been thinking since the minute Liz walked into the house.

"We're slaves to our divas," Matt remarked.

"Don't listen to them, teacher," Liz said to me.

"I'm afraid I might be too young to be your teacher," I replied.

The others burst out laughing.

Liz tried to defend themself. "Depends on what kind of teacher."

"Even then," I said, knowing my sarcastic comments might get me into trouble.

Liz gave me a withering look. "I'm being bullied. I cannot wait to finally open my fashion bar in New York and not talk to you again."

"What's a fashion bar?" I asked.

Liz paused. "A bar where you can buy fashion."

"Wouldn't the clothes get filthy?"

"I won't allow poorly behaved people in *my* bar."

"You're poorly behaved," Matt remarked.

"Kiss my sugar butt," Liz replied.

I was used to Mina's creative linguistics, but this banter was coming fast. I wanted to go back to my books, back to Sherlock Holmes – even back to hallucinating. It was less mad than this. Still, I was determined to persevere. For the case, of course. Not Matt.

"Has Matt told you about his obsession with the Queen of England?" asked Liz.

I made the connection. Perhaps I could keep up with this banter after all. "Yes, he played me one of his songs."

Matt laughed, but suddenly he lost his balance and reached for my shoulder.

"Is everything okay?" I asked.

"Yes, I'm just not quite fit yet."

This is what you get for ignoring doctors.

"Maybe you should go home and rest?" I said, hoping Matt would suggest that I accompany him back to his house. The little time we'd already had alone was probably the most beautiful of my life. But alas, he shook his head and we marched on.

"He's very stubborn," I said to Bev.

"If you want to call it that. I call it unhealthy people-pleasing. Based on what he said about you, you're definitely a stubborn one," she replied, finally taking the gift from me.

My hands immediately reached for my cigarettes. "I may be a bit stubborn, but I can also be kind. Every now and then." I lit a cigarette.

"Do you know how many people die from smoking each year?" said Liz over their shoulder.

"Seven point one billion worldwide," I said.

Liz looked back briefly. "What a treasure, marry him. He's smart and handsome," they said to Matt, linking arms with him.

"You're like a living Wikipedia," Bev said, looking at me like I was from another planet.

"I think Andrew is overwhelmed by you all," Matt noted, laughing.

"So, Andrew, how do you feel about karaoke?" asked Liz, but before I could give my horrified answer, a figure walking along Camden Market caught my eye.

I recognized him immediately: the man with the bowler.

The sum total of my sport ability surfaced in the desire to run – not away from him, but after him. Breaking from the group, I crossed the crowded road and approached the man with determination.

He turned around and looked at me in shock. He had a moustache, and I was absolutely sure it was Watson.

"What are you doing?" shouted Matt from across the street. "Andrew?"

Watson ran off. It appeared he was fearful of being drawn into the case.

I took off after him. Watson was more athletic than I expected. I chased him through the stalls in the narrow corridors until a pram stopped me. It happened in a fraction of a second. I flew directly over the pram and fell on the hard ground. The woman pushing the pram scooped up her baby and screamed. Luckily, the child had not been harmed.

I raised my head. Around me, people gathered and pierced me with their gaze.

"What's going on with you?" asked Matt. He sounded upset as he sat down next to me.

I looked at him in shock. "Did you run after me?"

He tried to gulp down air and nodded.

"The man…the bowler man was there. I wanted to talk to him."

"The bowler man?" asked Bev. To my surprise, she didn't seem out of breath in the least, even though she still held the heavy gift in her arms.

"A man he's seen here before," Matt replied.

Liz sat down exhausted on the ground. "I usually ask for a number," they said with a heavy breath.

Matt looked at me anxiously. "Andrew, there was no man in a bowler."

"But I saw him."

"There was no one there," he said softly.

"I saw the bowler man," I whispered. Then I realized exactly how mad I sounded. I wiped the sweat from my forehead and got up again.

People around me were still staring. I reached for my wallet, opened it, and held it up in the air. "Police. Please keep walking," I said, and the crowd gradually dissipated. I had always wondered if that would actually work.

Matt was still sitting on the ground. I stretched out my hand to him, and he pulled himself up. He stopped, and we held hands for a moment. I almost wished I had never met him; this brief touch triggered more feelings than I could bear.

"For a police officer, you're pretty slow," Bev said.

"Maybe he's the kind of policeman who drops his trousers for a few pennies," Liz remarked, winking at me.

Fortunately, my face was already flushed from the running.

Resuming our course, we went in exactly the direction I had come from, because the pub was in the immediate vicinity of the Camden Town Underground. Upon entering, Liz made sure everyone in the room looked at us by shouting, "We're here!" towards the bar. We went to one of the tables on the side and placed the gift in the middle of it. The room was dark and fuggy.

"Where are Michael and Toby?" asked Matt.

When I looked around, I wondered at the choice of venue. I had assumed we would go to a club or gay bar, not to a pub crowded with tourists. I supposed this was the least harrowing option.

Bev looked around. "They probably need more time than usual now."

Liz came to the table with four beers. "It's their party, they should be here," they said before emptying half their pint in one go. "More people without access to my world-famous New York fashion bar."

"Stop being so impatient," said Bev.

"I'm not."

"You are."

"Guys…" Matt interrupted. "I can't drink today." He gave me his beer, so now I had to drink two.

"Thanks," I said, worrying about the night's outcome already. I took a sip of the half-stale beer and looked around. The place might as well have been an airport.

"Are you comfortable?" asked Matt.

I nodded. He still seemed worried and tired, his eyes were still bloodshot, and although he was prone to acts of protest art in Trafalgar Square, he seemed to be the type for quiet evenings. It made me wonder why I'd found him in front of a club in the middle of the night. While Bev and Liz fought over who was most impatient, I tried to discover more about Matt.

"What had you been doing the night I found you?"

Matt seemed uncomfortable with the question. "I met with Brayton," he said in a muted voice.

The answer made me feel awkward. "Where was he when I found you?" I asked.

"I wasn't in the club or anything. We had met at an Airbnb, but we had a fight and I wanted to go home. *Anyway*…I guess it's what you have to put up with when you're in a relationship."

In the case "The Adventure of the Second Stain," a French newspaper reports four days after the murder that Madame Henri Fournaye stabbed her husband to death in a rage. She is said to be pathologically jealous because of her Creole origins. While I certainly reject the sexist and racist undertones, I could in that moment completely understand the unbearable pain of jealousy.

Matt got up and headed towards the bar. As soon as he was out of earshot, Liz leaned over to me. "Anything you want to know, darling?"

I scratched my cheek. "About fashion?"

"No, gorgeous." Liz tilted their head. "About Matt."

"It's a normal date thing to do," Bev clarified.

"I…I don't really know what to ask."

Bev turned to Liz. "Remember when we wore the most outrageous outfits and asked Matt how he felt about it? And we knew he was so embarrassed, but he didn't dare say anything?"

"Oh, how could anyone forget that day. He wanted to sit in the darkest corner of the bar, but we sat down by the entrance." Liz laughed. "I guess that's what you get if you don't speak up."

"Why couldn't he just tell you?" I asked. "I feel that he's somehow always in a state of alarm."

Both turned their faces towards me.

I looked down at my glass. "Not that I…"

Bev sighed. "He is constantly afraid of losing people. Everyone has their weakness, I guess."

"But the thing is," Liz interrupted, "when he meets people who take advantage of him, it usually doesn't end well. Like with that mayor. Always the same pattern."

"I mean, we know him, and yes, we poke fun sometimes, but it's never to hurt him," Bev said, signalling that Matt was coming back.

"What's his favourite film?" I asked in a hurry.

"*Casablanca*," Bev whispered.

"Really?" I suddenly had an enormous smile on my face.

As soon as Matt was back at our table, Liz engaged Bev in a conversation and both turned away.

"It's always been like that between me and Brayton," Matt said quietly to me as he put the drinks down.

The room around us got even more crowded, and I became increasingly concerned that Matt was harming his health by being there. He winced as he sat back down.

"How did you meet? I'm sure it's not easy to get into those circles."

"Well, I'd love to say we met at a charity gala or press gathering. But truth is, we met on a filthy sofa in a shady gay bar." Matt laughed, covering his mouth with his hand. "I had no clue who he was!"

I had to laugh too. "When was that?"

"We've been together, if you can call it that, for about a year. But *anyway*, we broke up the other night."

"Then why did you leave the hospital for him?"

"I always think that people will change. That I'll get my happy ending after all."

"Maybe that was part of your happy ending," I replied, feeling a warm buzz rising up in me. Knowing he wasn't absolutely sure about Brayton made me feel insecure, though.

"Here come our daddies," Bev said cheerfully, rising to walk towards the entrance.

"Time to round up the usual suspects," I said.

Matt's eyes lit up. "You like *Casablanca*?"

"One of my favorites," I said, looking at the door. A brown man in a wheelchair came in, followed by a tall, pale man. I immediately noted the elbow patches on the short man's jacket. Suddenly I didn't feel so out of place. I finally looked more modern than another person in the room.

"Hi. I'm Michael, and that's Toby," the man in the wheelchair said once he was free of Liz's hug. He reached out his hand. I was gaining serious expertise in handshaking; this time I didn't even suppress a scream.

"You're Matt's guardian angel," said Toby. He took me into his arms.

Plank again.

"We were just talking about it," Michael said. He and Toby seemed to be older than the rest of the group, which I welcomed.

"What's Matt doing here? Has he left hospital again?"

"Again?" I exclaimed.

"I might have done this before," Matt said, tapping his fingers on the table. This was something I often did when I was nervous. I noticed the repetitive noise was not bothering me.

"Back then you snuck out, took a train, and were sent right back in an ambulance," Bev said with a laugh.

"Look what we got for the baby!" Liz said. They handed the gift over to Michael.

By now, all eyes in the room were on our group. I wished again that I could have spent the evening alone with Matt. I wanted to show him who I was, but that was hard to do with these extraordinarily noisy people. I felt the sudden urge to learn how to tap dance. Just to gain his attention.

Michael opened the box excitedly. "Food, diapers, and toys? And *The Golden Girls*? Although, it will be a few years until our child can watch it. You're all perfect."

"False. *I'm* perfect," said Liz. "The others were far from involved. I'm getting more to drink. Who wants another drink?" They took off their jacket. They had tattoos. I should have figured.

When Liz went to the bar, Matt leaned over to me, smiling proudly. "Michael and Toby have been parents for a few months. I'm a godfather now."

"What's her name?" I asked, deducing *her* from the pink box.

"Mary," Michael said.

I would have liked to mention that the wife of the good Dr Watson was also called Mary. After solving the case in *The Sign of the Four*, he married a former client of Holmes: Mary Morstan. Sometime between 1891 and 1893, Mary died under unknown circumstances, and Watson moved back in with Holmes for a while. Without Watson, 221b was not the same place. He remarried, but the name of his second wife remains unknown. Sometimes I wonder if she existed at all.

"A beautiful name, right?" asked Matt, noticing I was in my own head again. He briefly stroked my hand.

"Yes, very nice," I replied, distracted by the touch. Looking at Toby and Michael sparked my desire to have my own family. They seemed like any other fresh parents I'd met in my life. Full of joy, deeply in love, and dead tired. There was nothing that confirmed my thesis that a family was something unattainable for me. Quite the contrary.

Liz was trying to get six glasses from the bar. I walked over, took three of them, and brought them safely over to the table.

"Keep him," Liz said to Matt, baffling me by drinking another pint in almost one go. "If you're in need of wedding outfits–"

"Your New York fashion bar…yes…" Bev said, annoyed.

"We'll see about that," Matt said. He smiled at me.

I swallowed and froze again.

"Where's the little one now?" asked Bev.

"Oh, she's with Michael's parents. It's kind of the first time we're out," Toby replied.

"I'm tired, but it's nice to see you lot again instead of full nappies," Michael joked.

"I've never met a family with two fathers," I said. "You must be very lucky."

"We are," said Toby, and he smiled at Michael.

"Toby is a teacher by the way," Matt said to me.

"I'm a history teacher, to be precise," Toby added, taking a sip of his drink. He had a soft, friendly face, and I could imagine that he and Michael were good fathers. With absolute certainty better fathers than mine.

"He can't go one second without spitting out historical facts," Bev said.

Matt had to laugh. "Toby, Michael, I meant to tell you: Andrew is Sherlock Holmes."

"Sherlock Holmes?" asked Michael with interest. "I love the series."

"Which one?" I asked.

"Well, the series. The BBC series."

I took a deep breath. There was not a series; there were only the original works of Arthur Conan Doyle. But if a defining series was to be chosen, then of course I would have named the one with Jeremy Brett as Holmes.

"I haven't seen any of the new series, if you mean one of those," I said.

My statement sparked silence at the table.

"Weren't you an expert in the field?" asked Matt. "Andrew was a lecturer," he said to Michael and Toby.

"I wasn't sacked for nothing," I remarked, raising my glass. "To all those who have noticed that life continues even after a fall." The others also lifted their glasses.

I didn't want to fully step out of my comfort zone yet, but what I had seen outside my box was intriguing. Mad but intriguing. I wished my father could see me hanging around without a tie in a tourist-infested pub with dubious queers drinking one pint after another. And that I maybe loved it. *Call it rebellion, father.*

"It's true about life continuing," Michael said to me. "I thought my life would be over if I was tied to this thing." He slapped his palms on the arms of his wheelchair.

"How did it happen?" I asked.

"I was a fireman. It happened at work."

"I'm sorry," I said.

"Don't be. Now I know that life has so much more to offer than two legs," he replied, taking Toby's hand.

"He finds a seat in every pub," Liz joked.

I guessed who had left the tasteless greetings card next to Matt's hospital bed, but Michael seemed to take the joke with good humor.

I felt that I must be close to solving my case.

I was far from it.

15

———◆———

The Daring Vegan

I didn't recognize it at first, but soon I saw the pattern: whenever I shared too many Sherlock Holmes anecdotes, Matt pulled on my jacket. Michael did the same with Toby when he went on a history tangent. Toby and I exchanged looks that said, *Let's drive the others crazy.* Luckily, the group quickly understood that we were doing it for fun, and they started throwing in useless facts themselves, which, I am very sure, were not necessarily true.

While I couldn't ignore my anxiety, I enjoyed the company of those around me that night. I didn't push them away, and I soaked up the atmosphere. I would have loved to preserve the moment and lock it up forever in a little box. Then I could take it out sometimes to remind myself I could make friends.

I didn't notice I was emptying one pint after another. It wasn't until I got up to smoke a cigarette that I realized I was already drunk. In that private moment, the thought of my lung cancer was suddenly more present than ever. I was scared. What would happen when I died? What would my last thoughts be before death? I wished them to be the most beautiful I ever had. Maybe even *I love you* or, as a Holmesian would phrase it, *You're wonderful.*

Outside, I slowly exhaled smoke and looked above. Aries was clearly visible, and the moon was in full shine. All I needed was a ladder to reach them. Then I could take a look at the world below my feet and finally understand it. Maybe the case was about learning to let people get close to me? I didn't know, but I hoped to find out soon.

"Fresh air?" a voice behind me asked.

Startled, I looked around. It was Matt.

I took another drag and blew the smoke into the cool evening air. "I had my last cigarette on the way here. A good sign," I said.

"What of?" He was smiling.

"I smoke more when I'm nervous or anxious."

"You don't seem to be either of those things."

"That's where you're wrong."

Silence followed.

"You're thinking about that night, aren't you?" I asked.

The streetlights cast an orange light on his pale skin. His hands were in his pockets, clenched into fists. "I don't…I don't want to ruin this evening by talking about that."

"But I can see that you need and want to."

His lips quivered. "I can't. Let's go back in."

I gently took his shoulder and turned him around. "Just say it. I don't mind. Scream at me or I don't know…curse. I have a great inability to feel offended by anything."

Matt walked away from the entrance. "You know, I don't understand this brutality. I don't understand what makes people want to destroy someone else's life," he said, kicking a stone. "And do you know what the worst thing is? Each of us has experienced something like this in some form, verbally or physically. You wouldn't believe what Bev has to go through every day when she walks through London. As if she were an alien. All she has to do is breathe to bother others. But anyway…"

His eyes were a deep abyss into which I sank. The cigarette in my hand gradually burned down without me taking another drag.

I looked around and saw the streets emptying. The tourists were leaving, and London began to reveal her second personality again. The city enveloped us in her bittersweet melancholy. It became quieter, and the cool air lay on my skin.

"Everything has been kind of different since that night," Matt said. "You know, it's mad. I feel broken." He rubbed his neck and wanted to step inside again.

I knew the feeling of wanting to run away from one's own feelings way too well. "What is broken can also be repaired," I replied.

A tear ran down his cheek. He turned away to hide it. I wished I had learned the art of comforting someone. I wished I had learned how to show compassion. I wished I had learned how to be human. But I just stood there as if I didn't care. Like a plank. Again.

"Imagine you have a vase," he said in a trembling voice. "And it's broken. You might repair it, but you'll know it's not as good as all the other vases. And every time someone picks it up too roughly, it will break again. That's why you don't touch it anymore."

I wanted to have the courage to take him in my arms. "Kintsugi," I said instead, trying to use words in place of touch. "A traditional Japanese method to repair ceramics. Gold powder is added to the glue so that you can see where the shards meet. It's beautiful. The repaired vase is therefore more valuable than it was before."

Matt turned back to me. His eyes were wet and red.

"I'm positive the police will bring those men to justice," I said as I rolled the filter of my burnt cigarette between my fingers.

"Oh come on, they rarely do. I know what was going on, and they don't care," Matt replied. He rubbed his neck again.

I longed to touch him with my own hands, but I couldn't. Between us was an insurmountable wall of self-doubt and fear. Although Matt had told me he and Brayton had broken up, I knew he wasn't really sure about his feelings. It's dishonorable to kiss a man who is still with someone else. I was helpless. "If they won't help you, I will," I said, smiling.

"Help how?"

"However I can. That charity performance, for starters. I remember the flyer well."

An ambulance drove past us, and we watched as it continued along the empty road.

"Something has to change in the minds of people, otherwise you can raise as much money and donate as much as you like and get nowhere. If minds don't change, it's only good on paper," Matt said, looking into the light of the streetlamp.

"You're doing quite well talking about what you didn't think you could talk about." I threw my cigarette down and kicked it out. In the farthest corner of my consciousness, I was hoping for a touch. With my pulse racing, I waited; it was as if I wanted to force it to happen through my silence. But Matt seemed rooted to his spot, and I was too paralyzed to do anything further. Holmes had told me I was in love, and I still didn't trust his observation. However, my heart was pounding and my knees were weak. As I was about to get another cigarette out of my pocket, I noticed Matt stepping closer to me.

"May I hug you?" he asked, his hand stroking my arm. His tone was that of an old-school gentleman. Maybe he was just copying me.

My hands were damp. I nodded hesitantly. I waited for him to move, and I didn't transform into a plank of wood. I longed for tea on a rainy afternoon in a cottage with his arms wrapped around me. *Is this a desire for intimacy?* The moment might have lasted seconds, but it felt like hours until he closed his arms tightly around me.

I remembered holding him in the street. Cold and motionless. I remembered his blood slowly dispersing over the pavement. I remembered being afraid he would die in my arms.

It was another cool night, but this one was filled with life. Death had never seemed so distant to me. Death could wait forever. There were people who didn't want Matt to live. People who didn't want us to live. But he lived just as I did, and in that moment, I felt more alive than I ever had before. We stood in a street and breathed, regardless of any others' convictions. We were insulated from all the looks and words they whispered behind our backs. The world around us had become invisible. Our hearts beat. Loud and fast. No matter what others thought of us or how disgusted they were. Our hearts beat in our chests like every other human being's, pumping life through our veins.

Matt's hands gripped the fabric of my jacket. He exhaled heavily, as if a load were falling from him. "I like your new look," he said.

"It was rather unintentional."

"I might have to get used to kissing a man with a beard."

Matt rested his head on my shoulder, and I felt his breath on my neck. I had never experienced such an overwhelming sensation. It almost forced me to my knees, but my body remained upright. I smelled his hair, and I wanted to swim in everything he was. In each of his words and in each of his movements.

My breath condensed in the air.

I closed my eyes.

All doubts ran from me in rivulets. My wall of fear was in danger of collapsing. I put my arms around Matt and pressed him firmly to me. Although my mind told me not to, my heart yielded to my desire. I felt the warmth of his body and his heartbeat as he nestled his head against mine. Forehead to forehead, we slowly began to sway. There was hardly any rational thinking left. My breath was shallow and calm. I carefully put my hand on his head and let it slide through his hair. Matt's lips touched mine. It was such a tentative touch that I couldn't tell if I had really felt it. He opened his lips and gently licked mine. Despite my fear of contact, I didn't shy away. Instead, I opened my mouth and felt him carefully with my tongue. A diffuse feeling wandered up my neck, a somehow-pleasant shiver. Very appealing, but also weakening. I pulled him tighter to me.

He smelled pleasantly sweet, and his skin was soft and warm. Sometimes you can tell the exact moment when an addiction starts. It was the moment I knew I was going to show him he deserves a man who doesn't just treat him like an option. Although my past had not prepared me to be the best person to reveal this to him, I knew that this time I would get it right.

He smiled and watched me with his sea-blue eyes as I grabbed his belt. It was as if I had completely dissolved inside myself. Everything was quiet. I felt like I no longer existed. The only thing I noticed were his fingers drawing circles around my waist.

He was putting a light pressure on me with his thumb. His other hand carefully slipped under my shirt and crawled up my back. Everything about him aroused me, and I wanted nothing more than to devour him completely.

I gently placed my hand under Matt's chin and raised it so our eyes met. "Here's looking at you, kid."

"And you said you weren't perfect." He kissed me again with tear-covered lips. "Why don't we go to my place?"

I took a deep breath and pushed him away gently. "It's not that I wouldn't love to. In fact, you should really not read my mind right now."

"I would say you're not interested, but I can tell you are."

"How much I would like to find out how accurate the name of Bikinki Bottom is … I…"

Matt laughed. "How about we fetch something to eat. Get to know each other first. I know a great falafel place around the corner."

I nodded. "I would actually love that." Although I only vaguely knew what falafel was, I was eager to get to know Matt.

It was like standing in a Christmas tree. The shop we were in must have been consuming half of London's total electricity. Everything flashed and glittered. I was still wondering what falafel was.

"You're a vegan?" I asked.

Matt finished paying for our meals. "Yes, for years," he replied.

Glancing around, I saw Holmes walk past the takeaway. *Why has he left Baker Street at this hour?*

"I've just got to pop out for a moment," I said, taking my phone out of my pocket to fake a call. Matt nodded and stayed at the counter.

I stepped outside. Holmes leaned against a wall just a few steps away.

"I'm in the middle of my case," I said as I approached him.

"You're still in doubt," he replied.

I decided to try and be more open. "I feel like I don't belong here."

"You know," he said, "Watson and I couldn't be more different, yet I share with him the love of everything bizarre and outside the conventions of everyday life."

"Maybe it's no different for me and Matt." I smiled. He had different interests than me, but in their essence, they were similar.

"Obviously, the young man may not be like you at first glance but trust my instinct when I say you have more in common than you think."

I'm getting relationship advice from Sherlock Holmes.

"So, you and Irene…"

"Irene who?" Holmes asked, dropping his pipe.

"Adler? Irene Adler?"

"I do have a lot of respect for this woman."

"Only respect?"

Holmes cleaned his pipe with his coat. "Respect, my dear Andrew, is the most valuable thing you can give to anyone."

"Wouldn't that be love?" I asked curiously.

"You might respect someone without love being involved. But never has there been true love without respect. Respect is the highest of feelings."

I looked at him, puzzled.

"I'll see you later, when you've solved the case," Holmes said. He walked around the corner and disappeared into the night. Or maybe just disappeared.

I was apparently closer to the solution than I'd thought. I went back inside the takeaway. It turned out that falafel consisted of fried chickpea balls, which, to my surprise, tasted very good. We sat on a garden set in the farthest corner of the shop, right next to a curtain hiding a sink.

"Are you having fun?" asked Matt, wiping sauce from his upper lip.

I wanted to touch his lips again. I wanted nothing more than to feel his body on mine. Instead of doing anything about it, I stared at him like a maniac.

"Andrew?"

I almost dropped my falafel. "Yes?"

"Are you having fun?"

"Very much so," I replied, taking a napkin. *I'm terrified, but I'm having fun.*

He looked at his meal in detail. "That's not the sauce I wanted."

"I'll go and ask," I volunteered, but Matt gestured that I should sit down again.

"It's fine. I don't want to cause any trouble." He took another bite. "*Anyway*...a man was killed just around the corner a few days ago."

I wondered at the abrupt change of topic. Perhaps Matt didn't want to discuss his inability to tell people unpleasant things.

He leaned over to me. "The odd thing is, the man had almost no blood in him."

"Then he bled to death?"

"No. There was no blood."

"No blood?"

Matt shook his head.

I took a bite of my falafel wrap and resisted mentioning Dracula Holmes. I could not resist mentioning regular Holmes, however. "No matter what or who it was, Holmes would solve the case," I said when I'd finished chewing. My shirt sleeves stuck to the unwashed table. The food was good, but was it worth the potential diseases?

"What would you say to Holmes if you could meet him?" asked Matt.

"I would ask him how he survived the fall." *Which is exactly what I did ask him. Don't mention that part.*

"At Reichenbach Falls?" asked Matt.

I was surprised. "You read some Sherlock Holmes?"

He looked at the stained table and smiled. "Maybe I suddenly felt like it."

"I signed up to Instagram to follow you," I said, taking my last bite.

"Why's that?"

"I suddenly felt like it."

Everything about him fascinated me. His movements and words had a magnetic attraction; they felt foreign but also strangely familiar. I didn't say another word. Silently, we sank into the world around us. For a moment there was neither time nor space, only the two of us in a sea of flashing lights.

I cleared my throat. "What would you say if you met—"

"If I met Holmes?" asked Matt.

I laughed. "No. If you met Elton John."

"Nothing."

"Nothing?"

"Nothing," Matt replied.

"Why nothing?"

"Because I would listen."

The answer surprised me at first, but then I remembered my speechlessness when I first met Holmes.

"You wouldn't have any questions?" I asked.

"No, I don't think so. I would have a question for Bernie Taupin, though, the man who wrote most of his lyrics." He wiped the rest of the sauce off the wrapper and licked his fingers. "I would ask why, although he loves her so much that he's sitting on a damn roof writing her a song with beautiful lyrics, he cannot remember if her eyes were green or blue. That has always bothered me."

I finally had the chance to land a proper joke. "But wasn't there a passionate song about blue eyes? Maybe he finally remembered after all those years up on that roof."

"Quite right! The rest is silence, I guess," Matt said with a laugh.

Again, the bowler man and the words on the junction box came to my mind. What I was trying to comprehend was too complex to ever grasp, yet it was more tangible than ever when I'd watched Matt lying on his sofa while listening to his favorite music. It didn't take words. The answer had crystallized at that very moment.

Holmes was right. Contrary to all probability and contrary to all expectations, I was in love.

"Meeting you was the best thing that could have happened to

me," I said, not daring to look up. The words just crawled out of me, and I didn't know if I had thought them or spoken them out loud. I raised my eyes. Matt's face revealed the widest grin I'd ever seen. *Out loud, then.*

"Same for me," he said.

We remained silent for another moment. My head was full of things I wanted to say, but I didn't have the courage to formulate them.

"Shall we go back?" I asked, to escape the situation.

We got up and left our rubbish on the sticky table. The scent of summer rain hung in the sultry air. I was still looking for words in my confusion of thoughts, but on that night something very rare happened: I was speechless. No weird comments, no useless knowledge, no Holmes fact left my mouth. I was silent. We walked close together, so that the backs of our hands touched. I should have turned my hand to take his; instead, I stuck it in my pocket and clutched my lighter.

When we arrived at the pub, Bev waved her phone back and forth. "Look at your stupid phone for once!" she shouted at Matt from afar.

"I need new friends," Matt said, so that only I could hear it. But he was laughing. "What's the matter?"

"The baby is beyond control," Liz replied, and they seemed bothered by the fact that the night was over. Liz's love for Mary had its limitations.

Toby laughed. "Mary won't calm down, so we have to pick her up. So much for a nice evening."

"I'll never do this family thing. What drama," said Liz, eyes glued to their phone. "Okay, darlings, I have a date now," they added, putting the phone back in their pocket and crossing their arms.

Michael looked at Liz in disbelief. "That was fast."

"Don't forget they're the Bermuda Triangle of London," Bev remarked.

I gave Matt a questioning look. He came closer. "Liz's body swallows everything," he whispered. I scrunched up my nose.

"I say!" Liz called out, and they left without another word.

While Bev said goodbye to Toby and Michael, Matt and I had a quiet moment for ourselves.

"I'm free tomorrow," said Matt.

"So am I." I looked at him, and for a second I could understand the thrill my teenage friends must have felt when they first experienced romance. It wasn't pleasant to realize I'd reached middle age before feeling it, but I was relieved that against all odds it was happening.

"Do you want to come over to my place tomorrow?" I asked. I almost flicked my lighter on in my pocket while fumbling with it.

Matt looked to the ground for a beat. With a broad smile on his face, he met my eyes again and nodded. "I would love to."

We parted, and I returned to my flat and lay awake in bed. The idea of seeing Matt again had blotted out all other concerns.

For a short time, I forgot what I would have to do first.

16

———

The White Interpreter

The next morning I sat in the hallway of the hospital, staring at the white ceiling. It was absolutely certain that I had cancer, but I didn't know yet if my death sentence was signed. I weighed how serious my condition might be: coughing up blood was likely not an indication of early cancer. Perhaps I was just a vampire detective who'd had an unsavory client for breakfast – a client who, contrary to all regulations, had eaten baked beans for his own morning meal.

The corridors were swept empty. Only a single patient passed me. She wore a mask and pushed an infusion bag in front of herself. A surreal moment. My legs were jiggling up and down. Anything would have been more pleasant than the silence that surrounded me in that sterile environment, because my thoughts were overflowing.

What if I only have a few days left to live? The shocking thing was not that the thought distressed me, but that there was someone I wanted more days with. I chewed on my fingernails. It was a habit I had given up years ago, which seemed to have come back. I tried to understand what was going on inside of me. *A future with another person? With a living person who would be by my side? A breathing human being I would actually let into my life?* I smiled. Maybe Mina was right when she said there was a living cell left in me.

My smile faded as the patient shuffled past me again. She looked like a shadow of herself and stared straight down the hallway. That could soon be me, emaciated and walking alone through the corridors of the hospital. I couldn't imagine losing my hair and revealing my poor health. There would be endless questions, intrusions. I thought again that I might choose a faster way out. Somehow the thought lacked conviction.

"Have a nice day," I said to the woman.

She stopped briefly, looked around, but did not answer. Instead, she just kept walking. I watched her until she disappeared into one of the lifts. The wait was unbearable.

Perhaps my lifelong unhappiness had to do with the fact that I'd set myself up against so many things. Against modernity. Against touch. Against socializing. Against charity. Against my boss. Against BBC's *Sherlock*. And against myself. Against who I really was. If you believe the universe is against you, you may mutate into a hypersensitive egocentric. You relate everything to yourself, you start unnecessary conflicts, and sooner or later you stop getting invited places.

As a distraction, I reached for one of the magazines next to me. A woman in Newcastle had apparently dated her nephew, who had also funded her breast surgery; a man from Bournemouth had fallen into a well and survived a full four days there thanks to a diet of insects; and a couple from Swansea had opened a sheep therapy center. I sighed and put the magazine aside. My gaze fell on another one buried deep under the mountain of paper. I pulled it out and saw the name *Elton John*. If I had to wait, I could at least prepare for my meeting with Matt. I flipped to the article, which revolved around an AIDS foundation. Although AIDS wasn't necessarily a conversation starter, I read on, hoping my knowledge would impress Matt.

At first, I ignored the movement in the corner of my eye. Then I saw it again. *I'm busy, Holmes. Stop lurking in hospitals.*

"Step up your game, bitch!" said Elton John, giving me a stern look from the page.

Oh no.

Oh please no.

Not another one.

I dropped the magazine on my knees and rubbed my face. Composing myself, I inspected the article carefully, but the image was friendly and static. I had to laugh out loud. My mind was short-circuiting. Just as I started to close the magazine, the picture moved again. I didn't dare look. Then I decided to trust my madness. I reopened the magazine fully. Perhaps I'd learn something.

"Buy some fucking flowers!" said Elton before disappearing completely from the picture. I wondered where he went and turned the magazine over. He was gone. *I've just been yelled at by a Sir.*

"Mr Thomas?" asked a voice from the doorway.

It was time to shed light on the dark.

I entered the consultation room and sat opposite my doctor. My eyes were lowered, and I tapped my fingers on my knee. My doctor's look communicated a slight reproach. Since my first appointment, I had cancelled all follow-up visits or postponed them for so long that they effectively cancelled themselves. Now I feared this behavior had brought me one step closer to my grave.

"Wonderful to see you," said my doctor.

I forced a smile on my lips.

He looked at his documents. "I would have liked to see you here earlier. It's unusual to notify patients of such a diagnosis by letter. We tried to reach you by phone."

"I lost my phone," I said, pressing my thumb so tightly into my palm that it hurt. I hoped my phone wouldn't immediately start vibrating.

"How do you feel?"

Apart from coughing up blood and hallucinating, I'm surprisingly well. "Actually quite good, except for the cough." The thought of dying tugged at me.

"We're going to have to do some more testing before we can start chemotherapy."

"Chemotherapy?"

"You were informed about it in the letter."

"I didn't finish reading it."

My doctor pushed his papers aside and started to write something down. "Displacement is a natural reaction to such a diagnosis, but if you want to live, you need to face the disease as soon as possible. I'll recommend a psychologist to you."

My heart was pounding wildly, my hands were wet, and my thoughts were blank. All that remained was a simple but very important question. "Will I be able to beat the cancer?"

"As I said, we're going to have to do some more tests, but you have a good chance if you start treatment right away."

"I'll survive?"

"The chances are good."

Good was not very good, and I already saw myself writing my will.

"What's next?" I asked.

"For further treatment planning, we need to know how far the cancer has spread in the body and what its growth properties are. We'll take you in for this from next week."

"So soon?"

"It's been almost three months since you first came here."

Again, I started chewing on my nails. I longed for a cigarette.

"What if I don't want to be treated?"

My doctor looked at me in surprise. "This decision is entirely up to you, but I advise you to go into treatment. If you're dismissing the seriousness of the disease, think of the loved ones in your life who would lose you."

"I…there aren't many."

He rested his chin on his hands and looked at me anxiously. "I'll give you well-intentioned advice. Speak to a psychologist. Going through this alone is tough." He pushed a note with contact details towards me.

"I'm aware that I'll die without treatment. Death is the only free choice a person has. Can't you even die these days if you want to?"

I could see what this was now. When I let my mouth run. It was a stress reaction.

"Do you want that? Do you want to die?"

I was silent because the answer was no longer clear to me. A few days earlier, I would have said yes; shortly afterwards, I would have ardently answered no. But at that moment, I was not sure. My mother came to mind, blossoming with music briefly before disappearing again.

"Whatever you decide, we will of course respect your choice. In any case, you can make an appointment at the front desk."

I nodded and got up, but I turned around at the door. "Can cancer cause hallucinations?"

"Pardon?"

"Can the cancer I have can cause hallucinations?"

"No, lung cancer doesn't." He rubbed his face. "I'm going to advise a CT scan of your head just to make sure."

After making an appointment, I left the hospital and decided to walk to Tottenham Court Road. I had to free up my head before meeting Matt. He shouldn't have to sit across from a man who was pondering whether he was worth going to chemotherapy for. Tottenham Court Road is the only street in the center of London that has the word *road* in it, but it's notable for another reason as well: it happens to be the street where none other than Sherlock Holmes bought his violin from a pawnbroker. One can soak up so much of London's energy by simply walking along the street that stretches from Camden all the way down to the very heart of the city.

It was definitely time for a hot comfort drink, so I went into a coffee shop to get a nice cuppa to go. Tea is the cure for everything, at least when you're British and believe nonsense. Inside, I was greeted by a familiar voice. Not Holmes, this time; it was Matt. Speaking from a screen right behind the counter. My eyes were glued to him while I ordered my tea. *Westend Street* wasn't anything I favored watching, but it had an involuntary tendency towards comedy which fascinated me. Christian, the character Matt played, was seemingly in distress over his broken car. A beautiful old blue Chevrolet. He got out to investigate. I took a sip of my tea. My tongue got burned. The car exploded. *They just killed my Cat.*

Back outside, trying to forget what I had just seen on TV, I walked past a flower stand and stopped. It was absolutely unacceptable to follow the advice of an ill-tempered photograph, but I didn't want to be threatened by Matt's idol again. No, this behavior was decidedly too much. I took a few steps back.

"What are you looking for?" the seller asked.

I glanced over the different cut flowers. "Something for a… meeting with a person," I said, rubbing my hand on my neck.

"A date?"

"No."

"For a birthday?"

"No."

"Your wife?"

"No."

"For–"

"I'll take one of each," I said in a panic.

"Excuse me?"

"One of each, please."

"That will…look colorful."

"One of each."

"Okay."

The seller plucked a flower from each vase and seemed unhappy about it. Maybe I had just insulted the honor of all gardeners, but I wanted to capture the one flower Matt liked most. The bouquet that was handed to me was a violation of good taste and uncomfortable to walk through the streets of London with. The seller tried to smile as I left, but I knew that she was murdering me in her imagination and arranging the funeral wreaths.

At Tottenham Court Road, I got on the 8 to East London and took a seat at the back of the upper deck. The bus was almost deserted. This was lucky, because I must have looked very lost with my gigantic bouquet and somber face.

"Do you know what Oscar Wilde said about good taste?" asked Holmes, sitting down next to me.

I looked at the flowers and tried to smile. "The best of everything."

"He bought you a watch."

"What are you saying?"

"Nothing, my dear Andrew."

We stared ahead. Holmes was unusually silent, and he looked strange on a bus with his Victorian outfit.

"How close are we to the solution?" I asked.

"Very close. A better gift would have brought us forward more quickly."

I sighed. "Flowers fit every occasion."

"These flowers fit no occasion. Why flowers?"

"I got a kind and well-intentioned piece of advice."

"Were you threatened?"

"No?"

Holmes raised his eyebrow. We sat in silence for a moment. *I guess my hallucinations don't know about each other.*

"Today it will be decided," he said.

"What exactly?"

"You'll know very soon."

17

The Friendly Intruder

I prepared for what others would probably call a date – something I would never have admitted this to be, though the word kept slipping into my head.

I was terribly afraid of the very concept because I had no clue what to do. When I met my wife, she made all the decisions and I simply followed. I never had to act on my own behalf or convince her to like me. She just did. Without me doing anything. It all went quickly from the beginning, and it was a love story that, from the outside, followed a Hollywood script. We were a perfect couple, except that I was gay. I'd never expected to connect as deeply with a man as I had with Christine, but the impossible had suddenly become possible.

When I walked past my study room, the typewriter grinned at me. I imagined Dracula Holmes' fangs. I feared I was at an impasse. The revenge publication had turned into a joke; it certainly wouldn't get me reinstated as a literature expert. The words I had written so far were sad proof: wickedly, majestically, dazzling? *Someone owns a thesaurus.*

Revenge had to wait. I needed to plan the day. However, my wardrobe made me despair. A black suit was too formal, a blue one too boring, and a grey one would look hopelessly dull. My light blue suit made me look like a teenager at prom, it was too warm for tweed, and I didn't even want to think about my white one. I'd bought it for my sister's White Night party and regretted it even before paying.

I sat down on the edge of my bed and stared into the open closet, having a sartorial meltdown. Finally, I opted for the dark blue one with floral lining, paired with a simple white shirt. After all, I had to appear relaxed. As I dressed, I felt a modicum of confidence returning. That's the power of the right cut, the right color. Maybe I'd been living in the closet for so long because I loved my suits. Except the white one.

My eternal companion was lying on my bedside table, and for the first time ever, I left it there instead of putting it in my pocket. The past, like revenge, would have to wait.

"I see you're prepared?"

"Hello, Holmes," I said, pondering how many shirt buttons I should leave open so as not to look too suggestive or too conservative. I decided that the limit was exactly three buttons.

Holmes had made himself comfortable on my bed and was wearing his silk pajamas. He seemed to have given the case over to me almost entirely – otherwise, he would not have behaved in such an idle manner.

"Have you ever had a date?" I asked, bothered that I had called it by its name after all.

"I beg your pardon?"

"A date."

"That's not my field of expertise."

"But you must have met someone."

Holmes' gaze darkened. "Not my field of expertise."

"Not mine either." I looked at Holmes in despair. He was, after all, the smartest man I knew besides me. Even if he had only Watson by his side, he must have a theoretical idea of the matter.

"In that case, I'm afraid we've come to a dead end," Holmes' voice rattled.

"A dead end? But you're Sherlock Holmes. You've got to have a clue."

"It has to do with feelings," he said.

I could see myself in him. "What are we going to do now?"

"Google?" asked Holmes.

We helplessly stared at each other for a while. Then I went to my computer to see what people usually did on a date. *If the world's greatest detective doesn't know what to do, maybe the internet does.* Holmes and I discovered that it is advisable to have a gift, as well as food and candles. Intimate acts were also mentioned, but I considered this inapplicable to my planned afternoon. It would have taken a lot of liquid self-confidence, and I didn't want Matt to see me drunk a third time. He might get the right idea about me.

I searched my kitchen drawers for candles and luckily found some half-burnt tea lights between the pencils and screwdrivers. Not particularly nice, but if candles were a must, then they would have to do. After all, I was a scholar, not an interior designer. My flat resembled a cross between a library and a museum of Victorian household objects. If London flats had one thing in common, it was probably lack of storage. Or perhaps bad insulation. So, my flat was always a bit messy and cold, and sometimes there was even mold. It's something one has to get used to when living in London, or in Britain generally.

The tea lights, now in four old glasses, were not much of an attempt at décor, but they were an accurate representation of my capabilities. Since toast and jam weren't suitable for the occasion, I decided to order food at an Indian restaurant around the corner.

When I was just about to light the last candle, the doorbell startled me. It took a movement composed of approximately thirty-four different yoga positions to not set my whole flat ablaze. *Consider all fitness for the year done.*

The person who walked up to my flat with hasty steps wasn't the delivery man at all.

"Mina, what a lovely surprise," I said hesitantly.

"I was on my way back home from the station and figured you might be in." She walked straight past me into the living room.

"Is it a complicated matter, because I'm about to have a…meeting."

She stopped, eyeing the candles and plates. "A meeting, huh?"

"Yes, it's a bit inconvenient right now. Could we maybe ta—"

"How are you, babes? Did you shag him yet? Oh, or is that what all this is prelude to?" She gestured at the candles and grinned.

"For heaven's sake! Could we please chat later? Though before you go, I should tell you that I think he might be interested in your organization."

She opened her mouth wide. "Shit! Really? You asked him?"

I nodded.

"Oh, god, dear Andrew, please don't fuck this up. How is it going between you two?"

"This morning I accidentally liked one of his pictures on Instagram."

"That's okay, I guess?"

"From 2012."

She seemed amused. "Not okay. Not at all. Please say there is more news. Positive news."

"I…we…" I was afraid Mina might faint when I said it out loud, so I waited until she sat down. "We kissed."

She stared, her mouth agape.

"He asked me to come to his place, but—"

"Gentleman, I know." She grinned. "But you wanted it, didn't you?"

I laughed. "Of course."

She dug around in her bag and placed a condom in my hands. "Just in case."

I quickly put it in my pocket.

"Why are you always a tiny bit inappropriate?" I asked.

"Pure entertainment."

"As much as I love you, I—" A knock at my door startled me. I opened it and looked into my neighbor's face.

"I cleaned up all the blood," I began. "There is no rea—"

He handed me two bags of takeaway. "I'm keeping an eye on you," he said, trying to peek into my flat.

"I didn't know you worked in the restaurant." *Smile Andrew, smile.*

"It's my restaurant."

"Oh, well, then it must be good."

"Why?" he asked, his face serious.

"Just because you're such a…friendly neighbor."

He nodded and left, but not without peeking inside one more time.

"Mina, did you know my neighbor owns the Indian place around the corner?" I asked, putting both bags on the table.

"Rudra? Yes, sure. We talked a few times."

"His name is Rudra?"

"How long have you lived here? You don't know your neighbors? Very you. Anyway, go on. You kissed. What else? Did he invite you to his yacht? Maybe a night at the Ritz?"

"I really shouldn't say this, but since you're an absolutely trustworthy person…"

"Absolutely. I only tell secrets to a small circle of people."

"Exactly, so, his ex is the deputy mayor of the City of London."

"No! You must be kidding! That's why you asked me to see if he followed Matt?"

I nodded. "And guess what? Brayton doesn't want it to be public at all. Not their relationship and certainly not the gruesome case Matt was involved in."

"I wonder why."

"Reputation, I suppose. But concerning the case, he doesn't want the police to sniff around and find out that it all happened in front of an Airbnb they had rented for a cozy date night."

"He's a member of the Conservative Party. How much worse can his reputation actually get?"

I chuckled. "He thought I was a lawyer and offered me fifty thousand pounds to not let the juicy details become public."

"Oh, shit! No way! Maybe *someone* should give Scotland Yard an anonymous hint."

"I do hope this someone isn't sitting across from me."

Mina smiled to herself.

"So, what's the matter, Mina? You don't usually drop by unannounced."

"It's about my parents' visit tomorrow. I just don't know how to tell them."

"I'm an expert in many things, as you know, but not this, I'm afraid."

"Sharing your true self, even with people you love, is hard. I just can't communicate my feelings when it comes to this." She undid her bun and shook her hair loose.

"Okay, I might be an expert on this after all." *A hell of an expert.*

She smiled. "When does Matt arrive?"

"He should be here soon, but it's fine. Dinner is getting cold already anyway. So, why do you want to tell them at all?"

Mina finally was opening up to me. At least a bit. "Because I want them to know who I am. What makes me the person I am. I want them to know. But I know they will despise me for who I am."

"They're still your parents."

"I know, but very traditional parents."

I thought of my own parents. Acceptance among family is not guaranteed for everyone.

"Was that the reason you moved out so early?" I asked.

She nodded. "They started setting up dates for me with random guys who had PhDs."

"I've got a PhD," I said.

"But not in medicine."

"Ah, they won't notice."

"I'm sure my father will. But be careful, he'll probably want to correct your nose."

I touched my nose. "No, I love my nose."

"So do I," she replied.

"You'll do great, I'm sure. You always find a way to fight against your inner saboteur."

"I just feel like I don't need a coming out. Like being pan makes it redundant," she said.

"If you feel like they need to know, you should let them know. That's what matters."

"Does it matter though?"

"I've felt so much better since telling you about me. That's all I can say."

She nodded. "I'll give you a call when it's done tomorrow, okay?"

"Please do. I'll come over with coffee and an emergency blanket," I said. Then I looked worriedly at the takeaway bags.

"You should transfer the food into bowls," she said.

Convincing.

"Oh, and ask Matt if he'd like to join us for Pride this weekend," she continued.

"Join *us*? I never agreed to go."

"I might need a party this weekend." Mina forced a smile to her face. "Right, Andrew. Have fun tonight."

"You'll be okay," I assured her before she left.

I turned on the radio. Another dating tip found in the depths of the internet.

"But what is your opinion, Sir Elton John?" asked a male voice over the airwaves.

I took the cutlery out of the drawer and laid it on the table. It actually looked quite nice.

"My opinion is that this table was arranged by a toddler. Absolutely horrifying."

Wait.

"You're not going to impress anyone with this cheap decoration. You should raise your standards."

I turned around a few times like a dog chasing its own tail.

"And the flowers…"

I quickly switched the radio off.

18

———

The Adventure of the Noble Bachelor

A few minutes after Matt was due, I started walking up and down the hallway. I was shaking and plucking nervously at my clothes. Anticipation and a pleasant tingling mixed with uncertainty. I had no idea what I was doing. Inviting someone into my sanctuary? I had visions of bolting from my own home in the middle of dinner. *The horror of it all.* Minutes ticked by. I started wondering if he had died in an accident on his way to my flat. I wanted to text him, but I worried that if he hadn't died in an accident already, he would once he started reading my text.

When I finally heard the doorbell, I froze.

After hesitating a moment, I buzzed Matt in. Then I waited by the open door. Before I could utter a word of what I had planned to say to him, Matt gave me a short hug. I smiled because I didn't care. Over the course of a few days, Matt had moved emotionally and physically closer to me in such small steps that I didn't turn into a plank in his embrace.

Matt took off his trainers, revealing socks with cockatoos in every color imaginable. I gave them a suspicious glance.

"Sorry, I'm a bit late. I met Mina outside," he said, putting his shoes neatly to the side.

I froze. *Did he just say Mina?* "Did she…what did you talk about?" *For over twenty minutes?*

"Just about the possibility of working together. You remember? Her organization and my theater group?"

"That's nice, I suppose." I swallowed.

"Absolutely. I think we'll do amazing things together. She has great ideas. No wonder she's your best friend." Matt grinned. "Of course, we talked about you as well."

"I got you some flowers," I said, handing Matt the terrifying bouquet in panic. Mina was a Pandora's box when it came to human interaction. I wanted to call her immediately and interrogate her.

He laughed. "I…wow…this is…"

"The most beautiful bouquet you've ever seen?"

"It's the most beautiful because it comes from you."

My face felt hot and I turned away.

Without being asked in, Matt led the way to my living room, and I followed him. He examined the space, and I waited for him to say it looked like a museum.

"I've only known you a few days and you've already invited me into your home," Matt said as if it was something absolutely unusual.

"Is there something strange about that?"

Matt shrugged. "I suppose I've gotten used to a bit more cloak and dagger on my dates."

"Well, maybe I haven't got as much to hide as certain other people you've been on dates with." *Audacious.*

Matt got the hint and smiled. "You can't help saying what's on your mind, can you?"

"I'm sorry."

"No, I like that you're so genuine. My life is filled with people who are only concerned with their own agendas. They're smooth. And most of them can't be trusted." He picked up my magnifying glass. "*Anyway*…my dates usually happen in random luxury restaurants. This marks a change."

"It's your first museum."

"It is! What is this?" he asked as he picked up one of the most valuable pieces I own.

"This is a miniature set of all of Shakespeare's plays. It's over a hundred years old."

He quickly put it back. "I love things like that. Wait, aren't you the man who didn't know 'The rest is silence?'" He smirked, and I couldn't help smiling too.

I also couldn't take my eyes off him as he examined my collectables in absolute amazement. People are such beautiful beings when they show you their passions. It's even more beautiful if you share a passion.

"Are these all the volumes?" Matt asked, looking at my editions of *The Strand*.

I hurried towards him. Nobody touches these without permission. "They are," I said, pulling one from the shelf. "You know what the most interesting thing is in these?"

"Holmes, I suppose?"

"To be honest, you can read the cases everywhere, but what makes these so special," I said as I flipped through the pages, "are the advertisements." I gently passed the volume to Matt.

"Drunkenness cured…It is now within the reach of every woman to save the drunkard…Can be given in tea, coffee, and thus secretly…" he read out loud. "This is hilarious."

"Here's another one."

"Fat folk should take Fell's Reducing Tablets…*Fat folk*? The Victorians were *shady*."

I pulled another volume from the shelf and passed it to him without saying anything.

Matt burst out in laughter. "Hoe's Sauce?"

"The source of appetite," I added, laughing. "Speaking of appetite…"

"Oh, nice. Takeaway," he said, sitting down.

"Everything's vegan," I replied, proud to have responded to a person's needs successfully.

"Why did you take everything out of the boxes?"

"I thought it looked a bit more decent."

He smiled. "You wanted me to believe you were cooking, didn't you?"

"Maybe," I said, and we both laughed. "What have you been up to today?"

"I was at the theater. But anyway…do you really want to know?" Matt asked, looking down shyly.

"Yes."

"I…okay…I went there to get a few things done for the charity play."

"What will it be about, exactly?"

He looked at me for some time and couldn't stop smiling shyly. "I'm not used to dates who like this kind of stuff."

"I like it too much, I'm afraid. Just wait. It will drive you insane." *Little did he know.*

"It's different monologues from people of different ages, sexualities, religions. It's all about their experiences of growing up queer, their joys and struggles."

"This sounds quite interesting."

"I expect you to be there, then?"

"Of course." I smiled. "Why do you do all this?"

"Do what?"

"Theatre, charity… Knowing your family, you don't really have to do this, do you?"

"It's my passion. Although, my family thinks exactly as you do."

"I – I don't think that way. I was just curious."

"Let me put it this way, knowing I have reserve assets gives me the freedom to do what I love to do. But I also want to give. That's why I'm initiating so many charity projects. The community has given me more than my family has ever given me. Love, for starters. Anyway, it's a matter of course."

"I wish more people were like you."

"That's the surface. I'm easy prey for exploiters. But that's another story," he said, and he chuckled.

"Do you have any plans for the future? Regarding all this?"

"I would love to direct a queer soap that everyone from grannies to Tories would enjoy. Something that makes our lives normal, not something sensational."

"I'd definitely watch it."

Matt smiled, covering his teeth with his hand.

Luckily, the amateur table decorations went unnoticed. I watched each of his movements. His way of holding the glass loosely in his hand and laying down the cutlery in order to gesticulate when speaking fascinated me. He had a lightness that I had never found in life. He didn't seem to care about etiquette or code. What I noticed, though, was an insecurity I couldn't quite grasp. Everything he did seemed effortless, but still he resembled a deer that could run away at any second. He also spoke every word without thinking first. In fact, he talked a lot, but I loved it. Until the topic turned to me.

"Did you enjoy last night?" he asked, pouring more wine.

"Surprisingly entertaining," I said with a smile.

"Why surprising?"

"As you may have noticed, I'm not really the type for such evenings."

"Then, what type are you?"

"No idea. I have no idea how to be myself. I don't know who I was and who I can be." I stopped. The words of my eternal companion had crawled out of me without warning. Instead of putting them on paper, as someone else had, I'd said them out loud. I swallowed.

"What do you mean?" asked Matt, shoveling the rest of the rice onto his plate.

I nervously rubbed my neck. "I've only told one person that I'm gay, and that was the day before yesterday."

Matt looked at me, stunned. "That surprises me."

"Why?"

"You're very confident. Someone who always says what he thinks. As I said earlier, it feels like you're the most honest person I've ever met. You're a disaster human who can't help being himself. I like that. A lot."

"I'm a good actor," I said, emptying my glass.

No words followed. A pleasant conversation had turned to silence without warning. The sound of my pulse in my ears left no space for clear thought.

"Me too," Matt said after what felt like hours.

I looked at him questioningly.

"I'm also a good actor," he repeated.

"Well, you trained at the Royal Academy," I said, assuming that Matt had made a joke to lighten the mood.

He looked unusually serious. "I don't really feel comfortable in my own skin either," he said. He stopped eating and pushed the plate away.

The moment had come: I had to practice empathy. I had to be up for this conversation. I couldn't joke or deflect. This wasn't the usual small-talk scenario; this was important. I rubbed my hands on my thighs. "How's that?" I asked, wanting to sound relaxed. *Progress.*

Matt took a sip of wine. "I don't like the way I look. I never have."

I was confused, because in front of me sat a man whose nature made me thaw. Everything about him radiated an indescribable beauty that I could not have put into words. Not only the way he looked, but also the way he spoke, moved, and dressed. I may not have favored the colorful socks, but I admired him for his sense of humor and light-heartedness.

"Growing up, I got bullied all the time for being gay, although I knew I wasn't. After that, I got bullied by men for being a certain type of gay. I've always been the fat gay boy or the weirdo who can't decide what he wants. No wonder I wasn't beautiful enough to be seen with the deputy mayor of London." He gave a bitter laugh.

"You're anything but fat," I said. "Not that there's anything wrong with fat."

"I'm thin for women, but fat for gays. Many gay men apparently have different standards, as you might know." He took his plate back and continued eating. "Everyone's either too skinny or too fat, too fem or too masculine, too tall or too short, too young or too old. Don't even *talk* about skin color."

I rubbed my hands over my face. "You know, one reason for my fear of coming out was exactly that. The labels. From all sorts of people."

"As if we're defined by our sexuality. Straight people are not defined by their straightness."

"That's true, but they also have the pressure of being a certain body type. Maybe humans are just cruel," I remarked, and I remembered my father. He never hesitated to enumerate my failures. I was either overdressed or looked like a beggar, too smart or too dumb, too cautious or too confident, too talkative or too silent, too childish or – in this case he never had a complementary term. "You'll never be a man like me," he used to say, but he never saw what I wanted to be instead. Although I'd always told everyone around me that my father didn't play a significant role in my life, I still compared myself to him every day. He was resilient, free from emotion, and a master in his field. Maybe the little boy inside me still wanted to become just like his dad to make him proud.

"Or maybe I'm just a gremlin," Matt said suddenly.

"Why are you saying that about yourself?" But I knew the answer well. After all, I was an expert in putting myself down.

"I was anorexic. But anyway…" Matt said.

The sentence hit me like the heat of a sudden explosion. He seemed lost, but I couldn't get myself to comfort him.

"When I was a teenager, it was something I could control. At least one thing I could do when my parents got their divorce. It was a real media circus, and everyone just forgot a child existed in the first place. Don't even get me started about *my* coming out. What did I get as my consolation prize? Severe panic attacks. Thanks for nothing."

Again, I felt Matt wanted to flee from himself. "How did you come out to them?" I asked.

"It was on my graduation day." He stopped and avoided eye

contact. "I invited my first boyfriend to dinner. I...I really thought they would be okay with it. But my father threw a tantrum in the restaurant and my mother cried about never having grandchildren. I'm their only child, you know. The relationship didn't survive long, and I dated a woman after that. My parents thought I had just been confused. There was no family gathering where my *confusion* wasn't part of the conversation."

"That's what you meant when you said you've been on a boat in a storm your whole life," I said, and I pushed the empty plates to the side. I hesitated. "Have you ever told them how you feel? And how you felt growing up?"

Matt shook his head. "No, I never found the strength to do it. I didn't know how and where."

"Maybe you'll find the right time," I said, stretching my hand across the table. "You're wonderful."

Matt put his hand in mine. Our fingers intertwined. A fire could have broken out in my flat and I wouldn't have noticed because I had lost myself in Matt.

He fiddled with the napkin in his other hand, separating each layer and putting them back together. "*Anyway*...I don't know why I'm telling you this. I'm sorry."

I took his other hand as well and made sure he looked me in the eye. "Because I asked you. And because you faced all that and got beaten up in the street, yet you're still going out there and taking chances. You live your life to the fullest, despite all obstacles, despite your family invalidating you, despite your career not going the way you hoped. You're the bravest man I've ever met."

"You know what a lot of people say at this point? Rich people have no obstacles."

"Money can't buy you respect or sincerity or love."

"Not at all, no."

I recognized the look on Matt's face. He tried to smile, but I felt that he didn't fully trust what I was saying. Once you have a concept of yourself, it's hard to believe that others don't see you that same way. That they don't see your flaws. That they don't see the parts of your body you find disgusting. That they don't see the same face you see in the mirror.

Matt got up, and I was sure he was going to put on his shoes and go. But instead he put his arms around me from behind. I looked up. In Matt's presence, I seemed to be the best version of myself, because there was no argument, no discussion, and the fear of touch had disappeared in an instant. I could think only of the blue eyes that looked at me familiarly. His smile had a warmth I had never seen in anyone looking at me. There was no need to analyze him or question his intentions. My guards, tasked with keeping me safe, quietly left, one after another.

I reached for a package on the table. "This is for you," I said, lifting it in the air.

Since my Google search had suggested bringing a gift on a date, I had found something to supplement the colossal bouquet. I didn't have to search long: it was immediately clear what the present had to be.

"You're probably used to much fancier presents, but…"

Matt tore the paper bag it was wrapped in and looked at me in dismay. "Your picture of Holmes?"

I nodded.

"But this must be awfully important to you? You're sure?"

"I'm sure," I said.

"Holmes looks very calm curled up in his chair, doesn't he? I wish I could be like him," Matt continued.

"You don't have to be," I said, standing up.

My heart beat louder, my breathing quickened, and despite my aversion to purple prose, I had to admit that butterflies were fluttering wildly in my stomach. I closed my eyes and gently put my lips on his. I waited for his reaction. When he got into the kiss, I kissed him emphatically. I put my hands on his hips and pulled him tighter. Matt put his hands on my neck. It felt beautiful, but it also scared me. I was close to a man – not only physically, but also emotionally. Something I had waited for my whole life. Matt carefully put his hand on my back and looked at me seriously. It was more tempting than I wanted to admit. I hesitantly stroked Matt's stomach with my fingertips, feeling goosebumps forming on his skin. We lingered for almost a minute. Then he took me by the wrist and stopped me.

"I think it's time for the dessert," he said.

"Is that a metaphor? Because I only have toast and jam and—" My mind went completely numb. The only thing I noticed was his hand caressing me. I struggled to keep standing upright. He pulled me closer, and I felt the warmth of his lips on mine. His hands slipped under my shirt and crawled up my back. Matt pushed me to the sofa. *Definitely a metaphor.*

When I felt his body on mine, we completed the first chapter of our story. At the start, the words came slowly to the page. Every one of them held more meaning than the ones before. Our eager hands typed faster and faster. They were hesitating but determined; then they got careless about grammatical exactitude. It was a hectic and interminable stream of consciousness. No punctuation marks, only the flow of language in a wicked manner. Everything I knew of literature dissolved into bright colors I had never seen before.

19

◆

The Curious Incident of a Hermit in Love

"Put that away immediately, Holmes."

The great detective dropped the book he was holding. "Andrew, awake already?" He bent down and retrieved the volume. Various maps and newspaper clippings, which I had carefully assigned to the individual chapters, fluttered to the floor. *The horror of it all.*

I was afraid the noise might have woken Matt; I crept back into the hallway to listen for him. *All clear.* "Holmes, I'm not alone," I whispered upon returning to the living room.

"This did not escape my powers of observation," said Holmes. While tucking papers back between the pages of the book, he paused to behold a replica of an article on the Hound of the Baskervilles. Sighing softly, he tucked it inside the front cover.

I snatched the book from him and put it aside. "How…how long have you been here?" *First he sees me in a towel, then he sees me in the middle of—*

"Long enough. I see you're getting on well. Beautiful. Very nice." He seemed scattered.

"Is everything okay, Holmes?" *I'm concerned about my hallucination's mental state. Naturally.*

"No. Well, yes."

"Yes, or no?"

"No." He sat down in his armchair and lit his pipe.

Holmes and I: two people who were absolutely not designed to talk about feelings. "Do you want to talk about it?"

He fumbled with his pipe. "Yes. Well, no."

I suppressed an exasperated sigh. "Yes or no?"

"Very well. I shall endeavor to...express my thoughts."

I nodded and sat down on the sofa. *Patience, Andrew, he's your literary hero.*

Holmes sat a moment longer. At last, he spoke.

"Am I real?"

My heart stopped. *Shouldn't I be asking* you *that?*

I had no answer. Was he real? When is something real? An awful lot of people thought god was real. And that was based on a book nowhere near as good as, say, "The Red-Headed League."

"Am I real?" he asked again. This time he looked me right in the eye. I could feel the look as it travelled all the way to my epigastric region. Where my breakfast should be now.

I hesitated. "To answer this, I think it is necessary to use evidence. What did Descartes say about existence?"

"Our thinking proves that something has to exist," Holmes said. A hint of his usual self-confidence had returned.

"And do you think?"

"Do I, Sherlock Holmes, *think*?"

"Well, there we have it. You're real," I said, hoping we'd neatly dealt with my hallucination's existential crisis.

"It's not that simple," Holmes said.

I sighed. "No?"

"There are books about me, on your shelf."

"And?"

"I haven't experienced some of what's written in them."

I took a cigarette, lit it, and sank into the sofa. "Haven't experienced *yet*," I stressed.

"Where did Watson get all this information about me? Many things in here are undoubtedly not accurate."

"You should ask him, not me, I suppose."

Holmes squeezed his eyes shut. "Can you make him appear?"

Sure, and why not conjure Moriarty while we're at it. "No," I replied.

"In case you meet him," Holmes said, "let him know that I do have significant knowledge of human anatomy, and my political knowledge is of good quality, self-evidently."

"I doubt that," I said, remembering cases in more detail than the detective himself.

Holmes gave me a frightening look.

"Say, Holmes…do you like bees?"

"They are quite fascinating creatures." Holmes' face brightened.

"Very good. That's good."

We sat for a moment in silence. "I'm afraid I'll only be real until I'm forgotten," Holmes said.

"That will never happen, Holmes. Not as long as I'm here. Trust me on that."

"What if you find something else more deserving of your attention? Perhaps it's better if I investigate with you from now on."

Is Sherlock Holmes jealous?

My attention was seized by the sound of the bedroom door opening. I looked over my shoulder, and when I turned back around, Holmes was still there.

Matt stood in the doorway with tired eyes and messy hair. He had taken the liberty of wearing my dressing gown. It looked so fantastic on him I couldn't object.

"It got cold without you in bed," he said, going straight to the kitchen to prepare breakfast.

I cupped my hand, breathed into it, and sniffed. Then I immediately went to brush my teeth.

"Did you find everything?" I asked when I entered the kitchen. He had. He had even found the teapot I'd put down about a year ago and never seen again. Perhaps he'd reached into my cupboard and pulled it from another dimension. He was so astounding that it seemed just possible.

"Where did you find the teapot?" I asked, trying to not pay attention to Holmes, who had followed me and now stood in the door frame.

"It just appeared out of nowhere, to be honest," Matt replied.

"Out of nowhere?" *Really, Holmes?*

Holmes looked at me with a triumphant smile.

I hugged Matt tightly and kissed his forehead. "Thank you."

He gave me a passionate kiss back and looked at me.

"What's going on?" I asked. My eyes met those of Holmes again, and I wished I could make him disappear with one blink. But he stayed. *Inconvenient.*

"You're beautiful, that's what's going on," Matt said in the softest voice.

My cheeks flushed. Some people have a scent in the morning that makes you want to stay in bed all day. Almost like a sedative. I was sedated. "It's nice that you stayed," I said, and I poured some orange juice. *Not you, Holmes, not you.*

Matt smiled and took the jam out of the fridge. "Haven't had sex for a long time?"

Holmes gave me a look of absolute terror and promptly disappeared.

I coughed up the orange juice. I laughed so much that I had to put down the glass. "How did you determine that?" I asked, pulling him close to me. Without waiting for an answer, I kissed him.

Matt sat down on the kitchenette and put his legs around me. When our lips touched again, he began to moan softly. He threw his arms around me and pulled me towards him so that he could sit upright. After a moment, our lips parted. Matt held me with his blue eyes. I shoved my hands under the dressing gown.

I rested my head against Matt's neck, laughing silently. I was overwhelmed by a joy I had never thought I could feel. Outside, it started to rain. The heavy drops splashed against the window, blurring the view of the large back garden.

Matt held my face. "You're doing me good…" he said before laying his lips on mine.

"And you me." *The pleasure of it all.*

"Is that so?" There was a shade of doubt in his voice.

"The fact that you're here means a lot to me," I said quietly, sinking into the blue sea.

Matt undid the buttons of my pajamas and slipped the top off my shoulders.

I cast a quick glance around to make sure Holmes was absent.

I was wonderfully happy.

I was terribly hungry.

And Holmes reappeared.

I stepped away from the kitchenette. "I…I need to go to the bathroom." *Sexy.*

As expected, Holmes followed.

"What on earth are you doing?" I asked, and I opened the window in hope that the street noise would drown out our conversation.

"Investigating."

"Investigating?" I walked up and down the room. "You're a millstone around my neck right now and not helpful at all, Holmes."

"I want to make sure the investigation is going in the right direction," he said. He began fumbling around with the artificial plant I hadn't cleaned for ages.

"Is this about our conversation earlier?" *All those years of wishing Holmes was real and look what happens.*

"We are drifting from the actual case. We need to concentrate, my dear Andrew."

"Isn't the case solved?"

The plant rolled out of Holmes' hands and into the wet bathtub, leaving little dust bunnies along the way. "Not even close."

"But you said it's about…love? To find love?"

"I'm not in the mood for guessing games," Holmes said, and his mood shifted.

"And I want to have some privacy."

"There is no privacy when we are on a case."

"*We?*"

A knock on the door. "Andrew, are you all right?" Matt asked.

I opened the door. "Yes, yes…I…" I looked around. Holmes stood in the corner with his arms crossed. "Matt, how about going on a walk?"

"It's raining."

"And isn't that romantic?" *Help.*

Matt laughed. "Okay, give me a minute to freshen up. Once you're, uh, done in there."

I smiled and closed the door again. "Can you at least look away while I shower, Holmes?"

Finally, he disappeared.

"When does something cease to exist?" I asked as we finally escaped my haunted flat.

Matt looked at me, confused. "I think when you die?"

"No, I mean…let's take Sherlock Holmes…" *What a coincidence.*

"Oh, you mean a fictional character? I suppose if no one remembers them anymore. What is forgotten no longer exists."

I opened my umbrella. "But won't there always be someone who remembers?" I asked.

"Not necessarily." Matt stopped, looked at me, and smiled.

"Hmm?"

"You're weird. I like that," he said.

"Weird?"

"Well, I've never had a date ask me about existence out in the rain, while said date is under an umbrella and I'm not."

"Oh," I remarked, and I quickly held the umbrella over him. "It's not the first time I've heard that I'm weird." Defensiveness flared up in me. How many times in my life had I heard I was different, that I didn't belong, that I didn't fit in.

"I don't mean that negatively," said Matt.

"Don't you?"

"No," he replied, smiling. "You're weird as in unpredictable, smart, and profound, almost like you're from another time. I'm happy I found you."

We passed the white houses in my street and headed towards Victoria Park.

"Strictly speaking, I found you. On the street."

Matt laughed out loud. "Yes, I'm a rescue."

"That you are, Matt the Cat." He was dismantling my walls stone by stone. Gently. Slowly. He just let me be me. And still he understood me. "It's good that you see me like that. That you like me."

"If I didn't, I wouldn't be out in the rain with you," Matt said. He pressed himself closer to me while walking.

No wonder Holmes never let love get to him. A love-drunk Holmes wouldn't solve a single case. His fine brain would be mashed potatoes. Just then a chill ran up my spine. I turned to see Holmes following us, soaking wet like a canal rat. I had hoped he would stay indoors.

When we finally reached Victoria Park, Matt's phone rang. As I stood uncomfortably close, I could hear every word.

"Hey, Brayton," Matt said. He shot me an apologetic look.

I tried to not listen, but now my curiosity was too great.

"I reserved a table at Le Gavroche, your favorite," Brayton said.

Matt smiled. "Oh, so you remembered?"

"That you love it there? Of course. Let's forget our little fight and have a nice dinner."

I kept holding the umbrella over Matt's head. I glanced at Holmes, who had started to shiver.

"Brayton, I…"

"Come on, it's a rainy day. There's nothing else to do, really."

"We could eat takeaway at your place and then have a walk in the rain?" Matt asked.

Holmes looked at me, confused.

I looked at Holmes, confused.

Brayton laughed at the other end. "Why would I do that, Matt? This is silly."

"I know," Matt replied.

A moment of silence. "Why don't we get you that Louis bag

you love so much afterwards? I'm sure I can squeeze in another hour between meetings for you."

A Louis bag? Should I have gotten him a Louis bag? What's a Louis bag?

"Listen, Brayton." Matt took a deep breath. "I don't want to have dinner with you, and I surely don't need a sugar daddy to buy me expensive things. First, I'm richer than your whole party. Second, I wanted the bag for Liz and not for myself. And third, I have never been to Le Gavroche, so it must have been someone else. As you remember, we were never out in public together. So, if you don't mind, I will no longer tolerate less than I deserve."

"We'll talk again tomorrow when you've calmed down," Brayton said.

"I'm walking in the rain and I'm happy."

"You do you, darling. Let's talk tomorrow."

"There is no tomorrow. Truth is, I've known you're an arrogant prick for a very long time, but I've stayed because I was afraid to be alone. I thought I didn't deserve better. But I do." With that, Matt hung up.

"What was that?" I asked.

"That was me realizing abusive love is not love in the first place. But *anyway…*"

I watched him delete Brayton's number and couldn't help but smile. Matt had finally told someone what he really thought. And he had done what I couldn't. Although I was brutally honest most of the time, I couldn't tell Christine the real reason our marriage ended. Suddenly, there was a desire in me to tell her the truth, but I didn't know when or how.

Matt took the umbrella out of my hands and closed it. "Let's walk in the rain," he said with a laugh.

"How was your dinner at Le Holmés?" I asked, feeling the water soak through my shoes.

Matt stood in the middle of a puddle. "It was a delight, my dear. And now let me buy you an expensive yoga mat to fix all our problems."

"Oh, I'm sure I can squeeze you between two meetings."

"But only if you buy me something. Something expensive, of course," Matt said, struggling to jump clear of the puddle.

"Let me help you with that," I said, and I ended up ankle deep in mud.

Holmes stood in the distance looking miserable. *Case solved?*

"You're hot," I whispered before biting Matt's lower lip.

"No one has ever called me hot. Sweet, yes. Adorable, sure. But never hot."

"Then it was time for it. High time," I said, beginning to freeze.

"I should apologize to Brayton, shouldn't I?"

"A friend of mine once said that respect is the highest of feelings. If someone has no respect for you, why should you have respect for them?"

"That friend was wise," Matt said.

"The wisest I've ever met." *Wise and obnoxious.*

"For me, that's you," Matt said. "Please stay in my life forever, in whatever way."

I breathed in deeply. "There's something you should know," I said. I didn't want Matt to sign up for something he wasn't ready to endure.

He pressed his hands tighter to mine, his wet hair hanging in his face. "What is it?"

I didn't know how to say it, so I just dropped the bomb. "I have cancer."

Matt was breathing hard; he was struggling with his feelings. He pulled his hands back and distanced himself from me. That was what I had always been afraid of. Another person's empathy towards me was a difficult feeling to process.

He looked up and swiped his hands over his eyes. "What kind?" he asked.

"Lung cancer. No surprise, I know." I tried to smile. "I wanted you to know that before we meet...before we meet more often. Not that...I mean, I would understand if–"

"I will help you go through this," he promised with tears running from his eyes. "This hurts."

"I'm sorry."

"Don't be. I'm glad you told me. You're not alone, okay? Whatever happens…"

"I talked to my doctor yesterday."

"Is it fatal?"

I hesitated. "He says there's a chance."

"Take it, please. And if you don't, I will make you."

"Now I have a reason to."

"You know what?" Matt said. "Now I feel really bad going to New York."

For a moment, we silently clung to one another. I had pushed this detail about Matt to the back of my mind, and it was not for me to decide what he could or could not do with his future. Yet it still hurt to hear he hadn't revised his plans to leave since meeting me. I wanted him to stay.

"Did I already mention you're hot?" I asked to lighten the mood, pulling him even closer to me.

Matt grinned through his tears and pressed his forehead to my chest.

"That you're probably responsible for global warming?" I continued.

"That's pretty cheap."

"So hot you've made the penguins go extinct."

"Why the poor penguins?"

I felt my phone vibrating in my pocket. It was probably Mina. I remembered I had promised to talk to her. However, instead of answering her call, I lost myself again in Matt's eyes. I was sure Mina could wait until evening. "If you'd existed in 1912, there wouldn't have been any icebergs and the Titanic would have made it to New York."

"The Titanic?"

"Yes, and do you know about the wildfires?"

"My fault?"

"All your fault."

"Are there any studies on this?" Matt asked.

"Absolutely, I'm an expert in scientific studies."

"Is that so, professor?"

I nodded. "Are my lips blue? I feel like an ice block."

"Okay, as romantic as this is…We should have a hot shower before we catch a cold," Matt said.

"Together?" I asked curiously.

"Of course," Matt said. "I actually never liked it, because of my…you know, *body issues*. But with you…I don't mind you seeing and touching every inch of my body."

"Good, because that's what I'm planning to do once we're home."

And home we went. Followed by the ever-present Holmes. I cast a final look over my shoulder at him. There was a darkness to his expression. A worried look. I wondered if he knew something I didn't.

20

◆

The Valley of Fear

I had my arm wrapped tightly around Matt's naked body and my face buried in his neck. I closed my eyes. The mixture of his sweat and cologne created an intoxicating smell. I never wanted to be without it again. He had dozed off, and I watched him sleeping. His nose was pointy and slightly turned up, and there were barely visible freckles on his skin. I ran my fingers along his jawline and smiled.

We were startled by a loud noise.

Matt grunted, and with eyes half closed he searched for his phone in the pile of clothes. "It's Bev," he whispered to me. "No, I don't think I'm coming to the pub today," he said into the phone.

I remembered I needed to call Mina back, but I forgot about it as soon as I kissed Matt's neck. "But I would love to," I murmured, knowing it would make Matt happy to see his friends.

He turned his head and smiled. "Okay. We're coming." Matt laughed. "Yes, you heard that right. We are coming." He hung up and turned his body to me. "You know," he said, "I think I've finally found my island."

When I heard those words, I knew the pub and Mina had to wait. I was absolutely sure she was doing fine. As always.

A few hours later we were back at the pub we'd visited two nights before. I was looking forward to seeing Matt's friends again. Having friends was now something I considered possible, even desirable. It was fun and not draining or frightening at all.

Liz and Bev were clearly having another argument, and almost everyone in the pub was looking at the two. My anxiety skyrocketed. *Maybe friends are a bad idea after all.*

"Calm down, you chickens," Matt said when we'd approached the table.

"I'm not a chicken. Look at her! She is!" Liz said, flapping their arms around like the bird they claimed not to be.

"Stop bitching about my outfit!" Bev shouted. "With your fashion sense, you'll never open your damn bar in New York!"

Her outfit was indeed extravagant, but she resembled a Christmas ornament more than any animal. I looked at a table in the left corner of the pub and saw that a group of girls were furtively pointing and glancing at us. Perhaps they'd recognized Matt's face. Or maybe they liked the show.

"Shots?" Bev asked, putting a glass in front of each of us.

I wasn't in the mood for hard liquor, but I expected it to make me relax faster. I regretted it the moment I swallowed.

"What are you going to wear for Pride on Saturday, Mr Bones?" Liz asked.

"Holmes, his name is Holmes," I corrected.

Matt giggled.

"Anyway. What will you wear?" Liz insisted. "I'm a fashion expert."

"Nothing," I replied.

"Oh, one of the nude ones. I once met a—"

"I'm not going," I interrupted.

Both Matt and Liz gave me a questioning look.

"Why?" asked Bev.

"This is weird," said Liz. "Because Matt already said you'd join him for brunch with his theater kids before we all meet up for the parade."

I looked at Matt.

Matt smiled. "I knew you would say yes, so I made plans for us."

"But I didn't agree to go. I don't want to go."

"Don't be silly," he whispered, leaning in as if I was a misbehaving child.

"I won't come," I repeated.

"Okay, kids, let's have more drinks," Matt said, rising and ambling towards the bar.

I was left without a proper conversation on the issue. Liz leaned uncomfortably close. "I heard you were together today *and* yesterday."

I cleared my throat and grabbed the shot Matt hadn't touched. "You heard that right." *Still tastes bad.*

"I bet my ass you had sex," Liz said as loudly as anyone could say it.

Bev rolled her eyes.

I wanted to escape. I did enjoy the company of Matt's friends, but I wasn't ready to casually talk about my feelings towards Matt, let alone our intimacy, with anyone other than Mina. Apart from that, I really wasn't comfortable being mothered by anyone. I was a grown man and not a naïve boy.

Luckily, Matt returned to the table with two giant pitchers full of beer. "Why are we here again? This pub is always so crowded." He took a sip of his beer and placed his free hand on mine. Of course, the little gesture was noticed by the others. But the worst thing was that the girls in the corner were trying to snatch a photograph of me and Matt.

I pulled my hand back and quickly poured a glass that I drank in almost one go. We weren't at home, unobserved, where vulnerability felt safe. We were on public display. And being on public display was a nightmare. *The horror of it all.*

"So, tell me *everything*," Bev said with her eyes wide open.

Matt put his hand back on mine. "We spent a couple of lovely days in Andrew's flat."

Liz rolled their eyes. "And?"

"We didn't leave, except for a romantic walk through the rain. That's all I can say," answered Matt, fixing me with his eyes.

"Look at you, you two lovebirds," said Liz. "Is this serious between you two?"

Matt squeezed my hand. "I wouldn't mind."

I turned to concrete. The alcohol started to take effect.

"What's wrong?" Matt asked.

"Nothing," I lied, continuing to drink.

"So, if this is serious…" Bev started. She paused and looked at Liz. "You finally broke up with Brayton?" she said to Matt.

"Finally? I thought you broke up the night I found…the night we met?" I asked.

Liz propped their head on their hands. "Don't worry, darling, there was never really anything to break up. Back and forth, forth and back. Matt has a heart way too good for this world…and that's the problem."

"I made it very clear to him that it's over," Matt explained.

"Just today?" I asked. I spotted Holmes sitting at the bar, drinking something that looked like a Pink Lady. *Leave me alone already.*

Bev took a long sip of her drink. "Better late than never. He was an empty shell. Just like everyone in your millionaire world. You can be glad you have us." She tried to put her glass down and missed the table.

Matt took her drink out of her hand. "Bev, maybe pause for a moment."

"No, really, what would you be without us? We're your family," Bev said, trying to hug Matt. He, however, declined.

"What a lovely sentiment tonight," said Liz. They took out their phone and started swiping.

Holmes stood up and almost stumbled over his coat.

What have I done to deserve all of this?

The alcohol gathered strength in my system. I switched from survival to self-destruction mode.

"I should go," I said, knowing I had better leave before things went downhill.

"Do you need the house for yourself tonight?" Bev asked Matt. "I could sleep at Liz's place."

"I think not. I have a date," Liz said.

"With whom?"

"I don't know yet," Liz said, swiping. "Someone."

"Okay. I'll sleep at Liz's place."

I shook my head and turned to Matt. "No, I…want to sleep in my own bed." *Introverts have rechargeable batteries and mine is empty.*

"Then I'll come with you," Matt said, linking arms with me.

"Alone!" I said far too loudly.

Holmes stumbled towards us.

Everyone in the pub turned their heads.

Matt pulled me to the side. "Why are you acting so weird and drinking like you want to forget today?"

"Aw, their first fight," Liz said, giggling and snapping a photo with their phone.

It was the first time I ever saw Matt close to losing himself.

"Liz, stop it!" Bev exclaimed, sensing something was up.

I emptied my glass. "I can't do this."

Matt looked at me, puzzled.

"Can we talk outside?" I asked, pointing to the door. And outside we went. I tried to walk like sober people walk, but the more I concentrated, the more drunk I looked.

Matt gave me a stern look when I lit my cigarette. "You shouldn't do that."

"What?"

"Smoke. You have lung cancer."

"And you technically still had a boyfriend when we hooked up. How can I trust you?" I tried looking at Matt as well as Holmes, who stood right behind him.

Matt laughed deprecatingly. "Why are you being like this all of a sudden?"

"I don't like you making decisions for me."

"I'm sorry…I…I guess I'm just not used to a healthy, functioning relationship."

That makes two of us.

Matt looked around. He must have sensed I wasn't looking at him only. "Truth is, I never had a proper relationship."

My old defense mechanisms kicked in again. "You told your friends private details." My heart was pounding. *Calm down, Andrew.* "So?"

"I don't want others to know what I'm doing…what we're doing."

"That's absolutely normal in a relationship," he said. "My friends are my family."

The word *relationship* made me feel unwell. Everything was going too fast. A train of emotions I couldn't stop was barreling towards me. "I don't think this is something I can do right now," I tried to explain.

Matt sighed. "What is this childish fight *really* about?"

I rubbed my face in agony. *I have social anxiety. I'm afraid of intimacy. I'm depressed. I have cancer. I cannot love you. You deserve someone else. You deserve to be loved.*

"I think we both make a great couple," Matt said as he forced a smile to his face.

"For you or your family? Am I the socially acceptable gay man that is less threatening to the heterosexuals? Do you need me for your portfolio? I don't want to play that role."

"What do you even mean?"

"Bev said I'm your parents' type, and now I believe so too. This is all going way too fast to be natural. Do you need me for the media?" My heart was pounding in my chest. My anxiety held my strings again and I wanted to run. My sweaty hands fumbled with the note in my pocket.

"It's going so fast because I finally found someone who makes me feel I'm worth *something.* You seemed like someone who actually cared and listened. Instead, you're just as ignorant and narrow-minded as everyone else." The train was unstoppable. "I was so close to loving you," he said, and he teared up.

I felt the same, but I was unable to communicate my feelings in a way that would make Matt understand. "I cannot give you what you need right now. I cannot play the happy couple part. I cannot. It's beyond my capabilities." I took a deep breath. "I'm sorry, Matt."

"I believe you. I believed everyone who said this to me before," he said silently. He rubbed his forehead. His hands were shaking. "But why doesn't anyone ever want to try?" He started to cry bitterly.

"Calm down," I said, noticing people around us were looking.

"Everyone I care for leaves me," he said, his whole body now trembling.

The situation demanded what I feared the most. Emotions and compassion. "That's not true," I tried to explain.

"Why didn't you just tell me earlier!" he screamed.

I glanced at Holmes. He shook his head. "You will ruin this case before it's solved."

Anger rose up in me. "Leave me alone! You follow me everywhere! Go away and mind your own fucking business for once! Leave. Me. Alone! I don't need or want you in my life!" I instantly regretted saying those words out loud.

I noticed Matt's breath getting shorter.

"I wasn't talking to you, I was talking to Holmes," I explained.

The door opened and Liz and Bev stepped outside. They hurried towards Matt. *Come on, Andrew, do something. Anything.*

"What's going on?" Bev asked defensively.

"It's just a fight, nothing more," I said. *Shut up, Andrew, and do something.*

Holmes disappeared. The one person who had always been in my way. Professionally, personally, and now literally.

Matt's knees got weak. He had to sit down on the pavement. He still couldn't breathe properly.

"He's having a panic attack again," Bev said to Liz, trying to comfort Matt.

Liz confronted me. "What have you done?"

"I've done nothing. He's overreacting. I was talking to Holmes...I..."

"Overreacting? Does this look like overreacting?"

"This…this is too much," I said, stepping away.

Liz followed me.

I stopped and looked at them.

"If Matt is too much for you, go and find less. But if you really care for him, you should tell him, *now*," Liz almost whispered before returning to the others.

For a moment I was rooted to the spot. It took all my strength to go back to Matt. "I'm sorry," I said, kneeling down in front of him.

His face was the angriest I'd ever seen. "Leave me alone," he said, almost unable to speak.

For a moment I thought I must have misheard.

Matt took a deep breath. "I really want you to go away, please."

"Andrew, I think it's better you go now," Bev said.

I stood up and left. I understood that I had to get away. As far away as I could. My throat hurt like hell, and I reached for my cigarettes. In addition to sadness, rage mounted in me. I should have stayed in my world. I should have stuck to what I knew I could handle. I'd been safe in my solitude, but more importantly, others had been safe from me. I felt a tear creep down my cheek, and it was like the last bit of life fleeing from me. I looked up, but the sky was dark; there were no stars visible. Stars held only empty promises anyway. After all, they had burned up just like me. I didn't want them anymore.

My feet carried me further and further into the night. My trembling hands took my phone out of my pocket, and I called Mina. It was late but technically still the day I'd promised to call her. The line rang for a long time, but she finally answered.

"Mina, I have to talk to you," I said. I sat on the windowsill of a shop, feeling like a little kid who had gotten lost. But I was just a grown man who didn't know where to go. I was glad to have at least one number I could call.

"Hi, babes," she said. "Wait, let me walk somewhere quieter."

The tear on my cheek had company. Loud noises on the other end. "I wanted to call earlier but we…"

"You promised."

"I know. But there was so much going on with me. And Matt."

"Kind of an arsey move for someone who considers me their best friend." The pulse of the city made it hard for me to understand her.

"I know, I'm sorry."

"But it's still today and you did call. I'm not a bitch. Well, you know…*sometimes*." She paused. "So, no hard feelings."

"Thank you," I said, beginning to freeze.

"Though, could you say you're sorry just one more time? I like hearing it from you."

I took a deep breath. "I'm sorry, Mina. I'm sorry." Someone shouting something on the other end interrupted me. "Where are you?"

"Wyndham's, we just got out. My parents and I saw a play."

"Your parents? That's…that's great." I sniveled. "Which one," I asked.

"*People, Places and Things*." Mina waited until an ambulance had gone past her. "I talked to Matt yesterday, but I bet he told you. He is such a cutie pie, really. Isn't he with you?"

I felt as if someone had squashed my lungs. "No," I said with effort.

"It's good to take things slowly, isn't it?" Again, a loud noise made it impossible for her to speak. "I came out to them. I came out to my parents," she said in a proud voice.

"Did it…" I said, trying to sound as natural as possible. "Did it go well?"

"Surprisingly well, actually. I don't know if they understand it a hundred percent, but they said they have my back and support me. Whatever may come."

The tears were unstoppable. "That is beautiful."

She muffled her phone. "No, Mum, wait a second," she said in a muted tone before speaking into the phone again. "Where are you, Dandy? Are you crying?"

My hands trembled as I led my cigarette to my mouth. I'd rarely experienced Mina in such a good mood. She deserved her happy night. I didn't want to disturb any person's happiness anymore. "I…no. I'm catching a cold, I'm afraid."

"Why did you call?"

I swallowed. "I just wanted to ask if you're up for a late drink."

"Sorry, babes. We wanted to go to that ice cream place down the street that makes it look like a rose. Can you believe that? Absolute magic."

"Okay, then have fun," I said, and my throat hurt. "You need to tell me more about your great day tomorrow, okay?"

"Thanks! I absolutely will! Talk tomorrow. Bye." She hung up.

Sobbing, I stepped into a pub across the street to hide for a moment. After a few quick drinks, I headed straight to the bathroom, went into one of the cubicles, and locked the door.

I sank to the floor and wished I had never come. It grew quiet around me. The only thing I could hear was the bass of the music, which penetrated the cotton wool of my ears like the beat of a clock. I remembered the watch and made sure it was still in my pocket. It was, and I took it out. My eyes tried to concentrate on it, but everything was shrouded in fog. I could have been a respected scholar. Instead, I sat drunk on the floor of a toilet cubicle in a filthy London pub. My hands encircled the watch. Although it was certainly not allowed, I lit a cigarette. This was exactly the sort of place that would have broken smoke detectors.

A knock on the cubicle door ripped me from my thoughts.

The door opened.

I looked up.

"Holmes," I said. I let the cigarette smoke escape through my nose. "What do you want?" I kicked the door shut in his face. *Come back with a warrant.*

"To talk to you," he replied.

Through the gap beneath the door, I could see that he, too, was sitting on the filthy tiles. He leaned his back against the door. I smelled his tobacco.

"The case has become unsolvable," he said.

"You know what? I don't care about the damn case anymore!" I was still trying to calm myself down, and my skin was burning.

"You're probably blaming me for the fact that we're now at an impasse," he said.

"No. No, not 'we.' *You* are at an impasse, and *you* are to blame. You are to blame for everything!"

"Calm down. We must look at the whole thing soberly. Viewed from a distance and excluding emotions, a solution can be quickly found. It would now be quite appropriate that—"

"Did you just ask me to calm down?" I interrupted him. *When did telling someone to calm down ever calm someone down?*

"You loved him, didn't you?" asked Holmes.

I hit my head against the wall. Every muscle in me tensed. I took out the little note. Again and again, I read the words and hoped to erase them. They had become a part of me that I never wanted to lose. I felt tears rising. I swallowed and took a deep breath. I wanted to leave the tears deep inside, but there was no stopping them. They ran down my face and onto my hands, which desperately tried to halt their flow.

"His name was Ian," Holmes said.

I pulled my knees tightly to my body. *I don't know what I am and I don't know what I want. I don't know who I can be and I don't know who I was.* The words Ian had written to me rang out in my head. I did love him. I loved him so very dearly.

"You have to face your past," Holmes said.

I put the note back in my pocket. The only thing I wanted to face was death.

"I want you to disappear. Forever. Your damn case is a shitshow. You're just a fictional character."

"That's what I'm afraid of," Holmes said. "I'm afraid that if I lose you, I will disappear. I don't want to be…dead."

His words sent shivers down my spine.

"If you want me to go, I'll say goodbye now," he said in a trembling voice.

"Just disappear!" I shouted.

Holmes stood up. "Goodbye," he said through the cubicle door. "I hope you'll solve the case anyway; otherwise, this farewell will be the last thing we say to one another. I guess it's our final problem."

And with that, he was gone.

I threw the rest of my cigarette into the toilet and got up. The blood flowed back into my legs, and I became dizzy. The stench around me intensified. I reached for the door, and my mouth filled with saliva. My breathing accelerated. I noticed my heartbeat slowing down, and everything around me turned a shade of blue. Despite the alcohol content of my blood, I knew what logically had to follow. A genius' mind cannot be fooled, even when it's highly intoxicated. *Why here?* I fell to my knees and held my head over the dirty toilet. After I had emptied out my whole body, I wiped my mouth with my shirt sleeve and dropped my hand heavily on the flush handle. I tried to breathe normally and suppress the urge to throw up again. I laughed and started to cry at the same moment. This wasn't what I wanted to be, but I didn't know how to change anything either. Legs wobbling, I got up and made my way out of the pub with determination. I could have just gone home to hide under my blankets, dwelling in self-pity. Instead, I decided it was finally my turn to tell the truth. If Matt and Mina were able to, so could I. It was time to talk to Christine.

21

—

The Final Problem

A cold splash of water on my face woke me up.
"What in god's name are *you* doing here? You gave me a
heart attack!" Christine, better known as my ex-wife, loomed over
me. She held a pink watering can shaped like a flamingo.

Apparently, I had fallen asleep on her terrace.

"It's the middle of the night! I thought you were a robber!"

"Hi, Christine," I said, trying to put on my best smile.

She gave me a questioning gaze. "So?"

I sat up. "I need to talk to you."

She put the watering can down and crossed her arms. "Why?"

In that very moment I wanted to grab her and hold her. I'd
missed her so much. Seeing her overwhelmed me with so many
different emotions that my body ached and my head was full of
buzzing bees. "Please, let me in, I need you," I begged, knowing
that there was absolutely no reason to let me in.

"Are you crying?"

"No," I said, crying.

To my surprise, she waved me in but didn't say a word.

The living room was still as I remembered. A light room beautifully
decorated with fresh flowers, blankets, and pillows. The scent of

roses mixed with the burned-up wood in the small fireplace next to the kitchen. There were candles everywhere, and Christine lit them as soon as she walked in. A routine she'd had ever since I'd known her. I took a seat on the white sofa in the center of the room. It all smelled pleasantly like home. I had lived in this house for years, and it only then occurred to me that I actually missed it. I missed Christine's warmth and big heart too. The strongest heart on earth, and I had managed to break it. She radiated the same warmth that Matt did whenever I met him, and I can say without a doubt that I still loved her.

Christine went to the kitchen and put the kettle on. "With milk?" she asked as if nothing had happened between us. But a lot had happened – a lot of silence and lies on my part. Sitting right there in the living room was something I'd wished for ever since. Lost for words, I closed my eyes and let the house infuse me, giving me the courage to speak.

A few moments later, she came back with two white mugs the size of planting pots. She sat down next to me and wrapped herself up in her oversized cardie. Her hair was up and her glasses were on, which indicated that she had been working late and probably hadn't gotten any sleep so far. We were much alike in that regard: a love triangle between her, me, and our work.

"Hi, Chris," I said with a lump in my throat.

She looked at me as if she suspected that her overworked brain was inventing me. *Welcome to the club.*

"Hi, Andrew," she almost whispered. She took a sip of her tea.

My body was tense. "I didn't know where else to go and started to walk…home."

Our eyes met. There was a calm certainty in hers. She knew I was anxious and afraid and that it was okay. She knew me like nobody else.

"It doesn't feel like home without you here," she said.

Hearing that made me tongue tied. Emotional intimacy was far trickier than physical intimacy. With Matt, both got mixed up, and I was beginning to understand why that was so challenging.

Christine took off her watch and put it on the coffee table. "It's a bit like the first time we met."

I finally started to relax a bit and smiled. "I was lost for words on that day too."

"I guess you just didn't think that anyone on earth would dare to correct you about something Holmesian."

I shook my head. "Never. It did impress me, though."

"What kind of people did you expect to meet at a Sherlock Holmes-themed conference?"

"The usual smattering of people with a little bit of knowledge," I replied, remembering it as if it were yesterday. It was a rainy and cold summer day. The conference was in a hotel in a small Cornish town called Boscastle. There were no hounds, but a dog followed us for about a mile to a pub. As we found out later, it was his scam.

"Why did we always think we were so much smarter than everyone around us?" she asked, trying to hide her smile behind her cup.

"Because we are?"

"Obviously."

We both burst out in laughter.

"You kept your humor, Andrew. That's good."

"You kept your beautiful smile," I said.

She averted her gaze. "Why exactly are you here?"

"I…I need to tell you something," I mumbled, not knowing if I was actually ready to finally tell her the truth.

"That you're gay?" she asked out of the blue.

"How did you know?"

"I knew for a long time, Andrew. When you love someone, you know them, through and through. Though what you know might end up hurting you."

"Why didn't you talk to me ever again?"

"Because you chose to lie to me. After all those years, you didn't trust me enough to tell me. I always thought you would come by and tell me eventually. But you never said a word."

"I'm here now."

"Almost three years later." She took off her glasses and let her hair down, gently running her fingers through it. No more work tonight.

"I was afraid," I said, holding on to my mug as if it could keep me upright.

"Of what? Of me loving you still?"

"Is that the case?"

She nodded. "Every day, every second. Every time I sit in the kitchen and remember how you ruined our first Christmas meal, or in the bathroom, where I see you showering while I put on my makeup. I miss you when I watch TV, because you had answers to all the questions, and you would somehow see all the mistakes in movies."

"As Holmes said, the world is full of obvious things which nobody by any chance ever observes," I remarked. But even a quote from our beloved detective couldn't stop the words that I feared hearing.

Her eyes grew wet. "The garden misses you. The roses have almost all died, since you don't take care of them anymore. This house misses you. Yes, I love you still, Andrew. I will always love you."

I stared down a tunnel. I hadn't been a terrible husband. She actually loved me. But I could never love myself while I lived in that house. All I did was drown in my own misery because I couldn't be honest with myself or her. I ruined her life in a way I didn't want to. I felt horrible. "I don't know what to say, Christine. I…" *I love you too. I want you to be loved. I want you to be happy.* The words died before I could speak them out loud.

She put her mug down and lowered her head as if she was waiting for me to comfort her.

A tear rolled down her nose, and it fell on her knee. Again, I was turning into a pillar of salt. Whatever misery I was in because of Matt, in this moment I could almost hear my heart break. I wanted to cry out loud but held my breath so Christine wouldn't notice. There was no air anymore. My heart began to beat out of sync. I wanted to completely disappear inside myself and just become nothing. I wanted to be nothing. Nothing cannot ruin lives.

After a few hours, I started for home feeling worse than I had ever felt. The streets were still dark and empty. White sandstone and red bricks were colored by the familiar orange light. Sirens howling in the distance intertwined with the soft fluttering noise of the trees in the otherwise screaming city.

"Where are you going, lad?" a voice called from the opposite side of the street.

I recognized the homeless man immediately. I hesitated, but I decided to go over and instantly crumpled next to him.

"Still not better?" he asked, handing me his ever-present bottle of booze.

I gagged just smelling it and handed the bottle back to him. "Obviously not," I said.

"You really need to do something about this, whatever it is that created this mess," he replied, a look of concern on his face.

"I will tonight," I said, taking the bottle again. But I still couldn't drink from it.

"You're not going to do something stupid, are you?"

"Maybe," I replied.

"Why's that?"

"I'm gay." *Well, guess I'm telling everyone now.*

He stared at me for a very long time, which made me feel uneasy.

I took a sip from the bottle and shivered as I swallowed the most disgusting booze I'd ever tasted.

"All this mess because you're gay?" he asked, unable to hold back his laughter.

"Do you think this is a joke?"

"No. No, not at all. Love is one hell of a ride. No matter who you fall in love with."

"This has nothing to do with love," I assured him. I lit a cigarette.

He gave me the "and we both know that's not true" look and started to chew on an old biscuit. His reaction to everything I was going through was to eat a biscuit as old as me. *A biscuit? Really?*

"Look at you. This has to do with love."

"There is someone who says he could have loved me."

"Could have? What, did you mess it up?"

"Oh yes."

"How?"

"By not being able to love him back."

"Not being able to or not wanting to?"

"Both? You know, I always thought my problem was that I'm not lovable. Turns out the problem is that people do love me."

The man shook his head. "If you give up now, this man will be left heartbroken. He loves you."

"I've broken too many hearts doing this love business. My ex-wife still loves me and is absolutely heartbroken, and I couldn't even take the man I love in my arms when he needed me."

He laughed. "The man who probably loves you too?"

I nodded.

"Your life isn't a mess. You can bring this back in order."

"My relationships have all ended in tragedies. I'm simply not capable of this."

"I'm sure you are. Who's got the keys to your heart?"

"Me?"

"Give them away."

"That won't help." *Heavy is a heart that holds a ghost.*

"Why's that?"

"I can't show my emotions. I absolutely blame my father; I was punished for showing them. I inherited this. I will never be able to change this. Turns out I'm just like him. It would take getting hit by a fucking bus to change who I am." I stood up as if an invisible force were pushing me.

"What, leaving already?" he asked.

I didn't even bother to reply. With shaky steps, I walked a few paces up the main road, hoping to somehow meet Holmes along the way.

"Holmes!" I shouted, and I heard my voice echoing back from the concrete buildings around me. "Holmes!" I shouted again.

He was gone. Truly gone. After what I'd said, I couldn't blame him.

I walked on. In the distance, the bright lights of a double-decker bus appeared. *I'm manifesting metaphors now.*

I looked back at the homeless man, who seemed to be pulling something off his face. He wasn't a homeless man at all. He was the man in the bowler. He was Watson. *I really am mad.*

The loud horn of the bus frightened the sleeping birds. They fled in panic from the branches of the trees. When the lights blinded me, it was already too late to step aside.

"It was a metaphor!" I cried. And in the final seconds, I looked through the front window of the bus bearing down on me. Elton John sat behind the wheel. Next to him stood Sherlock Holmes, who directed him to hit me.

"NORBURY!"

I was catapulted through the air. I landed on my back, and an indescribable pain exploded throughout my body. I looked at the stars hovering above me. From then on, everything was black.

22

—◆—

The Curious Woman

In my delirium, I wondered if the good Dr Watson had felt similar pain at the Battle of Maiwand in 1880, when he had suffered a serious shoulder injury. "Originally," one should add, because in *The Sign of the Four*, the shoulder became a leg. Probably it was a small oversight by Arthur Conan Doyle, but not a few tried to conclude that, if this pain wandered, Dr Watson had returned not only with an injured shoulder, but also with an injured psyche – the pain in the leg was imaginary. Poor Watson must have lived through horrible things while serving. However, I think the description of imaginary pain is unfair: psychic pain, as I well know, is not to be underestimated. Despite all the conspiracy theories, I persist in believing that the author made a mistake and continued with it so as not to cause further confusion.

But it was clearly my shoulder that was injured, because when I woke in the hospital bed, I could barely move my upper body for the pain. I was wrapped in a weird bandage, and I was shocked to see that my shirt sleeves had been cut off. This was one of my favorite shirts: the collar and the insides of the cuffs had a beautiful and unique pattern. How dare they save my life and not that of this wonderful shirt.

The bed I lay in smelled like a hotel bed, but this vacation was involuntary. Or was it? I didn't remember much about what had happened, but I had the sense that I'd placed a bet. Had I won or lost? My head was exploding from the previous night's excessive alcohol consumption. My mouth was unpleasantly dry. I coughed into my hand, and to my horror there was blood. Unfortunately, the bus hadn't knocked the cancer from my lungs. I grabbed a tissue from the bedside table to clean myself.

Despite everything, I felt strangely happy and relaxed – two states of mind which made me skeptical. Whatever they had given me for the pain, I probably could have used it a few days earlier. Before my brain was torn to shreds.

I carefully scanned my shoulder. It had to be a fracture, because I couldn't find any signs of surgery. I continued to feel the swollen area but could not detect a broken bone. So, it was a bruise, which I found fascinating considering a bus had hit me.

I looked at the white ceiling and was no longer sure if I had deliberately stepped in front of the bus. Had it been an accident? After years of theorizing about other people's suicides, I realized I must have done it with full intent. My pickled brain must have wanted to tell me something. Probably that I needed to change immediately, but even at this point I didn't understand such an obvious explanation. All I knew was that I had driven myself to the abyss until the jump didn't seem so bad anymore. Or to be precise: *I'd rather get hit by a bus than talk about my feelings.*

I closed my eyes and tried to sleep. Dozing off, I imagined being in front of a fireplace with my notebook and pencil. I saw myself scribbling something on the paper. There were four dancing men, and I tried to figure out what they meant.

"Awake, young man?" said a weak and grumpy voice beside me.

I turned my head carefully. *Maybe she's a hallucination.*

The woman in the next bed was so small and thin that she could have been well over a hundred. I wasn't aware that men and women could be accommodated together in a room, but upon consideration, I realized that the NHS was, as always, completely on the rocks. I ignored her and tried to bring back the image of the dancing men.

"When I was your age, I wasn't allowed to sleep that long. I'd had four children by that point," she said.

No, she's too chatty to be a hallucination.

"Good morning. I'm Andrew," I said, resigned.

"My second-born is called Andrew," she replied, trying to sit up slowly. "I'm Harriet. The hip."

"The shoulder," I said, tapping the bandage.

"I know. When they wheeled you in, they were talking about your encounter with a bus. Seems it just clipped you. Lucky."

"Yes, lucky."

"I imagine you gave the driver a fright, though."

That's when Sherlock Holmes, Elton John, and the bowler man came back to me. I winced and fell silent. I looked at the ceiling again and hoped she would follow my example. At her age, she couldn't have long to live. I decided to wait.

The medication I was on caused my eyes to close after only a few minutes. Although the image of the dancing men didn't return, I had never felt so at peace with myself. I wondered if that was a normal state after attempted suicide, but there was another explanation, of course: a chemical one.

"They gave you morphine," Harriet remarked.

"How do you know?"

"I looked at the infusion bag."

I inspected the drip and saw how small the label on the hanging bag was. The old woman must have been very close to me in order to decipher its script. How peculiar does one have to be to approach sleeping strangers in hospital? This wasn't a case for Sherlock Holmes; this was a case for the Met.

"You got up for that?" I asked.

"I was curious," she replied, smiling good-naturedly.

She would have made the perfect killer. Old, friendly, and frail. At night, she'd sneak over to the beds of strangers and inject poison into their infusions. You could never know when your last day would come, but surely nobody would suspect a woman who could barely walk after a hip surgery. At least you'd have a realistic chance of running away from her. Another case for Dracula Holmes: *The Slow Chaser.*

"You have very soft skin," she said.

I turned my head so quickly I felt a sharp pain in my shoulder. There must have been an expression of pure horror on my face. She had *touched* me? Without permission?

She laughed out loud. "It looks soft, I mean. I don't touch sleeping patients. But I admit that I would have been happy to secretly wash you. You smell like a pub toilet."

Her deduction was perfect.

She stared at me for a moment. "They said something else about you."

Please don't let it be anything Holmes-related.

"Did you mean to do it?" Harriet asked.

"What?"

"Did you intentionally step in front of that bus?"

I paused. "I don't know."

"You don't know?"

"No."

"But you were there?"

"I still don't know."

There was no sane way to explain that I was shouting at Sherlock Holmes in the middle of the night because he'd disappeared after I insulted him in a pub toilet, so I stepped in front of a bus driven by none other than Elton John to kill myself without actually wanting to kill myself. They probably don't even make a greetings card for that.

Harriet pulled two needles out of a drawer and began knitting.

"Then it was probably intentional," she said, without looking up from her knitwear. "You know, I usually have a room all to myself," she continued quickly, precluding my reply.

"I'm not going to stay long," I said.

She looked up in horror. "Your shoulder got kissed by a bus. Of course you should stay for a while. Your company will do me good."

"What about your children? Are they not coming to visit?"

She laughed out loud. "No. They've turned their backs on London."

"That's a pity."

"Actually, it's not. I never wanted to have children. Do you have children?"

I shook my head.

"Would you like to have any?"

"I would love to, yes."

"As a man, you can choose," she said.

I closed my eyes, breathed in deeply, and considered stuffing the ball of yarn into my ears.

"Today it's the same as it was in my time. Just look around. Having children is a trend. Women who don't want children are pitied or declared ill," Harriet said grumpily.

"How many do you have?"

"Six, and I didn't want any of them."

"How did you endure that?"

She put her knitting needles aside, and finally the repetitive noise stopped. "May I give you some advice?"

My mind screamed no, but I said yes.

"Live your life to the fullest, the way you want it, before you become an old bag like me," she said calmly, taking the needles back in her hands.

"Are you in love with your husband?" I asked.

She snorted and, to my delight, put the knitting needles back to one side.

"Of course not. Glad he's dead. I loved George from the shop."

When she said his name, she smiled, and the grumpy old woman turned into a young girl.

"He's dead, too, as it happens," she added.

"If you could see George again, what would you do?" I asked.

"I would pack my bags and move my hip out of here as quickly as possible. A new car simply begs to be driven."

I laughed.

Although my shoulder hurt so much it almost paralyzed me, I had to get out of the hospital. I had to talk to the real man I had wronged, but first I had to talk to the imaginary one. I didn't know how to locate a fictional character, but I was sure that you could find anything in London if you searched for it long enough. If you could drink coffee in a Victorian toilet at the Attendant, dance on a clown's grave at Joseph Grimaldi Park, and adopt monkey brains at the Grant Museum, you could surely find Sherlock Holmes somewhere.

I carefully sat up on the edge of the bed. Every cell in my body screamed, "Don't do it!" but I tried to walk anyway.

"You look terrible," said Harriet.

"Thank you," I replied, sitting down again. The pain was so severe that I saw black for a moment. I looked at my dirty clothes. Another suit had shuffled off this mortal coil, not to mention the shirt. I could smell myself, which is never a good sign.

I tried to get up again.

"You should stay. You'll be let out soon anyway," Harriet said, fumbling with her jewelry.

"But I have to find him," I said in despair.

"Who?"

"Sherlock Holmes."

"Did the bus hit your head as well, love?"

"Not at all," I replied, leaning down at her bedside. "He's my friend, you know." I tried to stand upright without holding on to the bed frame but failed.

"Sherlock Holmes? Your friend?"

"Mad. I know," I said, managing to walk a few more steps towards the door.

Harriet shrugged. "Nothing really surprises me anymore. Pumpkin in coffee, plastic hips, and cadgers in suits."

I wasn't offended by her assessment of me. Although the past few days had been full of pain and drama, they had also been the best days of my life. I had finally gotten my wake-up call.

"Oh, I'm very weird, but I like it that way, and that's what I want to tell him. I owe him my life," I said, knowing what needed to be done. I coughed again and tasted the blood in my mouth. *This should not be how it ends. This cannot have been my life.*

"Then off you go. What are you waiting for? Find him," she said, turning back to her needles.

I was just walking out the door when she said something else.

"I have something that belongs to you. Thought I'd take care of it. I don't trust those nurses."

I looked at her inquiringly. She opened her hand, and I recognized the item immediately.

"That's your pocket watch, isn't it?" she asked.

I had already feared it lost. Relieved, I took the watch that Matt had given me, and a sense of remorse and shame overwhelmed me. Sadness rose up, but I swallowed it down.

"Thank you very much. It's very important to me," I said. A tear ran down my cheek. I was losing control again.

"Of course it is. Do you know what a thing like this is worth? You only get something like this from someone who is very close to you. As close as two people can be," she said, winking at me.

I could only nod without a word.

"The engraving is beautiful," she remarked.

I stopped. "Engraving?" I turned the watch around and didn't see any.

"There, on the side. I might be old, but I'm not blind," she said.

I looked more closely at the sides of the watch. I wondered why Matt hadn't told me about it when he gave it to me, and I was even more surprised that I hadn't noticed. I had thought it was some kind of twining décor. Harriet was a real detective.

"What does it say?" she asked.

I laughed. "I thought you said you're not blind."

She, too, had to laugh.

I read it out loud. *The smallest act of kindness is worth more than the grandest intention.* I stared at the watch. It was a quote by Oscar Wilde.

"You know, Harriet, I never wanted to kill myself. I wanted to kill something inside myself. I'll make sure it dies, because I want to live. Harriet, I want to live!"

"Then why the hell are you still here, love? Off you go! Find Holmes and make things right!"

With each step, my shoulder pounded with pain. I felt like an inmate who was about to break out, hoping not to be seen by a nurse or doctor. When I left the building, I tried to orient myself at first. I had no idea which hospital I was in, but it wasn't hard to tell. It was St Bartholomew's Hospital, known simply as Barts to Londoners and Holmes fans. The oldest hospital in Britain, and also the very place where Holmes and Watson met for the first time. I couldn't shake the thought that Holmes himself was responsible for me being brought here.

I had to get hit by a bus to realize what my case meant. In hindsight, I had been too stubborn and narrow-minded to recognize the simple solution. It's worth the effort to look beyond yourself, outside your bubble. You might learn something. I certainly had. And I needed to find Holmes as soon as possible; it was the only way I could prepare to talk to Matt. If Holmes wouldn't come to me, I just had to go to him.

Like a zombie, I limped through the busy streets until I reached a tube station, trying to keep my arm as stable as possible. Every little movement stung like a thousand needles. To make matters worse, I had to fight against overwhelming fatigue. I couldn't manage my search alone in this state. I needed my Watson. Not the man in the bowler, no. Mina. She was the only one who could help me find Holmes. She was my friend. Despite the pain, despite my head continuously falling to the side, despite dozing off a few times, I miraculously managed to get off at the right stop.

I hesitated on Mina's doorstep.

I looked for my cigarettes, but they were gone. One should probably stop smoking when one is coughing up blood, but I was too nervous to let go of my old habit.

"Do you want to go in?" a woman next to me asked. She

unlocked the door and let me enter. I looked exactly like I'd been vomiting in pub toilets and getting hit by buses, but it was Hackney, after all. They were probably accustomed to it.

With my face distorted by pain, I climbed step by step and finally reached Mina's door. My heart was pounding. I felt almost dead. My fingers hovered over the bell, and all words escaped me. Instead of pressing the button, I knocked. Nobody seemed to be home.

I let myself sink to the floor. "Mina, let me in!" I demanded, but I heard no noise from inside. "Okay then, let me die in front of your door!" I leaned against her door and stared into the hallway. "Mina, I need you. Please, let me in," I cried in the most dramatic voice I could pull off.

Finally, I heard steps behind the door. When it opened, I fell on my back and looked up at her. The pain shot from my shoulder into my legs. I could tell by her outfit and wet hair that she had hurried out of the shower.

"Hi, Mina."

She stared at me in pure horror. "Oh shit. You look like you've been run over by a bus."

I laughed. "That's exactly what happened."

"What?"

"I've been run over by a bus," I said, trying to sit up again.

"What? Seriously?"

"Seriously."

"Andrew Thomas. You're a disaster," she said, kneeling down next to me. She shook her head. "Dandy Andy, you smell horrible."

"I know."

For a moment, she stared at me, speechless.

"I have to find him, Mina."

"Who?"

"Sherlock Holmes."

23

—◆—

A Scandal in Hackney

"What on earth have you done?" Mina asked, shaking her head next to me on the sofa.

"If I only knew," I replied. "You'll think I'm mad but—"

"Believe me, I already think you're mad."

I looked at my arm in the sling and saw that it had taken on the colors of the universe: blue, red, and black. No matter what my next steps were, I knew I had to accomplish them before any appendages fell off.

"I talked to him. I talked to Holmes," I said.

"You talked to Sherlock Holmes?" She looked at me with a mixture of fear, incredulity, and anger. "You mean Sherlock Holmes, the detective from the books?"

I nodded.

"Shit, what actually went wrong with you?"

"I'm completely clear in my head," I assured her, trying to straighten my shirt with one hand.

"It doesn't make any difference anymore," Mina said, helping me with my buttons.

"I'm just trying to save what can be saved," I said. "I talked to Christine last night."

Mina looked at me, puzzled. "Okay. This is a lot of information in five minutes."

"I was drunk and went to our house. It was good to finally admit the truth."

"I wonder why she let you in." Mina finally had the semblance of a smile on her face. "I'm glad she even recognized you."

I tried to look remorseful when I explained to her what had happened. This remorse, so unusual for me, had almost devoured me over the past day. "So, I left him there. Having a panic attack. His friends were there but…God, I acted like a complete and utter arse. And Christine says she still loves me."

"After all you've done?"

"She knew I was gay."

"Ouch."

Big ouch.

Mina clutched a pillow over her stomach. "You should talk to Matt again sober. You can talk this through. If not you two, who else?"

I nodded. "Tell me about your talk with your parents," I said to change the subject.

She took a deep breath. "This is…I…There are far more important things right now. I mean, look at you."

"No, please tell me," I insisted.

"I don't like to get emotional," she said, burying herself in a blanket.

"I know, neither do I, but I did, and it helped."

"You know, it helped me. It helped when you confessed your feelings, when you trusted me enough to tell me. I think that was the final push I needed to tell my parents. So, thank you, although you're not as good as me at doing the queer business." Finally, she smiled.

"To put it like Les McQueen, it's a shit business." I laughed. "Now how did it go?"

"So, we had a nice high tea at the Café Royal and I just told them." She put her hair up in a bun. "Just like that."

"Don't tell me you came out to your parents surrounded by gold, mirrors, and flowers while having high tea. *Just like that?*"

"Sometimes you got to jump in at the deep end."

"A *very* divaesque deep end."

"Babes, what else did you expect from me?" She undid her hair again, not being satisfied with how her bun turned out. "Seems like I was more afraid than I needed to be. My father even apologized for his attempts to find me a handsome *male* doctor, and my mum asked if I needed new clothes. Which was hilarious, of course, but I guess it's just new for them."

"I'm glad it turned out that way."

"So am I. It turned out to be one of the best days we ever spent together. I finally was myself around them."

We sat in silence for a moment.

"Are you ready for the ultimate show?" I asked.

She sat up like a little child and clapped. "Oh, I am! Bring it on!"

"Holmes gave me a case. My case. I was supposed to solve it," I said, pulling a thread out of my cut shirt sleeve. I needed to buy new shirts as soon as possible. *Later. Priorities.*

Her excitement faded. "You're serious about this, aren't you?"

Of course I was serious. I tried to explain that it wasn't really Holmes, but she didn't fully understand what I was talking about.

"How does this work, exactly? You talk to his…spirit?" she asked.

"No. With him. I'm sure I'm making him up, but I see him and talk to him."

"Do I understand this correctly? You sent him away, and now you want to find him?"

"Yes. Because I solved the case," I replied. "I have to tell him to know if I'm right."

"And you can't just…you know…make him appear? It's your brain, isn't it?"

"No. I don't know why, but it doesn't work that way. I have to go find him."

Mina looked at me inquiringly. "How do you plan to find a

fictional character you've been having imaginary conversations with?"

I explained my assumption that if I visited some of his favorite places, I would find him again. This was the sum total of my plan. But I was sure he wasn't gone. Beyond needing his confirmation that I was right, I couldn't live with my conscience if I didn't tell him I'd solved the case – and if I didn't thank him. After I found him, I would settle the matter with Matt. I didn't have a plan for that, but if I found Holmes first, he would certainly have some advice. This Sherlock Holmes was a part of me, after all. It would have been very strange if my second self, my alter ego, didn't have any clever ideas. Holmes was right that to really solve the case, I needed the most important figure. And that figure was Matt.

"How am I supposed to understand this?" asked Mina. "You and Holmes are like Dr Jekyll and Mr Hyde?"

"That's the way it is, I guess."

"What was the reason for Matt's panic attack?"

My legs jerked up and down. "I had a fight with him."

"Why?"

"He clearly wants a relationship with me and I panicked."

"*You must be kidding me!* That sexy and intelligent cat wants you to be his boyfriend and you panic?"

"That's exactly what happened, but I talked to a homeless man about it and now I get what's wrong with me."

Mina laughed. "Right. Years of me telling you what the problem is and a homeless man makes you see it in one night? Ha. I love you!"

I leaned back and looked at the ceiling.

"Shit, I can't pretend any longer," she said suddenly. "I have to tell you."

Not more news. Please.

She took out her phone and held it under my nose. "I'm afraid a lot of people know what was going on last night."

I had broken the internet. *Again.*

"Someone even snatched a photo of the fight," Mina said.

"This is not good. Not good at all."

"Here they're calling you an aggressive intruder, and here they're saying you're his lawyer."

"Can't they just not write about me, please?"

"You know what, Dandy Andy? I should start writing about you."

I smiled. "I'd be lost without my Boswell."

"Your what?"

"My Watson."

"What an honor, Mr Holmes."

"Holmes in distress," I said, looking at the state of my suit again.

"I think I still have old clothes from David here. You shower first, then we'll think about finding Sherlock Holmes. Now there's a sentence."

I looked at my shoulder. "I'm afraid I might need some help." My arm was aching, and the hand attached to it was almost numb. This next part was going to be humiliating.

"God damn. I hate you, Andrew," Mina said, taking my good hand.

"I hate you too."

I was sure it was because of those words that she gave me David's lilac t-shirt and strange beige trousers. If it hadn't all been for a bigger purpose, I would have refused to touch them. The fabric alone was appalling, never mind the form-fitting cut. Mina convinced me it would be better than walking around in rags. I questioned that, but of course she was right. And having already faced Holmes in underwear, these clothes were no worse.

"Isn't this outfit too pastel for your taste?" I asked, hoping she would give me something else to wear.

"Shockingly pastel!"

Mina had such a pragmatic way of undressing an almost immobile man that I got slightly worried. After all, such practice was not learned in the office.

"Can this go in the bin?" she asked in an emotionless tone. She held my clothes up.

"You can still patch those trousers," I replied.

"So, everything goes in the bin," she said, throwing the bundle into a corner. She scanned me. "Not bad for a man your age."

"My age?"

"Yes. I hope you can get out of your underwear alone," she said. Luckily, I could.

When I got into the shower, all I managed to do at first was let the water run down me. Any further movement hurt too much. Slowly turning so the water could reach every sore inch, I realized I shouldn't have left the hospital. My injured arm had swollen to a disturbing size, and the fingers of its dependent hand were not just numb – they no longer moved. They looked like tiny sausages. In a desperate attempt to wash myself, I caused the bandage to fall from my shoulder, and I could see the full extent of the devastation. I felt sick at the sight of it. *Don't fall off yet.*

"Do you need help in there?" asked Mina through the door.

"No. I'll just wait until I'm dry." And I did. For half an hour I stood in the bathroom. It wasn't until the moisture left my skin that I tried to get back into my underwear through a remarkable acrobatic act. I asked Mina to come in and help me with the rest of the clothes.

"I desperately need painkillers," I said. I sat exhausted on the edge of the bathtub.

"And a new bandage," Mina added.

I was now dressed in lilac and beige. Despite my aversion to spring colors and synthetic materials, I found it surprisingly pleasant. I would never have exchanged these clothes for my suits, but with a hangover and bruised shoulder, they were just the right thing to wear.

"What is this?" asked Mina, holding a rust-brown note in her hand. "I don't know who I am and I don't know–"

"Nothing. Just a piece of paper," I said, ripping it from her. The quick movement made me clench my teeth.

"Who wrote it?"

"Nobody, actually. No one." I put my eternal companion into the pocket of the ghastly but comfortable trousers.

Mina walked into the hallway. "So, where do you want to start your search?" she asked as she put on her shoes.

"Well, nothing outside the center is an option. We don't have enough time for that."

"That doesn't necessarily limit our search, does it?" said Mina. She tossed some things into a backpack and helped me get my shoes on.

She was right. Even today, Sherlock Holmes fans from all over the world make the pilgrimage to London to follow in the footsteps of the master detective – and there are many such footsteps to follow. London is littered with locations from Doyle's stories, from the hospital where Holmes and Watson first met to gentlemen's clubs and grand hotels. I didn't know where to start. His home would make a likely option, but this, as Holmes connoisseurs know, proves to be a little difficult. Sherlock Holmes lived at 221b Baker Street, a fictional address in Conan Doyle's time. Back then, Baker Street was numbered only to 85, and this was not extended until 1930. The place where 221b Baker Street is today would have been Upper Baker Street at the time of the Sherlock Holmes cases, and in fact the true address should be 239. So, the legendary building is not real – it only became real later. Nevertheless, tourists and locals flock to 221b Baker Street today to visit the Sherlock Holmes Museum, a Victorian house modelled on the one described by Doyle and often mistaken for the actual building.

"We could visit some train stations, pubs, restaurants, and hotels," I said, knowing that we would only scratch the surface. "And, of course, St Bartholomew's Hospital." *Pray they don't recognize me.*

"So, I'll put on more comfortable shoes," Mina said. She picked up a different pair.

If you could find yourself, then you could probably also find a part of yourself that you projected on someone else. It had to be possible. I had to be able to solve this. My intellect couldn't have become that rusty since getting sacked.

Mina stood tapping her leg, her shoes in her hand.

"I'm ready," I said.

She hesitated. "Andrew, I don't think it's going to work like this." She dropped down onto an armchair. The shoes fell to the floor. "Do you have any cigarettes?"

"No, I smoked all of them yesterday or lost my last pack."

She exhaled. "I hate to smoke the stuff without tobacco." She rose and briefly disappeared into the bedroom.

"I thought you quit?" I shouted after her.

"I still have tobacco!" she called from the other room.

"Here we go," I said with a sigh.

"Hush, you," she said, opening a window.

"I'm not going to take drugs under any circumstances. I mean, aside from the ones I'm already on," I said. She looked at me. "From the hospital," I clarified.

While I had to admit that it would be easier to find Holmes under the influence, I didn't want to fog my mind in broad daylight.

"You know yourself better than I do, but don't you think it might help get you in the right frame of mind?" she asked, calmly rolling the paper. "You're always so stubborn. When did he appear to you?"

"When I wasn't expecting it. A lot of the time I was drunk."

"You see."

"Actually, I believe I've been drunk since I was sacked," I said.

Mina took a lighter from the table next to her and lit the rolled paper. A sweet smell filled the room. I watched her lips as the smoke slowly crept out of her mouth.

"I should have known you never quit," I said. I tried not to inhale the smoke. Images of Camden Market and hippies flashed through my head.

"I did. For a few weeks," Mina said, laughing.

I tapped my fingers on my knee, longing for a cigarette. "How will this help us?"

"If you see more, you can find more," she said before taking another drag. She held in the smoke for a long time before slowly letting it escape.

I thought about the past few days. *I got sacked. I fell in love. I'm permanently drunk. I have cancer. I'm inescapably gay. I was hit by a bus. Now I'm chasing a fictional character through London.* These had been the worst and the best days of my life at the same time, and I didn't know what was imagined or real about any of it.

I laughed out loud. *What have I been doing with my whole life?*

"What's going on?" asked Mina.

"I went mad. It's horrible. I love it. Maybe I should…" I said, pointing to the joint in Mina's hand. I was curious to see if she was right about it helping.

She handed me the joint, and I took a drag.

"This doesn't mean I approve of drugs, Mina," I said. "It burns my throat." I coughed.

"Fasten your seatbelt. It's going to be a bumpy night."

"That reminds me, we haven't watched *All About Eve* in ages." I coughed again but didn't taste any blood. I really had to stop smoking, in any case. And I supposed I would eventually have to tell Mina about the cancer. Another day.

"You just want to help me because your organization needs Matt," I joked.

"No, I want to help you because I love you and want you to be happy." I looked at her sternly.

"And factually my organization is dead without Matt's help."

I couldn't stop laughing. We both wanted to chase Matt.

Mina stretched out on the sofa and tapped her phone. "You know that I believe in the supernatural."

"I do, but how will that information help us? Last thing I need is more imaginary creatures ruining my inner peace."

"As if you ever had inner peace, babes. You always had inner confusion, nothing more, nothing less."

She was definitely right about that.

Mina put her phone down. "We have to sort of summon him up."

"How?"

"Well, if he's your spirit or whatever, then we need…"

I thought about blood, hair, and candles. Things from various horror films which never seemed to fail.

"Things related to the last few days," she concluded.

"So, blood, hair, and…falafel?" I asked, laughing. I imagined Dracula Holmes arranging falafel on the floor to conjure a departed soul. *The Case of the Dead Vegan.*

"What about Matt? What's the kitten like?"

"Unusual."

"We need more," she said, again tapping her phone. "We need music!" She held the joint, giggling. "And don't come here with your weird classical tootling."

"Classical music is not–"

"To me it is." She laughed.

I took the joint back. The pain in my shoulder was finally getting better.

"Give me your phone." I ripped it out of Mina's hand and tapped on various apps until I finally found an internet browser.

"What are you doing?"

"Music."

I tried to find the song Matt loved, but I couldn't remember enough about it. My thoughts were a colorful potpourri of the last few days, and there was little room for something immediately helpful. Then I remembered Patrick Procktor. Luckily, Google seemed to know what I was thinking, and at last I found the album. My inability to use modern technology ended in a wild chase through the depths of the internet that led me to YouTube. I panicked and tapped on a random suggested video. Not the song. Instead, I faced the arch-enemy of anyone uncomfortable with showing emotions. Love songs had most emphatically never been my métier; however, this version of my most feared category of music confused me so utterly that I kept watching and listening.

Mina looked at the phone. "Shit, what *is* that?"

We watched a clip of Elton John in a Donald Duck costume playing "Your Song." We both burst out with laughter.

"Is Matt the Cat a fan?"

Although her question wasn't funny, I couldn't stop laughing. "He is as obsessed with that musician as I am with Holmes," I said, breathless.

YouTube was still presenting us the finest selection of Elton John live performances when Mina suddenly stopped giggling. "We have to be careful not to summon the wrong person."

If you only knew. I imagined Holmes wearing a flamboyant feather suit, heart-shaped glasses, and glowing platform shoes. I doubled up with laughter.

"Calm down, we're conjuring spirits," Mina intoned.

I put the phone aside and let YouTube run in the background. Matt was the core and origin of my dilemma, so I tried to visualize him in front of my spiritual eye as best I could. He was such a strange ingredient in my life, but one that could make it so much sweeter.

"Ideas, we need ideas," I said, leaning back.

"I know, I know. Why don't you search Baker Street? Where the museum is."

"Because it's a bloody museum, and it's not the Baker Street from the cases, you ninny."

Mina finished rolling a cigarette and handed it to me. "No reason to curse, Dandy Andy. Are we going to chase your spirit now?"

We were. But Sherlock Holmes would not be the only spirit we encountered that day.

24

—◆—

The Empty House

We took the Overground to Stratford and from there continued on the Central line to St Paul's. As we got on and off, I was reminded of my injuries courtesy of various passing people who bumped into me.

"What's so special about the hospital?" asked Mina, trying to ignore the noise of the train.

"That's where they got to know each other."

"Who?" she asked so loudly that a group of men turned to us.

"Holmes and Watson," I whispered.

It's an unwritten rule that you don't talk on the Underground. Should one break this rule, one normally gets dark looks from the rest of the passengers, followed by a tense and hostile atmosphere. This applies to all public transport in England: do not speak, and preferably do not breathe. Just stop existing. It's a British hobby.

We walked down King Edward Street. As we approached the hospital, I glanced around. I was half expecting orderlies to jump from the shadows and forcibly detain me. Stepping in front of a bus surely counted as being a danger to oneself or others.

We walked in, still giggling about what we were trying to do.

"The emergency room is in the back," said a woman in the entrance area. She pointed at my arm.

"Oh, no, I'm okay," I said. My arm might look frightening, double its usual size and almost falling off, but I did feel surprisingly well.

"Have you seen Sherlock Holmes around here?" asked Mina, who still had a broad grin on her face.

"A man about my size, long coat, possibly wearing a deerstalker," I added.

"Sherlock? Sherlock Holmes?" the woman asked in disbelief.

We both nodded.

She checked her computer.

"No, he's not a patient. He's a detective. You must know him," I said.

"Do you think this is funny?"

"Yes, because I'm baked," I said. I held on to the desk. "I'm baked like an apple pie."

The woman was done with us. "Should I recommend psychological services or call security?"

We preferred to leave the hospital before we were expelled from it. Being arrested was the only thing missing from the list of incredibly stupid and avoidable things I'd recently accomplished.

"She was in a bad mood," Mina said as we stepped through the glass door and into the street.

"What if she just wanted to hide the fact that he was there?" I asked.

"Dandy Andy, you're thinking like a real detective. Maybe we should go look and–"

I held her back. "We really shouldn't. Maybe later?"

Mina nodded, and we headed towards the Underground. We grabbed a coffee and way too many snacks at a nearby Pret. I wondered what Holmes would think of Pret.

"Where to next?" Mina asked, absorbed in the act of opening snack wrappers.

"We need to take this more seriously," I said.

"Andrew, we're doing everything we can."

I nodded. She was probably right. How could anyone take

a search like this seriously? This was purely a case of madness. Maybe that title was fitting after all. I tried to think of a place Holmes could be found at that time of the day.

"Waterloo," I said. "We'll get off there next."

"Waterloo? Why? I hate Waterloo."

"It's mentioned in several works. I can't think of anything better right now." I hurried to catch up with Mina, who had begun marching ahead. "John Openshaw had to return from Waterloo to Horsham but was murdered before he made it, Helen Stoner took the first train to Waterloo, Sir Henry Baskerville arrived from Southampton at Waterloo and–"

"Andrew!"

"Yes?"

"I love you, but I don't know these people, and I really don't care. Is there a place they went together often? Holmes and Watson?"

I thought about various locations all over London. "Café Royal and Simpson's."

"Well, then let's go to Piccadilly Circus," Mina said, walking down the steps to the Underground. Again, we were greeted by a warm wall of stuffy air, and my shoulder was back on the battlefield.

Café Royal was a restaurant on Regent Street in London which opened in the second half of the nineteenth century. It was a popular meeting place for writers, artists, politicians, and even members of the royal family. Oscar Wilde was one of its regular customers. In December 2008, Café Royal was closed, and the entire historical inventory was auctioned off. Everything had to go to make room for a luxury hotel. Luckily, the "Grill Room" was largely preserved and was renamed the "Oscar Wilde Lounge" after the renovation.

In "The Adventure of the Illustrious Client," an assassination attempt is carried out on Sherlock Holmes in front of the café. The two attackers manage to escape through the back entrance. In the same case, Sherlock Holmes and Dr Watson meet twice in Simpson's during the investigation of Baron Adelbert Gruner, the man who planned the assassination attempt. Located in the building complex of the Savoy Hotel, Simpson's is one of the oldest restaurants in London. In "The Dying Detective," Holmes suggests that he and Watson meet at Simpson's after giving their testimonies. So, these two locations existed at the time Doyle wrote.

As expected, the Underground was overcrowded. To make matters worse, we had to change at Oxford Circus on a Friday afternoon – something one should under any circumstances avoid. This also applies to the rest of the week. At Piccadilly Circus we exited into the fresh air, if you could call it that in London. What Times Square is to New York City, Piccadilly Circus is to London, only in much smaller dimensions. The massive illuminated advertisements for current plays and various large corporations flickered ahead of us, and it was hard not to look at them. Under the colorful lights, the world of Sherlock Holmes was as far away as earth is from the moon.

"Where do you want to go first?" asked Mina.

I thought it was wise to start with the Savoy, as the Café Royal was right on the way to the world-famous Paddington station, which I had set as another destination.

On our way through the crowds, Mina suddenly stopped.

I almost stumbled over an innocent dog. "What is it?" I asked, looking at her. She was laughing at a newspaper box. The headline about the upcoming Brexit vote wasn't of much interest, but an article right under it indeed was: *Date night corruption scandal – Deputy Mayor Hughes arrested in Nightclub Bohemia for attempted cover-up of the Lewis case.*

"Someone must have given the police a hint," Mina said.

"*Someone?*"

She resumed our route. "Everyone gets what they deserve. And we deserve to be guests at the Savoy."

The Savoy is one of London's most prestigious and opulent hotels. You don't just march into it unless you're an international celebrity with a credit card and no limit. Its first manager was none other than César Ritz, who later founded the Ritz Hotel, which suggests what kind of place it is. A simple room here costs over five hundred pounds a night, which is about half my monthly rent. The only way for people like me to enter one of the buildings is to visit the Savoy Theatre.

We stood in front of the large white building and looked up in awe. I cursed the fact that I wasn't wearing a suit. Mina looked as if she'd come fresh from Brick Lane. We smelled of cigarettes and cannabis.

"Do you have a plan?" asked Mina.

"Not really."

"We could simply go in and look around. Pretend to be tourists who got lost," she said.

It wasn't a particularly thoughtful or good plan, but it was the only one we had.

We went to the entrance of Simpson's and hesitated.

"Shit, what are we actually doing here," Mina said. She walked through the door without warning. I reluctantly followed her, feeling like a sinner trespassing on holy ground.

I had only seen the interior of the restaurant in pictures. The original was even more beautiful, but the renovated space still inspired awe. The dark paneling and wonderfully designed ceiling stucco made the space feel like a different world. There were rooms that told stories, and this was clearly one of them. In the past, women had to use the dining room on the upper floor, which was done in pastel colors. The rule was dropped as early as 1984.

As soon as we set foot in the restaurant, a waiter approached us. "May I help you?" he asked in a tone that said we'd better leave.

"Oh, pardon. We're looking for a friend," Mina said with a French accent.

I had to turn away to hide my laughter.

"What does he look like, your friend?" the waiter asked, stern but still friendly.

"He's about the size of him," Mina said, pointing to me, "slim, has a distinctive nose. Probably wearing a long coat and a deerstalker."

"Well, if you don't mean the man beside you, then you must

be joking. The one you're looking for hasn't been here for over a hundred years." He winked at Mina.

I was surprised by the man's patience. He'd definitely had more experience dealing with eccentric people than the woman in the hospital.

"But now I have to ask you to leave," he added, holding the door open for us.

We went out again and bent over with laughter.

"What was that?" I asked Mina.

"That, dear Andrew, was my best French."

Unfortunately, I hadn't spotted Holmes among the guests. Maybe it was impossible to ever find him again. I contemplated giving up because it seemed my mind wasn't in the right place to see him anymore.

We walked back over to Piccadilly Circus and towards the Café Royal.

"Scene of your coming out party. What's our plan this time?" I asked.

"I go in and distract everyone. You go to the café and look around."

I stopped her in front of the revolving door. "I don't know if that's such a good idea. What if we get banned?"

She turned around. "Can you afford anything in there?"

I had to admit this was a good point. We stepped through the door and were amazed by the large entrance hall. It was lined with white and beige marble. On the left and right were fireplaces with fresh flowers on their mantels. While I stood with my mouth open, Mina ran purposefully towards two employees in uniform. She acted drunk and mumbled incoherent nonsense. Her performance had nothing elegant about it, but it was a clever tactic to distract the staff. I seemed invisible. Either it was Mina's striking performance or the lilac flowers that framed the room. Lilac is the new camouflage.

I approached a door at the end of the hall. Beyond it was a lavishly decorated room framed by mirrors. Some guests glanced up at me, probably wondering who had let the peasants in. I looked around but couldn't find what I sought. After bathing long enough in the critical eyes of the guests, I went back to the hall. Mina gave a signal, and we left the hotel.

"And?" she asked.

I shook my head.

"And for that I got banned?"

"You got what?"

She laughed. "So, we can't have our honeymoon here anymore."

"You can't have yours here, but I could still stay the night with my husband," I corrected her, and it felt strange to have said it. Another marriage had never crossed my mind before.

We went down a little passage between Jermyn Street and Piccadilly Circus called the Piccadilly Arcade. It's a beautifully designed side street with unique charm. A strange place to feel overcome by hopelessness. We were getting nowhere.

About to give up, I recognized a familiar face in the group walking towards us. I glanced at Mina, but she was busy looking in a window to see if she'd got something stuck between her teeth. *Perhaps every gay man has to hallucinate Elton John at least once to become a member of the community.* Maybe he was the leader of the Gay Mafia after all.

"I bought flowers," I remarked.

"You didn't buy flowers, you bought a disgrace," he said.

I looked around, but nobody else seemed to notice what was happening.

"When did you forget to think, Andrew darling?"

"I…what?"

"You need to think!"

"I'm always thinking."

He sighed. "Not your fucking therapist." Then he disappeared into the crowd.

"And what now?" Mina asked.

"I need to think," I said. Everything around me was way too loud. The different voices, sounds, and smells distracted me. I knew where I needed to go. "The Museum of London. That's what's next."

Mina wasn't happy with that. "Back to the bloody east? What on earth is it about you and that museum?"

"It's my thinking place."

"Of course, my special snowflake has a thinking place." She continued walking to the Central line. "You, Sir Dandy Andy, can top up my Oyster tomorrow. Trust me on that."

Luckily, it was just a few stops to St Paul's and a short walk to the museum. Otherwise Mina would have eaten me alive.

"Can we look at Roman London first?" she asked when we entered the museum.

"No!"

We went down to my sacred place, the Victorian high street. The place I went when I needed to think clearly. I had never taken someone with me, but I trusted Mina.

"How do you expect to find somebody or something here?" she asked, looking around.

I didn't know, and we decided to cancel the search when I couldn't find an answer. The effect of the drugs had subsided, my arm was in a lot of pain, and I was prepared to accept that I wouldn't be able to tell Holmes I had solved the case. I would have to figure out how to talk to Matt again without him. *The horror of it all.*

While Mina was looking around the old shops, I sat down in the bar. Fortunately, I had the place to myself. The beautifully decorated mirror behind the bar reflected the outside shopping windows. I could tell they had replaced a pair of mittens with another one. I must have been a lonelier man than I thought to recognize such change. *Or just unapologetically gay.*

"You're looking for Sherlock Holmes, I suppose," said a voice next to me.

I jumped and looked to the side. There he stood: the bowler man.

"He will be at home in Baker Street as usual," he continued.

My mouth went dry, and I couldn't speak a word.

"I apologize for my extremely inappropriate behavior at Camden Town a few days ago." He doffed his hat and turned to go. "Good afternoon."

"Good afternoon," I replied, watching the man until he disappeared down the indoor streets. By now I was absolutely sure he was Dr Watson.

Mina walked into the bar. "Have you seen a ghost?"

"I know where we have to go," I mumbled, still stunned.

She sighed. "Where to now?"

I winced. "The first place you suggested, actually."

"Are you kidding me? Please tell me this is a joke. The bloody Sherlock Holmes Museum?"

"Sorry to break the news, but that's the place. Even if it's just a museum, and even if the actual address is number 239, we have to go. We have to go to Baker Street."

25

—◆—

The Baker Street Regulars

We took the Circle line towards Baker Street.

"What exactly do you want to say to him when you find him?" asked Mina.

I tried to support my arm and ignore the pain. "I want to tell him I've solved the case and I'm grateful to have met him."

"Grateful? What for?"

I smiled and didn't answer. By now it was evening. We rushed over, and fortunately a man in a police uniform was still standing in front of the entrance.

"They close at six," I said, looking at my pocket watch. "It's ten minutes to six."

"What now?" asked Mina.

"I don't know, you always had a plan," I replied. We crossed the road.

"Are you still open?" I asked the man in uniform cautiously.

"We are, but you'll have to be quick. Don't forget to buy a ticket!" he shouted after us as we entered the building.

The museum has three floors, not counting the attic. The Victorian building is lovingly furnished with pipes, laboratory equipment, and of course a violin.

We walked directly up the steep, narrow staircase to the first floor, where Holmes' bedroom and the study are located. I looked around carefully.

"Is he here?" asked Mina, who had already touched and moved about all the objects in the exhibition. Never take children to a museum. Especially, and I remind you again, if they have a pen and you're near a balustrade.

"Obviously not," I replied, gesturing for her to put the magnifying glass back in its place.

"How do I know how it works with your hallucinations."

I breathed in deeply. "Mina, don't annoy me now."

"Or what?"

"Or we will never find him."

"That's madness!"

"Obviously?" I browsed through a stack of newspapers on Watson's desk. The room was crammed with relics, all of which were draped in detail. The study looked as if he and the great detective had just left it to pursue a new case.

I felt heat and noticed a warm glow to the room. I looked at the fireplace. Cold and dark a few moments before, it now burned. Even the candles on the magnificently equipped dining table were lit.

"I think they were both here," I said. The notes on the Camden dancing men were on Watson's desk. He had drawn a big question mark next to *the rest is silence.* "The candles are burning, and the fire is going."

Mina looked around. "The fire? What are you talking ab—" She stopped short. "Oh, I mean, *right.* Sure. Of course it is." After a few beats, she began pawing at more exhibit objects. "And look here! The pipe is still warm." She handed me the pipe that Holmes had smoked during his visits to my flat.

"Thank you, Watson," I said. "Thank you for all this here."

"Of course, Sherlock." She smiled. "So, if they were just here, we must have missed them."

I lifted my head suddenly and fixed my eyes on the ceiling.

"What?" Mina asked.

"Footsteps."

Mina looked up too. "Okay, so maybe they're still here."

We walked quietly up to the second floor, where Dr Watson's bedroom is located – right next to that of Mrs Hudson. Perhaps it was she who was still at home, preparing everything for the return of the detective and his companion.

"There's no one here, huh?" Mina whispered.

Our search had started to feel like getting a tiny piece of eggshell out of a yolk. The more aggressively you try to grab the piece, the faster it slide through your fingertips.

I leaned against a wall and slid down in desperation. "What am I doing here?"

Mina squatted in front of me and took my hands. "Don't give up now you've come this far."

"This is further than any psychiatrist would approve of."

"Psychiatry can wait. I'll drop you off when we're done."

I snapped to attention, hearing noises again.

"More footsteps?" Mina asked.

"I hope that's not the wax figures."

Mina opened her eyes wide. "The what?"

"The wax figures. On the third floor."

"You must be joking."

"I'm afraid not."

"Your brain is creeping me out a little, frankly." Mina closed her eyes and breathed deeply. "I'm John Watson and I'm not afraid of anything or anyone. I am John Watson and I–"

"Mina."

"Right. We have to keep looking. On to the wax figures."

Up we went. Luckily, we didn't find any characters alive on the third floor, but to our regret we didn't find Watson or Holmes either.

I stood between the figures and must have looked as pale and old as them. "Mina, I give up."

"You're right," she said, crossing her arms.

"I'm a failure."

"I know."

"Great."

"You're such a whiny uphill gardener."

"I beg your pardon!"

Mina walked towards me and grabbed my shirt. David's shirt, rather. I was prepared to end up dead in lilac among the wax figures – perhaps more of a Stephen King title than a Doyle one.

"Listen, barmy twit, your life is going in the exact right direction for the first time! So, stop acting like the airy-fairy gay bellend you are and set this straight!"

"But I quit the whole straight thing."

Mina loosened her grip and busted out laughing. "Move, Dandy Andy! The game is about!"

"Afoot!" I shouted as I followed her down the steps.

We were walking past the study again when I came to a complete halt. It took Mina a moment to realize I was no longer following her.

"What is it?" she whispered. She turned around and tiptoed back to me.

"The candles are out, and there are plates on the table."

I carefully looked around the corner towards the fireplace. It was dark and cold again. I shied away, breathing hard. "Someone's there."

"Who?"

"Not Holmes. Well, it is a Holmes, but not the right Holmes." I looked around the corner again. "Yes, that's the wrong Holmes."

The man who had made himself comfortable in the study had a receding hairline and was as stiff as a statue. His mastery of the method of deduction surpassed even his younger sibling's. Although he is rarely mentioned in the canon, he is often portrayed in film adaptations as simple, haughty, and gullible. I had no interest in finding out what Mycroft Holmes was really like.

"Well, talk to him," said Mina.

"Definitely not."

"Why?"

"This man is way more intelligent than Sherlock Holmes; I don't want him to be in my head."

Mina looked into the room. "It's empty," she said.

"No shit, Sherlock."

I stepped back to the stairs. I had no idea why my brilliant mind was seeing Mycroft Holmes. Maybe I needed to fight some kind of final enemy to get what I needed. However, I really didn't want to face this living computer.

"I think if your mind is making this all up, there's a reason you should talk to him instead of his brother," Mina said.

She undoubtedly had a point. It had to make sense somehow. Until this moment, all my hallucinations had made sense, however ridiculous they had been. I took a deep breath and walked back towards the study entrance. Mina gave me a push, and I was suddenly standing in the middle of the room.

"Sorry. My brother is indisposed," the elder Holmes said, without looking at me.

I approached him cautiously. The old wooden floor creaked under my feet. "When will he be back again?" I asked. *For the sake of everyone in the room, I hope it to be soon.*

This time Mycroft looked at me. His eyes had something frightening in them. His suit was the most exquisite I had ever seen, but it seemed ready to burst from his weight.

"When he finishes his current case," he replied, folding his hands under his chin.

I don't know why, but his gaze made me question everything I was and everything I had ever experienced. I don't want to say that I felt fear at that moment, but it must have been something very close to it. It was remarkable how, without conversation, someone could drive his companion into a dialogue with himself just by staring at him. I thought of Matt and how I had done everything wrong that I could have done wrong. I was sorry, and I wished nothing more than to be able to put it right. The left corner of

Mycroft Holmes' mouth lifted slightly. I interpreted it as a kind of smile. He had probably been in my head all along, keeping to the shadows, unlike his brother. And it hit me: I was never like my hero; I had been Mycroft Holmes all along. Sitting there in his arrogance, he reflected back all of my failures, the perfect summation of my old character. But now that I'd changed, I could see the differences. *Does he bathe with rubber ducks too?*

I closed my eyes and remembered. I remembered the blood, the hug, the gift, and the longing to be close to him. Close to Matt. I could hear him, smell him, and feel his arms wrapped around me. It was very real in a strange way. I was startled when I opened my eyes again. In front of me sat Sherlock Holmes, with a victorious smile on his face. The fire glowed brightly again.

"Excuse me. My brother can be terrifying. Just never let him get too close to you."

"I…I didn't."

"Good," Holmes said, folding his hands under his chin. "I need to thank you."

I looked around, confused. "Thank *me*?"

"Yes, indeed," he replied. "You helped me. I was afraid of being forgotten. Of, in effect, dying. I no longer have this fear."

"I told you, you will never be forgotten. You're a legend."

Holmes had a weird spark in his eyes. "I am, indeed. But this was my last case. I'm ready for something new. I plan to–"

"Keep bees on a small farm upon the South Downs?"

"Indeed," he said, giving me a confused glance. He picked up a book from the table, titled *Practical Handbook of Bee Culture, with Some Observations upon the Segregation of the Queen.* "Why are you here, Andrew? Surely not to talk about bees?"

"I solved the case."

Holmes raised his eyebrows. "Well, what was the case?" He lit his pipe.

I hesitated. "My life. It was about my life."

Holmes looked at me inquiringly.

"It was about saving my life. I was giving up. I was one hundred percent convinced I would die. Either of cancer or by my own hand before the cancer could get me. I was afraid of what's to come. I need someone to help me through the very hard times ahead. Someone who is more than a friend. Someone I can finally be honest with. Someone I don't have to play a role for. Someone who loves me. That's where Matt comes in."

"It took you almost too long to realize this," he said, looking at my blue arm. "The last part is still missing."

Holmes was right; I knew I wouldn't be able to endure the next part alone. Fear already devoured me night after night, and I could only guess what it would be like if I went into treatment. The coming battle required another person to fight by my side, but I feared that this was too much to ask for – even from someone who had offered.

"You once asked me how I survived the Reichenbach Falls," Holmes said. "The question now is: How will you survive?"

"I don't think I need to survive."

Holmes smiled. "Why is that, my dear Andrew?"

"Because just like you at the Reichenbach Falls, I have to die without dying."

I knew it all along. I knew I was going to die. I had thought it would be cancer or suicide, but it was the third option. Change is a kind of death.

"Quite right. To start anew, something has to end."

"How do I pull off the trick?"

Holmes calmly smoked his pipe. "Take what the last few days have given you and use it. You have a voice, so use it. Do what your old self would have never dared."

"He has never been a man for great speeches. Unless he's talking to himself," said a serious voice behind me.

I looked around and saw Mycroft standing by the window. He would make a great Dracula Holmes.

I fled from the room and rushed down the stairs.

"Andrew, wait!" Mina shouted after me. "What did all that mean? So you did want to kill yourself?"

"I have cancer!" I yelled happily. "I'll explain everything later!"

"You *what?*"

"I know what I have to do."

I have to say everything out loud. I have to stop talking to myself.

26

―

A Question of Identity

It was good to wake up in my own flat. My own bedroom, my own bed, my own pajamas. The Holy Trinity of a hermit. Admittedly, I did wake several times during the night and check that I wasn't in hospital, sleeping next to a homeless person, or getting prodded by an old woman with boundary issues. I wouldn't have been surprised. There was a woman next to me, but she was snoring louder than any man I had ever met.

This day would be something special; I knew that, and I had respect for the tasks set before me. I pulled the blanket over my shoulders and rolled to the side. If I had been told a few days ago what I was about to do, I would never have left the flat. Or rather, I would have left the flat and then the country, adopting a new identity along the way. But as the last few days had shown, I wasn't particularly gifted at doing the things that Sherlock Holmes could do. I'd always thought I could, but I wouldn't be putting my skills to the test anymore.

I carefully placed my feet on the floor so as not to wake Mina. One of the wooden planks creaked loudly. I stopped. Mina turned over, briefly opened her eyes, and closed them again after yawning.

After leaving the museum, we'd spent the rest of the evening in my flat, forging a plan for the next day. Mina had shown herself willing to let alone my hasty confession about cancer, sensing that it was too much for me to go into right then. "We'll certainly be discussing this later, though," she said. "You're not dying on my watch, babes." She was, however, very interested in my conversation with Christine, probably an easier topic. For her.

We focused on the plan and the three things it needed: cigarettes, painkillers, and courage. Luckily, I'd already bought the first two ingredients, but I was still hoping for the third to fall from the sky. *Where does one buy courage?* The liquid kind was out of the question this time.

I moved cautiously towards the bedroom door. The doorknob squeaked quietly as I turned it. The day would be challenging, but I wanted my future, my happy ending, whatever it was to be. Moving forward isn't always pleasant. Sometimes it's like a summer ride in the Underground at rush hour. You hope to arrive at your stop quickly, but it's dirty, uncomfortable, and confusing on the way there.

I put on my dressing gown awkwardly; my arm was still rather lifeless. Intense pain chased through my limbs. I clenched my teeth. The painkillers had a positive effect, but they didn't make my arm more mobile, and they certainly didn't relieve the pain completely.

I went into the kitchen, opened the window, and lit a cigarette. Next to the sink sat a half-empty cup of tea from the previous evening, and I took a sip from it. Even cold tea was better than no tea at all. I exhaled smoke into the morning fog. Condensation had formed at the window, and it was dripping down right in front of me. I hoped that Holmes would show up, but he seemed to have disappeared from my head. I felt I might still be able to find him if I tried again, but I knew even that feeling wouldn't last. I had solved the case. I needed to die without dying. Or in other words: I needed to kill off the rest of Holmes' brother inside of me. It was time to change. It filled me with joy but also with a certain sadness; the spirit of the past few days would soon be irrevocably gone.

Early mornings have something special. As the city slowly wakes up, it is strangely quiet. It is cold, and the spirit begins to wander. I stuck my arm out of the window to avoid scattering ashes in my kitchen. A few drops of water fell from the window onto my skin. My head sought words that could express what I wanted to share with Matt. After the impression I had left, they had better be the best words I had ever uttered. I closed my eyes and breathed in deeply. The cool air spread in my lungs, and I coughed up blood again. I felt the water drops slowly running down my forearm. It was time to dream without sleeping. I threw the cigarette out of the window and went to my study room.

Dracula Holmes – By Andrew Thomas. The fleeting fog revealed a skinny figure at the Florentine fountain. My tired eyes seemed to wickedly betray me, but there he majestically stood with his long coat fluttering in the dazzling moonlight.

I laughed, ripped the paper from the typewriter, and tossed it in the bin. After a while, I started anew: *How I Learned the Trick – By Andrew Thomas. Walking outside the University of London, I knew the disaster could no longer be avoided. It wasn't a "this train will split at the next station and you just sat down with your meal deal" disaster, but it was equally inconvenient.*

"What are you doing?" asked Mina as she stepped into the room.

I turned around. She looked funny with my shirt on and her black hair all piled up like Big Ben. "Working on my revenge publication," I replied.

She stepped closer. "Is this about you?"

"I guess so." I stood up.

Without warning, Mina gave me a tight hug. "I'm afraid of losing you."

"Don't worry, I'll be fine."

"Don't say that as if your diagnosis is nothing."

"I know, I'm afraid too. But the story I write will have a happy ending. I promise. You know why? Because I'm not alone."

Mina let go and smiled. "No, never." She paused for a while and looked at me. "Let's get this day started!"

"We still have time," I explained, following her back into the bedroom.

"You've said that for far too long. Think of your plan."

I sat down on the edge of the bed and dropped back onto the pillows – something not recommended after an accident like mine.

"It's such a shitty idea," I said.

Mina leaned over me. "First, pay attention to your choice of words, young man, and secondly, the plan is brilliant."

"I'm not the one who curses all the time." I covered myself with the blanket. "As if someone is going to listen to me," I mumbled.

"Just one person will need to listen," Mina remarked. "What would Holmes do?"

"Take drugs and hide at home?"

"I'm not very familiar with the stories, but I don't think so." She threw a pillow in my face. "Andrew Thomas, get up! Don't you let another person ruin your day! Get up and ruin your own damn day like a grown-up! Change your life!" She disappeared into the bathroom.

Change my life. By talking. About my feelings. Not my strength – but maybe it didn't have to be my weakness either.

"What if I fail?" I shouted after her.

She opened the door for a quick moment. "We'll always have Paris, babes!"

With a deft rolling motion, I got out of bed. One thing I could say with absolute certainty on that morning was that the day ahead would bring change, either positive or negative. Either I would win back Matt or leave the country. But Mina was right, regardless of anything that might happen, she and I would always have the memories of the past few days. It was an unforgettable time, and nothing could change that. Just like Rick and Ilsa had Paris in *Casablanca*, we had London and weed.

Mina was humming a melody when she came back into the room. She picked up her clothes.

"That isn't funny," I said when I recognized the song.

Mina laughed. "Come on. 'I'm Still Standing' will be the hymn of the day." She continued to hum.

"Stop it. Just because Matt likes this sort of thing doesn't mean I do."

She came towards me, using her toothbrush as a microphone and singing the chorus.

I grabbed the toothbrush. She stopped singing.

"I need some Chopin now," I said.

Mina rolled her eyes. "You, Sir Dandy Andy, need to get some clothes on and move your butt out of this flat."

I was tempted to note she was still only wearing my shirt. "Do you even know who Chopin was?" I asked.

She sighed. "Chip chap whatever what." She started to get dressed right in front of me.

I turned around, opened my wardrobe, and traced my fingers along the various fabrics.

"Which one do you want to wear today, Mr Bond?" asked Mina as she tried to squeeze herself into her skinny jeans.

"I would be a horrible Bond."

"All of England knows that." Mina sat down on the bed. "But you could be a Bond girl."

"Only if I could wear a bikini like Honey Ryder." The idea of a pale, hairy man in revealing swimwear stepping from the ocean waves made me smile. The looks on people's faces would be priceless.

I opted for a white shirt and a black waistcoat. A combination that promised me attention. Finally, I was able to recognize myself in the mirror again. My face was shaved, my hair was combed, and my clothes were without any holes, dirt, or lilac.

Mina fetched her bag and put her sunglasses on her head. "All right, Mr DeMille, I'm ready for my close-up."

"We're in London, Mina, not Sunset Boulevard." I looked around for the pocket watch and found it on the bedside table. Next to it was my eternal companion. My hand automatically reached out to pick it up and put it in my pocket. Although it had a tragic past, it might have been my lucky charm after all. I was ready to go.

At Tottenham Court Road I woke Mina, and we got on the Northern line towards Camden Town. My arm was pinched between a little blond woman and similarly-sized man, and I wasn't sure if they'd stabilized it or worsened my injury.

When Mina and I had freed ourselves from the carriage, we swam with the crowd to the escalators. We rolled past various posters advertising shows and theatrical performances. Outside, I saw a familiar sight: the woman from Westminster who'd been collecting for HIV education. Apparently this was her new spot. I stopped in my tracks, pulled out ten pounds, and handed it to her. It felt like fate.

"Here for more pens?" she asked.

"No, to do something good," I replied. *But one more pen wouldn't harm anyone.*

"I cannot believe my own eyes," said Mina as we continued down the road. "You are properly freaking me out now."

"Don't be afraid of change, Mina," I teased.

"So what do you do if Matt won't leave the house?" she asked.

"At some point today, he'll go out. It's early enough we won't have already missed it. Worst case scenario, I'll start a fire," I said, and Mina laughed.

In fact, we waited about an hour, hiding across the street from the house where Matt and Bev lived. Huddled on a low wall behind an old Volvo, we watched everything that happened. It was markedly less exciting than the stake-outs on TV.

We waited. Nothing happened. Not even a dog walked past us. The usually busy street seemed deserted that morning. Luckily, the Volvo stayed put, otherwise we would have been exposed. As the minutes ticked by, the pressure built within me. Finally, I burst in a most unexpected way.

"His name was Ian," I said.

"Whose name?"

"The one who wrote the note. The one you found yesterday."

"Ian?"

I nodded. "I met him at university. That was almost two decades ago," I said, making sure the note was in my pocket.

"What is Ian doing now? Are you still friends?"

I shook my head. "He's dead."

"What happened?"

"Nobody knows for sure. He was found lifeless in his bed."

"Pretty clear, isn't it?"

"Probably," I replied, and I was glad that silence followed. The unspeakable is not real unless you squeeze it into words, and I still wasn't fully ready to talk about him.

I was looking for my cigarettes but couldn't find them. I took a deep breath.

"He had fallen in love with me," I said. I regretted it the moment the words came out of my mouth.

"Were you in love with him too?"

"We were friends."

My lighter fell to the ground, and Mina handed it back to me.

I tried to explain. "I knew he wasn't doing well, mentally. I didn't want to get too involved. At the time, everything was just too confusing."

"That sounds typical."

"It was different," I assured her. I was lighting my cigarette when Mina patted me on the bruised shoulder. I screamed silently. "Why are you doing that?" I whispered.

Just then, I looked at the front door and saw Matt leaving the house. My breath deserted me, and it was hard not to go over to him.

"That's him, right?" asked Mina, and I nodded. My fingers stuck to the filter of my cigarette.

His hair was different from the last time we had seen each other, and he didn't seem to be in any pain while walking. I was glad to see he was doing better. To our surprise, Matt crossed the street and walked straight towards the Volvo.

I held my breath.

As he approached us, I was reminded that he was the most beautiful man I had ever met. Mina pulled on my shirt to rip me from my thoughts. Like children playing a game, we crawled and hid in front of the car.

"Let's go to the door," I said, noticing that I had dropped my cigarette in the rush.

"Wait until he's around the corner. If he finds out he's forgotten something, he could come back," Mina replied.

We knelt for a moment in front of the car, then carefully moved to the house. I wondered how my legs could still carry me, because they felt like cotton wool and needles. My instinct told me I'd better run away, but while I was mentally preparing for the next conversation, Mina pressed the doorbell.

It was too late. I looked into Bev's petrified face.

"What does he want?" she asked Mina.

"He wants to apologize," she replied.

"No, thank you. I'm pretty sure the *aggressive intruder* has already sold all his information to the media," Bev said. "Don't try to make more money out of this." She tried to slam the door shut.

"Wait," I pleaded, keeping my foot lodged between the door and its frame. The heavy wood pinched and hurt. "I didn't say anything to anyone. I promise."

"Honestly? Then what do you want here?" asked Bev.

Mina signaled that I should say something.

My fingers nervously pulled on a thread in my pocket.

"I love him," I said.

Mina looked at me like I was a ghost. The door swung open. "What?" Mina and Bev said simultaneously.

I looked at my shoes. "I fell in love with–"

"Matt?" asked Bev. Her facial expression said she had just found the answer to the question of life and couldn't believe it herself.

"I can't believe those words just came out of you," Mina remarked. "That was more than I expected. I mean, you're actually *saying the words out loud*."

"Oh my god," Bev said, still looking shocked. It was as if a wax figure were speaking. "You. In love. With Matt? After your display the other night?"

"With him it's almost as beautiful as being alone," I said, looking down at my shoes.

"Is that a good thing?" Bev asked Mina.

"Yeah, he's romantically challenged." Mina could barely hold back her laughter.

"I'll say."

"Wow." Mina reached into my pocket and took out the cigarettes.

Bev still wasn't moving at all. The only thing that shifted was her hand, which gestured to Mina for a cigarette. Mina lit two and handed one over to her.

"Wow," Bev echoed, looking at me with a questioning glance. "He has a gentle side," she said to Mina, who nodded.

"Yes. Surprising."

"Can you stop talking about me while I'm standing here?"

"No," they replied at the same time.

Contrary to all my expectations, Bev asked us in. Matt was at brunch with his friends from the theater. The brunch he'd invited me to once upon a time.

"I suspected something like this," Bev said from the opposite side of the table. "I just wondered if you'd realized it yourself – or if you'd be able to admit it. Everything about you literally screamed: I love you, please stay forever."

"Really?" I asked.

"It was the elephant in the room. The flaming elephant," said Mina. She took one of the chocolate bars from the bowl in front of us.

"The only things missing were heart-shaped balloons and pink fairy lights," Bev remarked.

I blushed, embarrassed to have turned into an open book. "Can I use your toilet?" I asked.

Bev pointed towards the stairs. "Up on the right," she said.

The whole time I was upstairs, I could hear the two women laughing below, probably about me. I couldn't blame them. Even I thought the proceedings had been funny; I just couldn't laugh about it. Yet.

On my way back, I stopped at an open door and carefully peeked inside. It was Matt's room. It might sound odd, but although I had met Matt only a few times, I recognized the room by his smell. The space was surprisingly tidy, and I had never seen a room so full of books and vinyl – except my own. I looked around. The bed was almost unrecognizable under all the piled-up blankets and sheets. It was nearly impossible to spot Hercules lying on it. She seemed to be in her favorite place in the house. And green appeared to be Matt's favorite color. Everything was either dark green or mint. There was a black upright piano next to the window. I smiled. Of course. If he played an instrument, it had to be the piano. To my surprise, he had a Sherlock Holmes collection lying on top of it. I squinted to see which case he was reading. It was "The Valley of Fear."

"I knew I'd find you here," said Bev behind me.

"I'm…I'm…sorry…" I stuttered.

"I heard you like detectives, so…" Bev joked on the way down.

We sat at the table again. Only then did I recognize the various painkillers lying on the side of it. Neither Matt nor I should be out and about, it seemed.

"I have a plan," I said while unwrapping a chocolate.

"Before planning anything, we should call the others. Liz should be on their way anyway," Bev said. She took her phone in her hand.

"The others?" I asked, but she was already leaving the room to make the call. I dropped my head into my hands.

"What's going on?" asked Mina. She folded the chocolate wrapper into a paper plane that crashed straight out of her hand.

"I didn't expect everyone to be here," I said. I was looking for another chocolate bar that I liked; I desperately needed sugar in that moment. "I just wanted to talk to Bev, get her help."

Mina put her hand on my knee. "Don't be afraid. We can do it."

I nodded and folded a paper plane as well. "I'm not good at talking about my feelings." *But maybe I don't have to be bad, either.*

Mina took my paper plane, threw it in the air, and watched it crash. "What would you have liked to tell him?" she asked, lowering her gaze.

"Who?"

"Ian."

The chocolate started melting between my fingers.

"You wouldn't carry that note around with you if there wasn't something that went unsaid," she continued.

"It's hard," I said through a mouthful of chocolate. "I told him I didn't feel the same for him."

"Was that a lie?"

I looked at Mina and took a deep breath. "It was." I swallowed.

"What was he like?"

I had never talked about him, and it felt strange doing so after so many years.

"He…he was clever, funny…he was very handsome," I said, smiling although I felt sad. "He gave me the note after…after he had confessed his feelings for me. Just a few days later, he was dead." I cleared my throat. "I wish I would have been honest."

"It's time for you to say what you really want to say," Mina concluded.

"Past time." I was finally ready to speak. And I was going to make sure that everyone heard.

27

━━◆━━

How I Learned the Trick

"Michael and Toby are coming too. I wanted to go to the parade with Liz later, but since there's news…" Bev said.

I was hoping to suddenly gain the power of invisibility. Both Mina and Bev seemed quite satisfied by the idea of watching me claw my way up a mountain, naked. Metaphorically.

"By the way, I'm his babysitter," Mina said to Bev.

"I'm Matt's housekeeper," Bev replied.

Mina looked around the room. "A bad one, I see."

"You should have seen it yesterday," Bev said.

It was as if I'd ceased to exist. *Finally*. Their conversation was interrupted by the doorbell. A hurricane raged through the hallway, approached me at a frenzied speed, and hit me in the face.

"What the– !" I cried.

"You deserve it," Liz said. A second later, they smiled at Mina.

"Hi, I'm Mina. Mina Advani."

"I'm Liz. Actually, Giorgio. Giorgio Romano, but that sounds too gay." Liz turned their head towards me again and lost their smile immediately. "What are you doing here?"

I was reluctant to challenge the muscles their tight top revealed.

"He has a mission," Bev said.

"A mission? To become the most hated man in the world on

our day of celebration?" Liz was waving a champagne bottle in the air, and I was afraid that the cork might pop and hit one of us in the eye. Or worse. *Don't ruin my suit.*

"Listen to what he has to say," Bev replied, trying to calm Liz down.

"I don't know about you, but I wanted to have fun today," Liz said, heading towards the kitchen. The bottle still swung back and forth dangerously.

"Come back!" Bev shouted after them.

"F-U-N," Liz spelled. They slammed a cupboard door. A loud pop rang out. "Fun," Liz repeated upon returning to the group. They distributed three full glasses on the table, put the bottle down right in front of my nose, and sat. With a gallant movement, Liz reached for their glass and emptied it in one go. Then they looked critically over its edge. Everyone was staring at me.

"He wants to get off with Matt," Mina said.

Liz didn't change their expression as they reached for the bottle. Once again, they drank their glass in one gulp. Bev started laughing.

Liz didn't think it was funny. "Did I miss something? What did I miss?" they asked.

"Liz, calm down," Bev said, still laughing.

"What do you want from Matt?" Liz asked.

"I want to be with him." The words burst out of me.

"What?" asked Liz, looking at the others. "He's serious, is he?" Mina and Bev nodded.

"I don't believe you, not after what you did to him the other night," Liz said, and I feared I was at a dead end with my plans. I had no way to prove just how serious I was. *Welcome to the "Yes, I'm actually gay and in love with your best friend" show.*

Liz, however, wanted me to prove something very different. "Recite one line of Madonna's song 'Vogue,'" they said.

Bev sighed.

"I guess the word 'vogue' might be in it," I replied. I had no clue about Madonna, and I didn't favor having one.

Liz's face grew even more serious. "Cher or Tina?"

"Liz, this is stupid," Bev said.

Mina laughed. "No. Go on, Liz." I gave her a withering look.

"Neither of them," I replied. "Do I have to be a walking stereotype to prove how I feel? Maybe a floppy-wrist?"

"Okay. Now everyone calm down," Bev cautioned. While she seemed to be getting nervous, Mina was enjoying the show.

"You have more glitter on you than all the exotic dancers in Las Vegas!" I said to Liz. My mouth was off and running again.

"You take that back!"

"Why would I?"

"Because you don't want me to tell Matt about the Admiral Duncan."

"I went there by accident," I protested.

"Weekly? You call weekly an accident? I knew I'd seen you somewhere."

Bev and Mina burst out laughing.

I pouted and took a deep breath. Luckily, I grasped the concept of giving in before the situation got even more uncomfortable. "I'm sorry," I said.

Liz rose. "I can't stand people like you. There are too many of you, and I can't bear that anymore." They crossed their arms.

I was helpless. How could a best friend ever forgive what I had caused Matt?

Bev took a deep breath. "I know he shouldn't have…but Matt told us about…he told me that…you know…that you–"

Everyone in the room fell silent and looked at me.

"Sorry," added Bev.

"I have cancer," I said, looking around nervously.

Bev breathed in deeply. "You have so much going on and yet it sounds like you mean what you say about Matt, if you're doing all this."

"I do and death was never further away," I said. I took the flag, put it over my shoulders, and knotted it on my chest. "I'm Captain Gay. Here to save the day!" The others were unsure if they should laugh.

"I need your support for what I'm going to do." I took off my jacket and looked at my watch. It was just before ten; the moment was getting closer and closer.

Expression grave, Liz came to me and gave me a sudden hug. It wasn't their usual wild invasion of private space but one that felt so genuine and understanding that I almost teared up.

"Disease or not, we're both here to live our best life while we can," they whispered, before turning into a loud sensation again. "I'll help you! But only if you guarantee you'll buy my whole collection once I open my fashion bar in New York."

I laughed and took a few sips from the champagne bottle. "If you sell suits, why not. Do you have more?" I asked, lifting the bottle. Bev nodded and pointed to the kitchen door. Alcohol doesn't make things better, but sometimes it makes things easier.

The kitchen was even more chaotic than it had been a few days earlier. Bev didn't seem to be the housekeeper she'd advertised. Everything was piled up like a Tetris game at level six, and the fridge smelled strangely like stale coffee. Luckily, I found a bottle of white wine between the cucumbers and puddings.

Meanwhile, Toby and Michael had arrived. I was surprised to see they had brought Mary with them. She was asleep, suspended in a large sling that Toby wore around his body.

"You sounded so excited on the phone. What's going on?" asked Michael. He grew visibly irritated when I entered the room.

"Where's Matt?" asked Toby. He protectively cupped Mary's head with his hand. She made a quiet noise but slept calmly.

"So, what is this all about?" Toby asked Bev.

"Our dear Andrew has something to announce," Liz said.

Toby and Michael looked at me with suspicious anticipation. To drag a family with a small child out of the house on such a hot day because of what I had to say seemed a little much.

I sat down and glanced around. "I don't quite know how I–" I rubbed my hands together.

"He wants to bone Matt," Liz volunteered. Bev hit them on the back of the head.

"Is that your announcement?" Michael asked me.

"I want to go to the parade. I want to tell him…I want to tell him I love him."

"You can't say it someplace else?" said Liz.

"No," I replied. "Look, I need to show him that I really mean this. I need to do this properly. I need to stop being afraid of…I just need to stop being afraid."

"What exactly are you going to do? Dance naked through the streets?" asked Liz.

"That wouldn't convince anyone," Mina laughed.

Toby stroked Mary's head. "That's a good plan. But how exactly do you envision having a chat with him while surrounded by thousands of people?"

I had to agree it was a fair point. I told them about my idea of talking to Matt at the start of the parade.

"I have a megaphone," Bev said out of nowhere.

Mary put her hand in the air. It almost looked like a fist proclaiming the revolution.

"I don't know if a megaphone will be necessary," I said.

"Of course it will. There's music. People talking, singing, and celebrating. You're going to need a megaphone, darling," Liz said, and they rooted around in a cloth bag and handed me a square of fabric.

The others laughed loudly as I unfolded the crumpled rainbow flag. "Another one? I'm sure one is enough for my start."

Liz laughed. "One is never enough, darling."

I tried to appear relaxed and smiled.

"Nice to finally have you among us," Michael whispered.

"Well, I guess I've always depended on the kindness of strangers," I said, glancing at Mina.

She leaned towards me. "Oh, Blanche."

I smirked.

"What will you actually say to him?" asked Michael.

I took a piece of paper from my pocket and waved it through the air. "You'll find out soon. Via megaphone, apparently. It's all on here."

Liz tried to snatch the paper from me but failed. Their hand fell loudly on the table. Mary woke up and looked at me with her big eyes.

"She'll have to eat something soon," Toby said.

"Are you not coming?" asked Liz. They let Mary clutch their finger with her little hand.

"No. You can't go there with a baby," said Toby. Again, Mary raised her fist in a strange way.

"You can go with them. I'm staying here with Mary," Michael said. "I simply don't have it in me today to face nearly ubiquitous wheelchair inaccessibility *and* crowds."

Toby smiled at him and loosened the knot of the sling and gently took Mary in his arms. "Do you have any spare wrist bands?" he asked Liz.

"Absolutely. You know most people are unreliable," Liz said, handing him one.

I wondered where Mina and I would be if the others were in the middle of the action. I certainly didn't want to get too much attention. Just Matt's attention.

"Here it is," Bev came around the corner with a megaphone. It was glittery and purple.

"I refuse to use this," I said.

She dropped the megaphone, walked out of the room again, and came back with an old wine box. "So that everyone can see you."

I wiped my wet hands on my trousers. *This must be a personal vendetta.*

Twelve eyes looked at me with anticipation – though two of them were probably just hoping I had a bottle of milk.

"Okay. I'm really doing this," I said, putting the bit of paper with my speech back into my pocket. I was overwhelmed, the white wine seemed ineffectual, and I knew that sweat stains were already appearing on my shirt.

"Give us a moment. We don't want to look like peasants," Liz said. They went upstairs with Bev.

My sense of order drove me to collect the glasses and bring them into the kitchen. I searched for a free space between the plates and empty takeaway boxes.

"It's very brave of you," I heard a voice say behind me. Toby closed the door. "I know exactly how you feel." He pushed aside some of the dirty dishes to make way for the glasses I held. He leaned against the counter and crossed his arms. "I have twins with my ex-wife. We still get along very well."

I was surprised by this revelation. "My ex-wife and I hadn't talked for a while, but we did yesterday. She loves me still and this doesn't necessarily make it any easier," I said.

"Is there a chance of getting back together with her?"

I shook my head.

"There was a time me and my wife tried again, but I met Michael. And I fell in love with another human being. With Matt, you didn't exactly choose the most inconspicuous way of coming out."

"That's probably true."

"At some point, I realized that you shouldn't try to be what others want to see. You shouldn't change for anyone or anything. Not for your family, not for your reputation, not for money. You have to live the life you want to live."

His words were true, but things seemed more complicated to me.

"So, you're telling Matt all your feelings in a place where thousands can listen in?" Toby asked, and my heart dropped.

"Well, yes."

"Why not take the chance and say something to everyone there?"

"Why would I do that?"

"First, Matt loves romantic comedies, and they all seem to magically end with a grand gesture, and second, everyone will listen anyway. Apart from that, I believe you have way more to say."

"My speech isn't really designed to be…well, a proper speech." I hesitantly pulled out my notes and handed them over to Toby.

He propped himself up on the counter and read what I had planned to say.

"Can you help me with this?"

"Let's make this a supreme romantic comedy ending," he said, pulling a pen from the inside pocket of his jacket. It was a nice pen. "But one with real substance."

Toby reminded me very much of myself. The only difference was that he knew how to act like a normal human being.

We heard loud steps coming down the stairs.

"I think it's showtime," Toby said. He handed me back the piece of paper.

Bev and Liz were wearing the highest shoes I'd ever seen in my life, and their outfits left nothing to the imagination. Their eyes shone through a profusion of glitter. Liz's cheeks sparkled just as much in the colors of the rainbow. I put on my jacket. Captain Gay and his gang were ready to fight.

"Do you have any glitter left?" asked Mina as we exited the house.

"What a question," Liz said, stopping to daub at Mina's face. "You too?" Liz asked me.

"For heaven's sake. No," I replied. I hoped that none of the color would land on my expensive suit.

I lit a cigarette and dropped another to the ground in my hurry. Stopping was not an option, as the others were moving towards the Underground at about thirty kilometers per hour. My cape was blowing in the wind. Despite the speed with which we moved, Liz was still able to distribute flags of different sizes to the others. I wondered what else Liz was carrying in their bag. Toby refused one, and that surprised me.

"Solidarity?" I asked him, feeling uncomfortable in public with my cape. I had become a walking rainbow.

He smiled and took one of the flags.

"He and Michael don't really like Pride," Liz said.

"Why?"

"Too much hustle and bustle," Toby replied. "I avoid big events. And they're difficult for Michael. Accessibility has a way to go."

I was afraid of standing out, but we didn't really get noticed in the streets or in the Underground. People around us were in even wilder outfits for the parade, and all eyes were attracted to them – even in a city like London.

"We're joining a larger group, his theatre folks. Matt organized it. He's a blessing," Bev told me.

"We're already way too late. He's tried to call me seven times," Liz said. "You're the usual mess again," Liz added, handing me a bracelet.

"What's this?" I asked.

"That's your way into the parade," Bev said.

"Into? As in we're going to walk in the parade itself?"

"Of course! Hurry up!" Liz shouted, storming up the escalator.

We tried to keep up. The air was heavy and unbearably warm. The sweat ran down my back. As we stepped out of the station, we were greeted by a huge crowd. It was loud. Smells of food and cigarettes hung in the air. I clutched my megaphone and didn't let Mina leave my sight. Liz called Matt to find out where he was. When I thought about how Matt would soon be standing in front of me, my heart beat faster.

"Shit, it's full here," Mina said, staying with me.

I looked around and remembered why I preferred romantic walks in the rain and quiet evenings with my typewriter.

"I know where he is. He's in a really bad mood," Liz said as we went through the security check.

We started making our way through the throng. Various groups had already gathered and waited for the parade to begin. I was sure that Matt's mood wouldn't lift when he saw my face in the crowd.

"There are more friends of ours in the group, so you'll get to know the rest," Bev said. "I hope it doesn't make you even more nervous."

I shook my head. Of course, it did. The crowd kept pushing us forward. There was no going back.

"Can't you just get him, and we'll all meet outside of this?" I suggested. I was having serious second thoughts about Toby's grand speech suggestion. Being judged by hundreds – perhaps thousands – of people can have that effect.

"I would say you should both stop a little bit behind the group so he doesn't see you directly," Toby said to me and Mina. I thought that was the right idea.

Liz gently pulled at my sleeve. "We don't have long until the mob gets moving. We need to find our group before the parade starts."

Mina jumped up and down. "God, that's going to be fun. I've never walked in the parade. Shit, that's exciting!"

"I'm not happy yet," I said, clinging to her arm.

"I love your friends already."

"These are Matt's friends."

Luckily, we found the larger group in time. The others gathered in the distance. Between us stood about a hundred people who danced and sang.

"I can't possibly give a speech here. Everyone will be annoyed," I said. I put the box in front of my feet. "The music is way too loud, anyway." There were speakers pumping music at an incredible volume from a truck right next to us.

Mina ripped the megaphone out of my hand. "We might just have a few minutes before everybody gets moving. So, you want to give a speech? Give a speech. *Now*." She climbed onto the box. I tried to pull her down again. "I'm too short," she said.

"Come on my shoulders," said a tall man next to Mina. She looked at him inquiringly. "I thought you had something to say," he continued, kneeling. Mina sat on his shoulders and clung to the man's head as he got up again.

I was petrified. Full plank mode. A lot of plans sound great before you enact them. Already, people were turning around and looking at Mina. I could only imagine what looks would hit me.

She switched on the megaphone. The sheer number of people pressing in around me kept me from falling to the ground.

"I have a friend," Mina began, and I hid my face in my hands. "He's the biggest asshole the world has ever seen. He cares about nothing and no one except himself."

My breathing got faster. A panic attack was probably on the

way. No chocolate bar in the world could have supplied me with enough sugar to avert fainting.

"He fucked up, and now he wants to apologize."

A few people around Mina clapped and drunkenly shouted.

"He wants to apologize to you, Matt Lewis," she said.

We discovered that everyone around us knew his name: all eyes darted to us, and it got unpleasantly quiet. I couldn't see if Matt had heard this introduction, but Mina's face spoke volumes. She seldom seemed intimidated, but this kind of attention was too much even for her.

I knotted my flag more firmly and climbed onto the box. It wasn't until I was standing above everyone else that I saw Matt looking right over at us. The music around me became quieter. I didn't know if I was just imagining it or if someone had lowered the volume in order to hear exactly what the freak in the tailored suit was going to say at a pride parade.

"The man needs a microphone!" a woman behind me shouted. The crowd agreed, clapping. Hundreds of eyes looked at me with anticipation. I didn't need a microphone; I needed to wake up.

Mina pressed the megaphone into my hand. "I…I'm good," I said into it. I could see Matt's stunned face.

With trembling hands, I searched for my notes.

"Hello…I…I'm Andrew."

Again, some clapped. Others laughed.

"It's true. I'm a selfish asshole."

I looked at Matt, who stood with his arms crossed. I hoped that most of the people around me thought I'd had drugs for breakfast. My voice was soft and trembling. I was just trying to speak up when a woman handed me a microphone down from the truck behind us. I tapped carefully to test if it was turned on. It was. My fingers searched nervously for my cigarettes.

Suddenly the music stopped. Only in the distance could I hear other beats and voices. The interest I was receiving showed me how many people knew Matt, and I realized that I hadn't taken this into account.

"Thank you," I said, smiling at the woman holding the microphone cable. "Actually, I had imagined fewer people listening to this."

The crowd around me laughed.

I took a deep breath and looked at my notes.

"The question I was asked most frequently when I lectured at university was whether the famous detective Sherlock Holmes and his companion, Dr John Watson, were more than just colleagues. I would like to answer with a counter-question: Would it make a difference? Would it change even one line?"

I looked around. I had clearly chosen a topic that few, if any, had expected. It grew quieter, and people looked at me in confusion. My fingers stuck to the paper.

"The answer is no. Why? Because a person's sexuality is what the person is, not who the person is. We all have our own stories, our own biographies, and the gender or sex of the one we love certainly doesn't affect our character."

Hundreds of eyes looked at me, and I didn't dare look in Matt's direction.

"What I want to say is that no one should be afraid to be who they are and to live exactly the way they want to live. I was scared. I was scared for half my life. But I shouldn't have been afraid. No one should have to be afraid to live and love. No one should live in fear of being beaten or insulted for things they didn't choose. We cannot choose our skin color, gender, sexuality, bodies, or the place we are born. But the fact that these things are seen as what defines us, that these things are the measurements of how much we're worth in this world, shows how much is yet to be done."

I looked at Toby, Liz, and Bev. Liz was already crying into a handkerchief. I glanced down at the edited portion of my speech. It was time to be brave.

"We stand here because we don't just want to be tolerated; we want to be accepted. We stand here for all those who do not dare to walk the streets at Pride this year, who have not yet come out or are afraid to do so. We stand here to encourage others, and I am happy to stand here for the first time today."

I swallowed.

Mina stretched out her hand to me, and I held it tight.

"I'm not going to say I've done a lot. That's just you. You are the ones who make a difference. In schools, in politics, in jobs. I have not done anything so far, but I would like to say that I will work together with you on the road that lies ahead."

My eyes fell on Matt. His face showed no emotion, and his arms were still crossed. My final words, though heard by everyone, were written only for him. And they were the truth.

"A few days ago, I met a very special man. He gave me this…" My hands rummaged through my pockets. "He gave me this flyer for a charity performance at the Young Vic next weekend. So, if you don't have any plans yet, you should all go and see him, and… donate for the LGBTQ youth…of course." My voice cracked, and I was shaking while I held the flyer up as if it was the Bible. "I would like to apologize to him. You're right; I'm ignorant and narrow-minded. But that doesn't change the fact that I know I would do everything for you. I love you without knowing exactly how or why. The only thing I can say for sure is that I don't want to stop. Not for one day, one hour, one second. I love you just the way you are."

I gently pushed the microphone away and got down from the wine box.

The music was turned up again. Some genius among Matt's friends put on "Are You Ready for Love" at full volume. Why didn't people listen to Bach at pride parades? I never found out.

People clapped and patted me on my shoulders, and I clenched my teeth in pain. Mina gave me a kiss on the cheek. "Damn shit, I almost cried because of you," she said.

"Sorry," I replied, hugging her.

Matt appeared in the crowd. He stopped and looked at me. I wondered what the odds were he'd just keep walking. Away. Here and then gone. Instead, he began walking in my direction.

Mina stroked my arm and followed the others.

The strange feeling in my stomach intensified. It was as if

only Matt and I existed. I moved my body impatiently back and forth while he waded towards me through the sea of people and discarded flyers. In an endless loop, I went through all sorts of apologies in my head. *Excuse me. I am sorry. That was stupid of me. I like theater.*

His steps grew faster. As if through a narrow tunnel, he got closer and closer. My stomach turned. I thought I was about to faint. I closed my eyes. I took a deep breath and expected to be shouted at.

Instead, I felt two arms wrapping tightly around me. I pressed myself firmly against Matt and buried my face in his neck.

"I missed you," he whispered.

It was a relief to hold him. "So did I."

"On a scale from one to ten, how uncomfortable were you up there?" he asked, running his hands through my hair.

"I did it for you, that's what matters," I replied. "But if you're curious, a solid fifty. But at least now everybody knows about us, and they can leave us alone."

"They won't."

"I know, but I don't care," I said, smiling.

"You're not ashamed of being seen with me?"

"No, if I'm ashamed of anything, it's myself. I was an arse. I have to apologize."

Mina and the others came over to us.

"Finally, not a phantom," Bev joked. Her glitter was by now all over everyone.

"So, Matt," said Mina through the tear-smeared glitter. "Are we business partners now?"

Matt smiled at her. "Hey, Liz," he said, letting go of me. "Do you need a ticket to New York? I heard the city needs a fashion bar, and I have business to take care of here in London."

Liz stormed towards Matt and gave him a kiss on the cheek. "I'll pack my bags today! Now, the rest of you kids come with me. Let's give these lovebirds some privacy, you dirty voyeurs."

Matt turned his face towards me, and I felt his cheek on mine.

Looking past him, I recognized a familiar figure in the crowd. Holmes stood among the crush of people with a smile on his face. A man like him smiled very rarely. He was probably smiling not because of me, but because he had solved another case. His final case. He nodded, turned around, and disappeared into the crowd. *You dirty voyeur.*

Matt took an envelope out of his pocket.

"What is that?"

"A letter, to my parents. Twelve pages telling them how I feel and felt. I guess now is the right time." He smiled and took my hands. "How about we start anew, get to know each other properly, slowly this time?

As the parade started, the crowd began moving forward with us.

"You mean without me being an absolute madman?"

"Yes, I'd love that." He stopped. "Why are you laughing?"

"I never thought I'd say this one day…but this world is wonderful and so are you."

And when our lips touched, a familiar voice appeared in my head: *I don't know what I am and I don't know what I want. I don't know who I can be and I don't know who I was. But I will find the one who kisses me as if there was never any doubt about who I am, who I was, and who I can be, and I will call this love.*

The pleasure of it all.

Author Bio

Yvonne Knop is a bi and nonbinary writer who dedicates their free time to extending the secret Gay Agenda. Although born and raised in the north of Germany, Yvonne's passion for Sherlock Holmes and Doctor Who, their sassy humor, and aversion to talking on public transport made them suspiciously British from early on.

As a natural matter of cause and effect, Yvonne moved to London in 2014 and started to write (a novel for the drawer). No word was written until 2017 when the sudden question of 'What if I could talk to Sherlock Holmes?' came to them.

Conducting PhD research in the world's most extensive Sherlock Holmes collection, located in Minneapolis, USA, was a great help for answering that question. The result was not a PhD, but their debut Novel *A Case of Madness*, originally written in German and in a bold move translated by the author themselves when nobody in Germany understood a word they were saying.

You can find Yvonne on Twitter and Instagram.

Author Acknowledgements

It would be bold to assume any book came to life without help. In fact, without help of the following people this book would be more dead than the flowers beside me – trust me, they are a fire hazard.

First, I would like to especially thank two people:

Laura Major, Mina's biggest cheerleader and pen-lover herself – for supporting me and believing in me, even when I already lost hope. Thank you for your patience, creativity, and craftsmanship. You will always be the Doctor to my Rose. And of course, I need to thank Simon at this point – my personal Stamford who introduced me to Laura.

And *Atlin Merrick,* without whom this book would not be in the hands of any reader now. She did the incredible by making me believe in what I am capable of. She pushed me to write the best version of this book I could have written. Thank you for your trust, support and guidance. Finding her and Improbable Press was the best that could have happened to me, and wouldn't have happened without Sarah Tollok who tagged Improbable under my post during #pitmad.

Second, I need to thank *Franziska, Inka and Camilla* for not only reading this work once, but multiple times during different stages. Please don't let anyone know about deleted chapters or scenes. They still haunt me at night. Special thanks also to Kate and Daphne, whose feedback was highly valuable.

Third, thanks to everyone else who has supported me. Be it financially, by reading the manuscript, or in any other way possible. Most of them belong to the CoNC (You know who you are, you sad bastards!).

My last words in this book are dedicated to my parents, my sister, my sister's family, and my fiancée. Thank you for always watering me, so I can bloom. I love you!

Off to throw out the dead flowers now.

Get More Great Stories

ImprobablePress.com

From ancient gods rising, to road trips on the trail of cryptids, from romance to mystery to adventure, Improbable Press specialises in sharing the voices and tall tales of women, LGBTQIA+, BIPOC, disabled, and neurodiverse people.

Come along for the ride.

Sign up for our newsletter *Spark* at improbablepress.com